ANNA & ELIZABETH

A Novel

Sophie Cook

Published by
Four Leaf Clover Editions
4000 Cathedral Avenue, NW 340B
Washington DC 20016
www.annaelizabethnovel.com

Library of Congress Control Number: 2015944053

ISBN: 978-0-9908054-0-3

PRINTED IN THE UNITED STATES OF AMERICA

First Edition

Book and cover design by Judy Walker
www.JudyWalkerDesign.com

To the memory of my mother,

Maria G. Cook

Who not only provided many of the details
of this story but imbued it with her vision –
faith in the endurance of personal relationships
and a clear-eyed view of her country's history.

TABLE OF CONTENTS

INTRODUCTION

When I was growing up, I felt as if a golden age had existed just before my time. As a young child I caught glimpses of it before the war. I lived in a large apartment in Budapest, Hungary, with my parents, my little brother, and my grandmother and her sister, my great-aunt. The beautiful city, with its river, bridges, and hills, lay all around us. Many of the houses were painted yellow. It now seems to me that there was a golden light everywhere.

My grandfather, who died in 1940, had a thoughtful face and a gold-white mustache. I remember him singing a Hungarian folk song to me *"There is only one little girl in the whole wide world / And that little girl is my dear turtledove. / The Good Lord must have had me dearly in his heart / When he created you just for me."*

I still love that song. Although we were of Jewish origin, it symbolizes how Hungarian we felt, part of the culture of that flat land. My family was middle class, not wealthy, and they were disillusioned by how little the country had changed after the efforts of my grandparents' generation early in the 20th century to bring about greater justice and equality. But my parents enjoyed their friends and the lively cultural activities of Budapest.

All that changed in the early years of World War II. Jews became non-persons, non-Hungarians. They had to wear yellow stars, couldn't attend public schools or public events. My parents lost their jobs. They had to train non-Jews to take over their livelihood.

But I didn't know all this. I only noticed that my parents spent more time at home, that we no longer had servants or a governess, that my grandmother cooked the meals and my great-aunt played with me.

In March of 1944, the Germans invaded Hungary, and deportations of Jews started. My parents told me that I, aged six and a half, and my little brother, aged three and a half, would have to leave home and pretend that we were Christian children, with false names. I had a cross on a silver chain around my neck and memorized the Lord's Prayer. What really shocked me was that my father had tears in his eyes. I had never seen him cry. I knew that everything had changed.

The period that followed, from the spring of 1944 till the liberation of Budapest by Soviet troops in early 1945, was terrible for Jews. Almost half a million were deported and killed. My whole family hid in a variety of places, and except for a short few days in November, my brother and I didn't see our parents. The Swedish consul's secretary hid us in her villa in the Buda hills, where her Hungarian servants reluctantly took care of us. We were glad when another Jewish family that was already there made us leave, but this of course presented our parents with another problem of how to hide us. We then spent some time in a convent in Pest. I liked the nuns, the rosaries and the smell of incense, and especially the company of other Jewish children, who were also in hiding. I recall looking at the statue of the Virgin in the chapel and wishing I could believe in her but knowing that I didn't.

Someone denounced the nuns for sheltering Jews, and they threw us out into the winter night, telling the oldest of the children how to lead us to the lethal Budapest ghetto, the starting point for deportations. Amazingly, my parents were notified and sent a Gentile messenger to pick us up. However, they couldn't keep us in their own hiding place and found a half-Gentile couple, friends of my father, to shelter us, through the bombings, until the end of the war.

I was old enough to know the danger, but I experienced that time as one of intense homesickness rather than of fear. The only time I remember crying was when I caught a snatch of classical music on the radio that reminded me of home. The people who hid my brother and me were not unkind. They were running risks by sheltering Jewish children while they themselves were subject to the privations of war shortages and increasing danger from bombs and shelling. But I hated them for burning the paprika potatoes we ate and for only providing toilet paper made of newspaper in the cellar, where we hid during the terrible siege of the city. Most of all, I hated them for not being my parents. Finally, the bombing stopped, and our cellar doors opened. We went out to find a city in rubble and Russian soldiers who gave candy to children. Then my father came to see us. He and my mother had survived, but my grandmother and great-aunt had perished, "unfortunately," he said, with that inadequacy of words to feelings that we all experience in the great tragedies of our lives. I knew that I could never go home again.

Slowly, my parents rebuilt their lives. We emigrated first to Western Europe, then to the United States. When we finally had our own home in New York, I lived surrounded by furniture from Budapest that my mother had brought out with great difficulty, by antique clocks and china, and by lots of stories. It took me a long time, however, to find out exactly what had happened to my grandmother and to my great-aunt.

I grew up, still longing for that old life that had disappeared long ago. I studied, married, then had my own children. Finally, I decided to try to reconstruct that way of life before my own and of some of the people I never knew. I went to the Library of Congress, did research, and asked my mother to check out the details that I imagined.

I discovered that many of the books I enjoyed stemmed from the same longing I experienced for a lost childhood world. Late in life, Willa Cather wrote about West Virginia, the place her parents left for the Middle West when she was little, as well as about her slave-owning forebears. Paul Gauguin as a child lived in Latin America but grew up in France. I'm sure the bright colors he put into his paintings were intended to reconstruct some of his memories of a lost paradise. Even sadness can haunt. Charles Dickens, who spent a short time in a workhouse as a child, wrote about poor children all his life. I think that the feelings that haunted me were the conflict between gratitude towards the people who made it possible for me to survive and despair about the world that didn't allow others to do so.

I was particularly intrigued by the friendship between my

grandmother and a woman from the countryside who worked for her, two women of different backgrounds and temperaments. Their relationship symbolized the way in which people can transcend their circumstances and the limits that events impose on the best of intentions. I knew that my grandmother's friend had tried to save her during the war but failed.

In this novel, the character of Elizabeth is based on my grandmother, whom I remember. Anna's character is based on several women from a small village who worked for my grandmother and became her friends. I knew the last of these women and still correspond with her descendants. My grandmother's friend wrote me beautiful letters for many years, always starting with the ritual good wishes for health and prosperity and expressing hope that there would never be another war, "which eats up the livelihood of the whole world."

Although I had these real-life models, I invented all of the characters, including Anna and Elizabeth, their husbands and children, not to mention their thoughts and words. The historical events are real. World War I and the revolution in Hungary in 1918 can be found in history books. And many of the details are real, such as the embroidery Anna would have been proud of or the noodle cutter that used to belong to my family, an early precursor of the Cuisinart.

When I finished, the past and the people still eluded me. But some of their stories came to life for me, and I hope, for readers. Because there were sad and difficult moments in people's lives, the past seemed even more interesting, although less idyllic than I first thought. The present isn't that different from the past, it's just that we find it hard to look at our current lives as a whole as we live them.

By writing this book, some of my longing for the past was stilled. I now live in the present in a new golden age. This world is not perfect, but my family and friends lead productive, peaceful lives, with their own struggles, achievements, and disappointments, like the people in this book. Some day, this world will also disappear and present a new generation with stories they will want to remember.

PART I ~ PROLOGUE

"We go back a long way"

CHAPTER 1.
Saving Grandchildren (1944)

"Can we talk now?" Zsuzsi asked in a loud whisper as she and her brother Tom hurried after their grandmother Elizabeth down the back stairs of her apartment building. The girl had been looking for reassurance all morning, from the moment when Elizabeth ripped off the yellow stars that their governess had so carefully stitched on her sweater and on Tom's jacket.

As soon as she finished sewing, the governess had put on her hat and coat.

"Well, no more working for Jews for me," she said to the children's grandparents, and left without saying good-bye to Tom and Zsuzsi, who were not sorry to see her go. But this morning, instead of allowing them to enjoy her absence and linger over their toast, jam, and cocoa, Elizabeth told the children that they would have to pack so as to leave before the eleven o'clock curfew restricting Jews to their house. Elizabeth said this after opening an official-looking envelope in the morning mail and passing it to their grandfather Frederic. He read the contents slowly and put them back in the envelope. He looked up at Elizabeth. She didn't say anything more, gulped her coffee, slammed cups and saucers on a tray and left for the kitchen.

"Pack? Why should we pack?" Tom asked their grandfather.

Instead of answering their questions, Frederic hugged each of the children and told them to obey their Grandmama. Then he took his medicine and went back to bed. He looked terribly sad.

All morning, Elizabeth, rushing to get out of the city, was unable to find the calm, loving tone she had always had for her grandchildren.

"Later, little one, we'll talk later," Elizabeth would answer Zsuzsi over her shoulder.

Her flustered preparations would have been disturbing enough, but a remark of Tom's made Zsuzsi go rigid with fear.

"I thought we had to wear these," he said pointing to his sister's discarded yellow star. "Isn't it dangerous to go without them?"

"Don't move, darling," Elizabeth said, as she snipped away at his jacket with little scissors. "It's much more dangerous now to be with them."

"But you haven't even told us where we're going," Zsuzsi wailed. "I want to stay here."

"To Kisbánya, to Anna. Would you like me to help carry your suitcases down the stairs?"

Both of them clung to their bags. Elizabeth knew they must be blaming her for pushing them out of her home. It had been their refuge since their father went to America and their mother fled to escape arrest by the Hungarian Nazis. Or they blamed her, as she did herself, for being old and frightened. But she kept going, and soon the three of them reached the tram stop. In the crowded car, Elizabeth pointed to a seat and the children sat down morosely.

When a man in the tram stared at Tom, Elizabeth's heart froze. Since March, Jews were no longer allowed to leave their homes after the curfew, and it was nearing noon. Tom, with his fine curved nose and deep brown eyes, looked Jewish. The law rewarded those who denounced Jews. Elizabeth jumped up.

"Children, this is our stop. Excuse us, excuse us," she mumbled as she hurried them off.

The tram clanked away, leaving them at a stop in an industrial suburb. Long empty streets stretched away in every direction. Zsuzsi sat down on her suitcase, wiping her forehead. A skinny dog came to sniff at them but left looking for food.

"Take off your jackets, children," Elizabeth said. "We'll take the next tram even if we need new tickets, and Tom, please stare out of the window. Zsuzsi and I will talk about her confirmation dress. You must have friends who have been confirmed?"

"No, I don't," Zsuzsi said. "Yes, Panni was. She wore a white organza dress."

"Well all right, we'll just talk about whom you would invite and your party dress," Elizabeth said.

They got on the next tram to the train station, and Elizabeth bought new tickets, counting out her money with care. It was only when the old coal engine shook them with reassuring regularity towards Kisbánya that Elizabeth felt calm enough to try to reassure the children. No one shared their seats on the long hard benches of the third class compartment.

"You'll love spending the summer in the country," she said.

"You'll love staying with your Grandmother Ignatius...You wouldn't like it in America..." Tom said, mimicking an adult voice. "Every time someone tries to get rid of us, they tell how we're supposed to feel."

Elizabeth looked at his hunched adolescent shoulders. Someone should tell these children the truth. But how far should she go? She leaned closer.

"When your mother left, she said to me — I want to live, so I can bring up my children. I urged her to go, to try to get to Palestine, because of her love for you."

Even as she said that, Elizabeth recalled that her daughter, Kate, also said that if she was caught, she didn't want the children to be brought up in America by their father. Elizabeth felt enmeshed in half-truths.

"If the police had arrested mummy, do you think that they would have hurt her?" asked Zsuzsi in a low voice.

"Yes, I'm sure," Elizabeth replied without hesitation. Kate had been working for an illegal Jewish organization, and the police were without mercy. "Anyway, I wanted to tell you about the time when your mother and your Uncle Andrew, at about your age, spent a summer with Anna and her children, Esther and Stevie. Look, I still have the paper knife that Andrew whittled for me." The knobby little knife that Elizabeth had hurriedly put in her pocket was wrapped in a faded birthday letter from Kate. It cheered the children to read the spelling errors of their mother's letter.

"We went on a hayride today and I nearly timbled off. Wouldn't that have been a disgrease? But it was fun. I miss you both, but not enough to want to come home yet. But I do wish you a very happy Birth Day, Mother dear, and as soon as I get a beautiful gift for you, I will send it."

"Was she considering an ugly gift?" Tom laughed. "That would be a disgrease, wouldn't it?"

"Disgrease, disgrease!" Zsuzsi sang.

By the time they walked to Anna's house, the children knew the names of long dead pet farm animals, of hiding places that Esther had showed their mother and uncle, and how Stevie had saved Uncle Andrew from a bull.

From Kisbánya's small railway station a narrow path led to the village. They walked through flat fields where wheat, alfalfa, and beets grew. The greenness of the crops and the tall cypress trees in the distance calmed Elizabeth's mind. From a distance, she could see women and children bending over their work. The men are gone, she thought, gone for good, frozen in the Russian winter, fighting by the side of their German allies. The war was now four years old, and even what little information she could get showed that the Germans were losing on faraway fronts. But that seemed to make them even more eager to persecute Jews in places that were still under their power.

The main street of the village was deserted. Only dogs and acacia trees guarded the low white-washed houses with their black, overhanging thatched roofs. Elizabeth pushed the gate to Anna's front yard without pulling the bell's rope.

"Quiet, Bodri," she said to the old dog. The children were impressed when he retreated.

Three doors opened from the covered walkway of beaten earth that ran along the house, sheltered from the sun by a trellis of grapevine. They went past the large bedroom, nearly filled by the plump featherbed on the bedstead, into the cool, dark kitchen.

"Anna or Joska will soon be home," Elizabeth said. "Anna feeds the animals and gets dinner ready by sundown."

"Could I have a drink of water?" Zsuzsi asked, going to the sink.

"They get water from a well here, you goose," Tom said. "Speaking of which…"

An angry rooster was about to peck Zsuzsi. She ran to Elizabeth, but the animal walked out again, bobbing his red comb. Elizabeth found a pitcher of water and poured it into two cracked mugs.

Elizabeth sat down heavily to wait for Anna. She smoothed back her gray hair and pulled down her black and white silk dress where her slip was showing.

"It's a different world, isn't it?" she asked.

The children pulled out their books from their suitcases.

It occurred to Elizabeth that Anna might not be able to hide the children. Her brother-in-law was active in the local Nazi party, and everyone knew about Anna's Jewish friends from Budapest. Except for exchanging a few letters, she and Anna had not been in touch since the war started. Was she asking too much of her old friend when she wanted her to hide her grandchildren from the new wave of persecution unleashed against Jews? Would Anna herself be in danger? Elizabeth found reassurance from her friend's kitchen, where every worn implement hung well scrubbed on its hook. Anna is resourceful, she thought. And we go back a long way.

They had been waiting about a half hour when they heard the front gate slam. Bodri got up to greet his mistress. Anna came in, wearing a long blue dress over her large frame, a black apron, and a kerchief over her head. When she saw Elizabeth, she looked startled and reached back to close the door behind her.

"Anna, I had no time to warn you that we were coming," Elizabeth said as she rose from her seat.

"These are strange times, Little Madam, there's no need to explain," Anna said and reached out both hands to her old friend. She turned to the children. "And you must be Kate's children, Tom and Zsuzsi."

"This morning, the Germans ordered all Jews to move to the ghetto, and I didn't want to take the children with me because people were being deported from there, I've heard," Elizabeth said.

"Deported, meaning what?" Tom asked.

The two women were silent for a moment.

"We're not sure," Anna said, "but you know that the Nazis hate Jews, even children. They are evil people and God will punish them, but until then we have to stop them from hurting you."

She offered her guests some jam-filled doughnuts on a painted platter.

"I don't have sugar to dust these, but the jam is sweet, from our own apricots," Anna said. "I'd like to keep you here with me, but it's too dangerous. It would be better if you stayed in some out-of-the-way little hamlet even if it's not as nice as my village."

She smiled, realizing that for these city children from Budapest, her village might not be much. They were silent, waiting for her to continue.

"I know," Anna said, after a few moments, "my sister-in-law Martha's people. I've known them for a long time and I would trust them with my own children."

She said that they were quiet old people, who had lost all their babies except for Martha and had become especially kind grandparents.

"When my godchild Theresa ran away from a cruel employer, they hid her, and it was only because her mother believed she had died that Theresa came out of her refuge," Anna said. "The old people would never say anything."

"What did the cruel people do to Theresa?" Zsuzsi asked.

"They beat her with wet reeds," Anna said.

"Like Nazis," the girl said, shuddering.

"I'd like to go back with Grandmama," Tom said, sitting up straight. "I'm not afraid."

"I can't even take you, darling," Elizabeth sighed. "The order that came in the mail today doesn't have your name on it, so we would be separated right away. Staying here would be much better."

"And you'll come to visit?" Zsuzsi asked.

"Whenever I can," Elizabeth said. She got up reluctantly. "I have to go back with the next train, your grandfather is waiting for me."

She kissed them both, quickly wiping off Tom's silent tears.

"Come soon, Grandmama," Zsuzsi said, her voice cracking.
Anna walked out with Elizabeth.

"Excuse me for not coming further with you, Little Madam,"
Anna said, when they reached the gate. "Someone might drop
by the house and I want to be here to explain our new young
relatives."

Elizabeth was pained at having no further say about her
grandchildren, but she had no choice.

"If anything should happen to me, here is an address for
contacting their father in America, at least until we hear from
Kate," she said, reaching into her purse.

"Nothing will happen to you," Anna said as she embraced her.
"No matter how terrible this war is, it can't last forever."

They walked off in two separate directions, two old women,
out of breath.

* * *

As Elizabeth hurried along the path to the train station, she
smiled, recalling how Anna was still calling her "Little Madam."

She had been a newly married woman presiding over
a prosperous household when she first met Anna, a young
maidservant fresh from her village and dazzled by the city. In those
far-off days, Anna addressed Elizabeth as "Honored Madam," and
said "I kiss your hands" whenever she greeted her.

Elizabeth, whose husband fought for greater equality for
working people, was proud to get to know Anna as a person rather
than just a maid. After Anna married and left Elizabeth's service,
she often turned to her former mistress in times of hardship.
Eventually, Elizabeth asked Anna to call her by her first name.

"Oh, I couldn't do that, Honored Madam," Anna had said.

But Anna started to call Elizabeth "Little Madam." Elizabeth
liked that affectionate, deferential, faintly protective title. She
noticed now that Anna spoke with a self-confidence that Elizabeth
had never heard before.

She and Anna had been divided by class, religion, and
character, united by respect and affection. Now that she was

so dependent on Anna's help, Elizabeth wondered: Who had protected whom during all those years? And was time the great equalizer or did it conceal land mines that could destroy their friendship?

The trouble with getting old, Elizabeth thought, is that your mind keeps going back to your beginnings. But it isn't just for the memories, it's to try to find meaning in the long journey.

Chapter 2.
Beginnings (1880)

Elizabeth was born on a clear April afternoon in the family house at the outskirts of the little town of Iglau, in Moravia. The house was built at the meeting place of town and country where a stream that powered the Schwalb family's factory rushed down from the mountains. The water gurgled over the unusual weekday silence of the machines, hushed in the expectation of the baby.

The family living room stood empty. The gentle ticking of a clock superimposed a human rhythm over the sounds of wind and water seeping through the French windows. A fire had been lit in the tiled stove and through the grate cast flickering shadows on the veneered panels of the furniture. The room reflected an earlier period, the simple style of the owners' parents, rather than the dark, heavy fashions of the 1880's. On the round table, blue-edged coffee cups decorated with golden roses and an ample-bellied coffeepot awaited the family and the doctor attending the birth.

Finally, a door banged upstairs, letting out the sharp cry of the newborn. Two girls clattered down the stairs, wearing long, dark blue dresses, embroidered aprons, high laced boots, and thick braids. The older girl, Hilda, who was eight, flopped down on the piano bench and played a few bars of Mendelssohn to celebrate that she could be noisy again. Clara, aged six, bent over her.

"You haven't practiced all day, have you?"

"I haven't practiced, I haven't done my stitchery, and I don't even know where my French grammar book is," Hilda replied, still playing. "Don't you love it when everything is discombobulated?"

Clara shook her head.

"I don't love it at all. I miss Mamma and I don't need a baby sister. I'm going do scales every time the baby tries to sleep. Move over if you're just fooling around."

Their father and the doctor came into the room. Emile Schwalb was a tall man with rich brown hair and sideburns. He wore striped pants, a velvet jacket, and a silk vest. His eyes were shadowed with a slightly dreamy sadness, but his mouth expressed skepticism and humor. Doctor Zoruba, a bearded, hunchbacked young man, was dressed in a worn suit. His eyes had a warm gaze behind his gold-framed glasses. He went to the piano and gently pulled Hilda's braids.

"Your mother is ready to see you, young ladies. But don't tire her, she's weak."

"And then, may we have coffee in the kitchen? It's so cheerful! Everyone's there, Augusta, Jiri the coachman, his daughter Martenka, and I don't even know who else," Hilda asked her father as she slammed down the piano lid.

"Of course," Emile said. "And when you are upstairs ask the midwife — Hilda!" he called after the girl who was almost at the top of the stairs — "whether she would like anything sent up to her."

Clara, dragging her feet, followed Hilda.

Augusta, the housekeeper, bustled in with coffee, followed by Martenka, a girl in peasant costume, carrying the coffee cake of raised dough, snowy with sugar.

"A healthy little girl and a safe delivery!" the housekeeper congratulated the father.

"Thank you, Augusta," he said. "Let's hope Elizabeth grows up to marry a man who loves textiles."

"Oh, never fear. Husbands are a dime a dozen, only the good ones are scarce. Enjoy your meal, gentlemen."

Doctor Zoruba spread out his white linen napkin over his lap.

"Are you disappointed that the little one is not a boy?" he asked.

"I say so, but I don't mean it," Emile answered. "I'm happiest in the company of women. The family firm will just have to fend for itself."

He sipped his coffee through the whipped cream. The doctor ate a lot of cake, quickly.

"Hilda has a nice spirit to her, she will tell her husband to take over your firm if needed." Zoruba said. He took another piece of cake. "I have to say, your wife is a courageous woman.

"Can you believe that when I realized how easily I might lose Louise," Emile said, "I found myself praying to the strange God of my Jewish ancestors, whose language I don't even know?"

The doctor put his square hand over his host's.

"My dear Emile, to me, of course, you are neither Jew nor Gentile, just yourself. But don't you ever feel the spirit of your race, the longing for your far-off homeland?"

Emile shook his head.

"I think of my ancestors in Judea as fanatical shepherds worshiping a dour God. No, thank you, I am happy in Moravia with its woods and meadows and doctors."

"I'm not. What is our country under the Hapsburgs but a shadow of her former self?" Zoruba said.

"Still," Emile sighed, "the empire has its merits: food from Hungary, industry from Bohemia, waltzes and mismanagement from Austria. And while I'm not a religious Jew, the empire has been tolerant to my people."

"I must look at my patients again," the doctor said as he rose, reluctantly bringing to a close their never-ending dispute concerning nationalism versus empire, democracy versus stability. "But I predict that before this little girl grows to be a young woman, we will have thrown off the Hapsburg yoke."

After Zoruba left, Emile sat back and lit a cigar. He, too, wondered what the world would be like when Elizabeth grew up. There would be progress, of course — greater self-determination for the nationalities, higher wages and shorter hours for the workers. But he doubted that the Hapsburg Empire, which had lasted for five hundred years, could be dislodged by democratic nationalists like the doctor and his friends.

His thoughts turned to Elizabeth's future. He had thought of giving his son, if he had one, a technical education at the

University in Prague or in Vienna. He vaguely hoped that she might be interested in something of that kind, since her older sisters had shown no interest in straying beyond their restricted curriculum. But he wouldn't influence her. The sap in the fruit trees, he thought, comes from the quality of the soil, not from the gardener's pruning. He ground out his cigar and put on his hat to walk to town. The birth of the child must be entered into the municipal registry under a flurry of stamps contributing to His Majesty's revenue.

Chapter 3.
Village Feast (1885)

Five years after Elizabeth's birth, the reach of the Austro-Hungarian Empire was as wide as ever. To the north of Austria proper, beside industrious Bohemia and Moravia, where Elizabeth was growing up, the Dual Monarchy included the flat plains of Galicia and the wooded mountains of Transylvania. Towards the south, a stretch of Dalmatian coast gave the empire access to the Adriatic Sea. The storks heading for the Hungarian plains on their homewards migration from North Africa would travel over Austrian soil as soon as they crossed the Mediterranean.

Of course, it made little difference to the storks who ruled the territory over which they flew, any more than it did to the people working the land. Landlords and taxes did not change with ministries, not even with the passing and crowning of emperors and empresses who were mourned and celebrated at great public expense. The lives of the villagers were tied to the eternal rhythm of the seasons, the good and bad harvests and the unchanging traditions of peasant ways.

It was to the outskirts of the village of Kisbánya that a pair of storks headed in the spring of 1885. They flew in the high open sky of the Hungarian plain, over a monotonous landscape dotted by thatched roofs, church spires, and tall well-poles, sticking up into the sky like black fingers. The low whitewashed house where their ancestral nest overlooked the tiny garden and vineyard was today the scene of cheerful commotion — a feast to celebrate Anna's birth. The little girl's arrival, late in her mother's life, was a source of joy because she could help her parents as she grew older.

17

Two little boys, dressed since dawn in their Sunday best and itching with boredom, were the first to notice the outstretched white wings flapping over the roof.

"Mother! Father! The storks are back!"

Rozsa, the Nagys' teenaged daughter, looked up from braiding her hair at the huge birds flapping their winds as they landed.

"Here's good luck for the coming year!" Mike, her older brother, exclaimed as he brought water from the well.

István Nagy, their father, who had been shaving his chin and curling his long mustache as he leaned over the rim of the well, followed the birds' flight without comment. His wife Zsuzsanna, slightly stooped, clutching her triangular scarf over her shoulder, was about to walk to the summer kitchen, which was far enough from the house to prevent fires from burning it down. Two neighbor women were helping to cook for the feast.

"Holy Saints of all the Heavens, I've lost the wooden spoon that never touches onion," she exclaimed. "Have you seen it, István?"

"Don't fret, woman," her husband said. "There are as many spoons here as anyone needs."

"Where?"

"Why, in that tree. Hundreds of spoons. Or perhaps you might say in Master Andrew's whittling knife, which will carve the spoons from the tree. Or, you might say, in the Heavenly Mind which guides his hand...."

"It might be better not to say any of these things," Zsuzsanna said irritably, "when thirty-five neighbors will soon be here!"

"Mother! Anna's crying!" Rozsi's face reappeared at the window. Zsuzsanna went back as her husband resumed his shaving.

Twenty years of marriage had not taught her to laugh at his wit, nor him to stop his sallies. However, Zsuzsanna considered herself a lucky wife because her husband did not drink or beat her. As for István, his view was that as long as the woman did what was expected of her, she could be as morose as she chose. Actually, Zsuzsanna had reserves of gaiety, but they rarely surfaced. A close succession of childbirths and miscarriages, followed by return to hard work in the fields before she recovered, had aged her prematurely. Poor health made her gloomy and fretful much of the time. However, as she rocked the baby, she babbled to it and a smile came over her face. Just then, the first guests' cart rattled up to the house. Anna again burst into howls, and it was as a crying red-faced package that she was shown off to the arriving guests. Master Andrew, the village carpenter, congratulated her father.

"A fine girl child, already doing her God-given duty of crying and pissing."

Soon, peasant carts of all kinds stood around the house, their owners helping down a swarm of children. The neighbor women were setting long tables under the mulberry trees shading the house. The earthenware plates and mugs brought by each family for its food added a variety of painted designs matching the colorfulness of their clothes. The smell of roast spring lamb wafted over the tables.

When the guests settled down to eat and drink, no one intended to get up before nightfall. Anna's mother held the swaddled infant in her arms. The young girls of the neighborhood waited on her, a rare occasion for Zsuzsanna. The hum of conversation rose and fell. It concerned beasts bartered, deals made and unmade, and long disputes concerning the genealogy of every person and animal mentioned, dear to the hearts of members of a close-knit community. But attention was focused on the meal rather than on talk. The guests made their way through the gulyás soup with dumplings, then the stuffed cabbage with smoked bacon and sausage, then the roast lamb, and, for desert, hand-cut noodles covered with walnuts and sugar.

As the sun sank over the horizon, the black shadow of the well's cross pole lengthened over the ground. The guests unbuttoned their vests and sat back with a sense of well being and of relaxation that was unusual in their hard lives. Although the Nagys and their friends were peasant proprietors, better off than the landless farm workers, their plots were small, and each generation subdivided them further, boys and girls sharing alike.

The village gypsy put down the bone he had been gnawing and leaned his fiddle against his shoulder. Slowly, he started to play the old songs of the region, transmitted from mouth to ear over so many generations that the melancholy Asiatic harmonies never disturbed the hearers. Anna's father reached over for the sleeping infant. She woke up with a start to hear her father's deep voice sing to her the song sung to sweethearts.

> *There is only one little girl*
> *In the whole wide world,*
> *And that little girl*
> *Is my dear turtledove.*
> *The Good Lord*
> *Must have had me*
> *Dearly in his heart*
> *When he created you*
> *Just for me.*

Girls and boys winked to each other across the tables and took up the song.

> *The Good Lord*
> *Must have had me*
> *Dearly in his heart*
> *When he created you*
> *Just for me.*

Zsuzsanna didn't join the song. Weary and a little tipsy, she put her elbows on the table, her head between her hands, and fell asleep.

PART II ~ ANNA

"That is the way it is for the likes of us"

Chapter 4.
Saint Anthony's Fair (1889)

Anna's father lifted the little girl high into the air and held her over the rim of the cart.

"Now, where do we put this little package?"

The cart was very full. Over a bed of hay, Anna's parents had placed a crate of chickens and goslings as well as some suckling pigs squealing in their tight container. The animals would be sold at Saint Anthony's fair, in a distant town, instead of the nearby village where the bi-weekly market took place. Surrounded by heads of cabbage, Alex and Joey, Anna's brothers, sat on a pile of sheep skins which had been accumulating for the occasion. Her mother was bringing embroidered pillows that she had made during the winter months. Anna's father put her down again.

"No, there's no more room, but it's just as well. I don't want to sell her anyway. I'd just as soon keep her."

Anna's mouth turned downwards to cry.

"Stop your teasing, István," Anna's mother, Zsuzsanna, said. "Can't you see that the child is taking you seriously? You are to sit up front between us, Anna. And don't cry. I don't want to wash your face again."

She returned to the house for provisions for the trip, coughing as she went. The early summer morning regained its beauty for Anna while she climbed carefully onto the driver's bench with her father's help.

"You look as pretty as a picture on a painted chest, "István said.

Anna knew that she looked nice. She wore red boots and two

petticoats under her skirt and an embroidered vest. Of course, her big sister Rozsi had worn six petticoats at her wedding last fall, but she could not climb up the cart with them, and her bridegroom had to lift her up and everyone laughed a lot. And that must have been the end of the laughter because whenever Rosa came to visit afterwards, she mostly cried.

The family finally got installed and her father cracked his whip. The horse they borrowed for market days took off. In the woods, the birds started to sing and the boys clamored for food. As the children munched the rolls that had baked in the night's ashes, they enjoyed the jolting of the cart and the prospect of the fair.

"How I hate this fork in the road," Anna's father said. "No matter how often I steer the sheep to the right when I take them grazing, half the flock will always go to the left."

"Look, Anna!" her mother exclaimed "Flowers and candles!"

A small stucco statue of the Madonna in a light blue gown, surrounded by fresh garlands and lit candles, sat in a niche provided by an old oak's trunk.

"That tree was hit by lightning and that makes it sacred," István explained in a sarcastic tone.

"You must admit that the Catholic shrines are much prettier than ours," Zsuzsanna said.

"Pretty, pretty" he grumbled, "that's what their religion is. They put it on on holy days, like Sunday boots over unwashed feet."

"Hush. Faith is faith," she said.

"I know, my soul, it's not easy for a girl who grew up with embroidery on every pillow to put up with our plain Baptist chapel when everyone else goes to the golden baubles of the Catholic Mass," István teased her. "But that's the way it is for us Baptists and not otherwise."

"Why does Mommy want golden baubles?" Anna asked.

Her parents laughed.

"I just want some more color in our chapel," Zsuzsanna said.

"Your grandmother was a famous tracing woman," István explained. "She drew the designs on those pillows there, so your

mother is used to a lot of curlicues. But she had to leave the
curlicues to marry me, and she feels homesick sometimes."

"So do I, when the Catholics gang up on us," Alex said.

Anna didn't quite understand all this, but she felt that she was
her grandmother's granddaughter from the pleasure she got from
the Madonna's blue mantle and the flickering candles cradled by
the old tree.

The cart moved on and the sun was almost as high as the
church tower when they reached the fair. Anna held tight to her
mother's skirt in the noise, the crowd and the seemingly endless
row of stalls and carts. The fair was much bigger than the market
she knew, and many people wore embroidered costumes that gave
a Sunday air to the crowd.

Alex, who had unhitched the horse and led it to a watering
stall, returned.

"There is a shooting gallery, a penny-candy stall, an organ
grinder...." he said, excited.

"Yes, but you can't leave the cart until the animals are sold,"
their father said.

When he finally allowed the boys to leave, Anna still clung to
her mother's black apron. Zsuzsanna put five extra pennies into
Alex's hand.

"These are for Anna, buy her what she wants. And don't lose
her!"

The children wandered off. First they bought candy made of
potato sugar. It was chewy and slightly fatty, but it lasted a long
time in one's mouth. There was a lot to see without letting go of
their other pennies: the carved horses of the merry-go-round, the
photographer who could turn whole families into stone with their
long sittings. Anna's mouth fell open at the sight of the sword-
swallower, who also ate fire. She still had four pennies after the
boys had spent all of theirs, when she saw what she wanted. At
a big table, girls and women told an old man their names and he
wrote them on wooden spoons with colored paint mixed with
glue. Then he sprinkled bright glitter over the letters and around
the rim. Anna could see girls leaving, happily showing off their
spoons that were not for use, just for decoration, and she poked

her brother.

"Ask him if I can have one for four pennies, ask him. And tell him how to write my name."

Alex got in line while little Joey complained. The line moved very slowly. The old man joked with giggling girls while he painted the spoons. The boys soon tired of the wait.

"Listen, Anna," Alex said. "Let's come back when the line is shorter."

She agreed reluctantly as he put her pennies in his pocket. The current of the crowd carried them on. The row of stalls ended at a little square with a tavern. Here, few people wore embroidered vests and the children looked pinched and mean, as if they never held pennies in their fists. They would have left, except that they noticed a circle of people watching something. Anna and her brothers joined them, thinking there might be another show. Two drunken men were fighting, rolling in the dust and cursing. Suddenly, one of them got free, backed up, and opened a pocket knife that flashed in the sun. The crowd roared, but the other man was already charging in a drunken rage and the knife jabbed into him again and again. It happened so quickly that only the wails of the woman who threw herself on the dead man made people realize that the fight was over. The murderer disappeared and disputes broke out on how the fight had started. The children left, shaken.

"He fell like a scarecrow," Joey said.

"Did you see how big his pocket knife was?" Alex asked. They had come back to where the old man with the spoons stood and Anna tugged at her brothers. Alex reached into his pocket and exclaimed:

"The pennies! They're gone! Someone stole them!"

Bitterly weeping, Anna threw herself at her mother at the half-packed cart.

"What happened, my lamb? Boys, what happened?"

"A murder" Joey said. "It was exciting. You should have seen that man's knife — as big as this," and he opened his arms to show.

His father's hand landed on his cheek.

"The devil is never exciting," he said. "Is that why Anna's crying?"

The boys explained, and István slapped both boys hard. Anna continued to cry, more quietly now, because the pennies were gone and so was her hope for a glittering spoon. Her mother reached into her apron pocket.

"Look what I got for you, my little lamb."

She handed her a heart-shaped honey cake, richly painted in multi-colored sugar. It wasn't what Anna wanted but she felt a little better.

On the way back, the cart jolted her from one parent to another as her feet dangled from the high seat. She still grieved for the wooden spoon, but as she rocked to and fro in the golden afternoon dust she fell asleep, dreaming of the old oak tree hung with many colored spoons.

Chapter 5.
Zsuzsanna's Geranium (1895)

The pond was dry and the harvest poor in Anna's tenth year when her mother died. They buried her in the early morning in the Baptist cemetery. Afterwards, István and Anna's brothers set out for the fields. They had asked Anna to bring out the midday meal as soon as it was ready.

Anna walked over to the summer kitchen and stood disconsolately, her large hands hanging by her side, her cheeks still streaked with tears. She felt desperately alone. The everyday noises of the yard and the bright sunshine emphasized the abnormality of her being here without her mother. The sight of her mother's geranium, wilting from neglect during the weeks while Zsuzsanna had lain in bed coughing blood, brought to the girl's mind memories of her mother providing her with small joys through which both escaped from everyday's work. She remembered how one day when she was bored, her mother had stopped kneading bread and had gone out to pick a poppy flower to make a dancing doll by turning down the red petals and tying them with string. When they picked cherries together, she made earrings for her from double fruits and when she peeled cucumbers, she always placed a cool peel on the child's forehead. Anna's mother seldom spoke and even more seldom sang, but by these small gestures she established a special friendship between herself and her youngest.

Anna had not had time to make many friends among the village children. When she was five years old, her brothers had given her a long stick and put her in charge of herding their quarrelsome geese. Sometimes, other little gooseherds joined her to sling stones into the river while the geese fed, but woe to the one who lost a goose or gander while they played. A year or so later, Anna could weed and hoe the vegetable garden by herself. Anna was nine when she learned to build a fire in the fireplace where all the meals were cooked, and only six months ago she had baked her first rolls. And now she must cook every meal, except for the breakfast of cold bacon and onions!

The sound of the church bell startled her. If that noonday dinner is to be ready, she thought, she had better get to work. She remembered how her mother, coughing and clutching her fichu around her shoulders, had moved steadily from task to task. Although she had fretted about small things and did not smile, the fire was always going, the bread baked, and the men folk came in from their long workday to a cared-for house and garden. That was woman's lot and now it would be hers. She felt her mother's spirit supporting her as she watered the geranium.

After the first few days she discovered that she was not as alone as she thought. The neighbors watched, and when they saw that she had set herself to the task of providing for her father and brothers, small tokens of sympathy began to appear. Master Andrew's wife came by when she just happened to have more bean soup than her family could eat. As she put down the heavy iron pot, she approved the well-swept kitchen floor and the boots that Anna had set out to polish for Sunday. Another neighbor's daughter appeared the next day on her way to the river.

"Give me your washing, Anna, my basket is light today and I don't want to miss a chance to stay and gossip."

Anna needed such comfort because she got little encouragement from her own family. Her father, who had made fun of his wife's gloomy disposition while she lived, now cast a dark spell by his own silence. Her older sister had married long ago and lived on the other side of the river. Her brothers escaped to the tavern as soon as their tasks were completed. In the evening, her father picked up his Bible, and Anna mended in silence until the darkness forced both of them go to bed.

One day, when Anna went to wash clothes in the river, a conversation stopped on her arrival except for a remark that she caught.

"Nagy thinks differently about this than anyone else does."

She wondered why her father, so taciturn, would disagree with anyone, but no one said more. Later that day, she took her basket with potato stew and a wineskin of young wine to her men folk for their midday dinner. Her father and brothers were already seated under the tree that provided shade near the wheat field when she arrived. An old shepherd sat next to them, smoking his pipe.

"Sure they killed the girl, kidnapped her and killed her," the shepherd said.

"But why would they do such a thing?" István asked.

"Ritual murder," the shepherd said with great emphasis, "ritual murder. It makes my hair stand on end to think of it. They need the blood of Gentile children for their holy festivals."

"Where did you hear this news, Master Valerian?" Anna's father asked.

"My Paul took the wagon up to market in the city and he stopped to see his sister who is in service up there," he replied. "She has good information, she works for a county judge, my Margaret. She overheard talk of his issuing an order to drive out all this vile Jewry from the province."

"But even if those Jews down in Tiszaeszlár committed this terrible crime, what does it have to do with old Samuel, who comes through the village selling old clothes?" Anna's father asked. "He didn't kill anyone, I'm sure."

"They're sucking the blood of true Hungarians, neighbor," Valerian insisted. "Did you hear that half of Count Almássy's estate was sold to a Jew because he couldn't pay the debt a Jew wanted repaid?"

Anna's older brother Alex spat on the ground to show that he was old enough to talk as a man to men.

"He doesn't pay his day laborers, how could he pay his debts?" he said. "I've heard it said that the count has never been seen sober in the memory of the village."

"Listen boy," the shepherd replied angrily, "God put the Hungarian nobleman on earth to drink the good wine and keep the gypsies fiddling. Who are you to ask a lot of questions?"

"And if God put the Jews on the earth to be usurers, why is that for us to question?" Anna's father interposed.

The shepherd got up.

"I don't know what your God says, neighbor, but the true Hungarians are getting mighty tired of the foreign parasites."

With that he whistled his dog and walked off. The boys ate quickly and went to sleep under their hats. Joey snored, his mouth open. István ate slowly, stopping to take long draughts from the wineskin. Anna felt fear at the thought of staying alone in the house all day now that she suddenly saw her Catholic neighbors as different and hostile to her as a Baptist. Her father looked up to see her shifting from foot to foot.

"Are you still here, little girl? You don't have to wait for the basket, we'll bring it home."

"Father," she said timidly, "Would you teach me how to read so that I can have God's word by me when I am alone?"

He looked at her thoughtfully.

"I don't know about that. Most husbands don't welcome that sort of dowry. If you want to learn, you should be learning household skills, and now that your poor mother isn't here to teach you...."

"I could go to town as a maidservant, like Margaret," Anna said.

"Not until those louts over there marry, so I can have a woman to look after the house," her father said.

Anna continued to stand in front of him.

"All right," he said. "I'll teach you what I can and when my old eyes fail, you can read the Bible to me."

She went home comforted by his newfound concern for her. In the evenings, as she sat on the bench outside the door while her father explained the parables to her, and the smell of the acacia flowers wafted through the air, she started to feel again the sweetness of the present hour. But maybe she would go to a city or town some day. She would get a maid's book, like the one Margaret had, with her name printed on it and the official stamps and seals of the county clerk on the front page. Then her service contract had to be written in the book, not just talked over by two housewives on their stoop. She felt that her roots in the village had been loosened by her mother's loss and the realization of loneliness.

Chapter 6.
Easter Sunday (1901)

The early spring had only changed the color of the sky when Anna set out to work on her father's potato patch. The potatoes grew where the hill started to rise, away from the flat land of the village.

The girl, walking in the early morning, saw that the new buds on the trees were still protected by brown casings, and that the dirt was gray and hard. Only the song of birds in the sharp air gave promise that winter would soon be over.

Anna was sixteen. Under her wool shawl, a black dress and apron set off her strong, well-developed figure. After her mother's death six years ago, she had become so accustomed to dark clothes that when her mourning dress wore out, she didn't replace it with a more cheerful color. Her pastor from the Baptist chapel, who was proud of the serious, devout girl, encouraged her sober taste.

When Anna left the house that morning, it was with annoyance at her brothers for saddling her with the care of the potatoes. The family owned an acre of wheat in the fertile area surrounding the village, and that marketable crop was all that the boys cared about. As for her father, he loved only his flock. Since his wife's death, whenever he could, he took off for the long days with his sheep, his pipe, and his Bible. But as Anna walked briskly towards the hills, her annoyance at the menfolk in her family gradually melted away and she forgot the clothes soaking in the tub and the other chores waiting for her at home. She thought with gratitude of the small potato field, all scarred now from dug-up tubers, which had fed them faithfully through the bitter cold.

When she reached the field, a young man turned around on the plot next to hers and put down his hoe. He was short and squat, with red cheeks and a friendly, open expression.

"Well!" he exclaimed. "Look at what the spring wind brought this morning!"

"Good morning," Anna said curtly.

He bent down, picked up a piece of stubble and chewed the end of it while he examined her.

"Don't tell me that you've come all this way and that's the only greeting you'll give me!"

"I didn't come to give you greetings, long or short," Anna said.

She tightened her grip on her hoe, thinking how far they were from anyone, and of the girls who had been tumbled on such fields, willing or unwilling, with a baby to show for it. But the man shrugged his shoulders and picked up his tool.

"If that's the way you feel about it, my beauty, that's the way it will be."

He went back to work, whistling a song.

Anna hacked at the dirt clods all morning and her neighbor kept whistling. He was pleased with his skill, occasionally repeating a trill to improve it. She had to leave before noon to fix lunch. When she looked back, she noticed that he turned his head for a moment, but neither of them said goodbye.

"Who is working the field next to ours?" Anna asked as she ladled out the midday soup.

"That must be the Joska of the Vas family," replied her brother Alex. "I heard that Tamás is getting too old and has agreed to share the crop with that family of church-mice, who don't own a thing in the world beside their bare hands."

"Did anyone bother you?" asked her father.

"Who'd ever bother Anna?" asked Joey. "She's about as welcoming as the locked gate to the newborn calf."

"Leave Anna alone," István said. "If she doesn't spend her time with the young people lazing around the bowling game every Sunday, as you do, it's no loss."

Anna felt guilty because she had, in fact, wondered what Joska Vas would look like with a bowling ball in his hand and a song on his lips.

She continued to work the potato field all through the week, and on most days he worked next to her. He was very strong and broke up the dirt faster than she did, but when it came to planting, she caught up with him because she worked steadily, without taking breaks. He appraised her work with his eyes but did not say anything. She would have liked to break the silence, but the kind of suggestive talk that he had started was distasteful to her, and it was the only kind that boys and girls in the village exchanged.

One day, after gently warming their backs all week, the sun shone bright and strong. Work became more enervating in the premature heat. Joska stopped whistling. Their awareness of each other became almost unbearable. As Anna planted the tubers at the end of the field, she bumped into Joska. He seized her and threw her to the ground. They struggled. Anna managed to grab his arms and to hold him away, a few inches from her chest. For a short time, their eyes held each other. She was aware of the blue sky above and of his warm breath. He released his hold and she wrenched herself free. Anna stumbled up and ran almost all the way home. That evening, she told her brothers that if they didn't finish planting the potatoes, they might starve next winter for all she cared. They glanced at each other, but her tone discouraged their questions.

As she tended the endless variety of tasks that the awakening earth brought with it, she gradually regained her composure. From time to time, she could still feel the warmth of Joska's breast beating against hers and her relief in the moment when he let her go.

Anna had never really considered the question of how or to whom she would be married. If her mother were alive, she and the older women would have been arranging a match for her for the past year or so. As it was, Anna assumed that God would provide. But somehow, she didn't think that what He had in mind for her was a man from a family that was large, poor, and Catholic.

On Easter Sunday, Anna put an embroidered apron over her black dress and tied her braid with a ribbon.

"Well, well," her older brother Alex exclaimed. "Whose heart are we trying to break?"

Anna shrugged. When they came out of the chapel after the Easter morning services, Martha, the girl Alex was courting, put her arm around Anna's waist.

"Come and join us, Anna, the games aren't fair unless everyone's there."

Tradition, on that day, sanctified the flirtations that went on all year. The boys squirted the girls they liked with cheap perfume or water. They also squirted the girls they didn't like, and there was a great deal of squealing and mock anger and threats of taking off wet clothes, threats that never materialized. When Anna and her family reached the square, the organized games started, with the winner choosing a kiss as a reward.

Anna saw that Joska was surrounded by girls pinning flowers on his hat. They cheered him on during the bowling game, but he didn't win. He joked, whistled, and overshot his mark. He did better at the horseshoe toss, but he lost to Alex. Anna was pleased to see little Martha reach up to kiss her brother.

The baker's wife, carrying a large steaming pot, interrupted the games.

"How about the dumpling-eating contest? These are the first fresh curd dumplings of the year."

Lots were drawn for the contestants, and they pulled up chairs to the table where the dumplings waited. Joska was among those chosen. He unbuttoned his vest, leaned back in his chair, and started. Methodically, he ate dumpling after dumpling, without speaking or drinking, to save his breath. At the thirtieth dumpling, only two other contestants were still at the table. One of them got up at the forty-second to wash down the food with white wine. Joska sighed, picked up another dumpling, and shook his finger straight at Anna as if to say, "Look at what I'm willing to go through for you."

She looked at Joska, with his sleeves rolled up and his cheeks puffed out, and she realized that he would bring sunshine and gaiety into her life. She smiled back at him, a happy, sparkling smile. When Joska won, girls clamored to kiss him, but he just pushed back his chair.

"I've already had my reward" he said.

Anna went home with joy in her heart.

Throughout the summer, they met often, at the well, on the road, and once they danced together on a feast day. They did not talk much because he was laconic, although he expressed himself well when he chose to. She became more and more sure that under his male bluster he had a warm, steady heart.

The village girls teased her about this slow courtship.

"He's so smitten with you, Anna, that he'll never propose!" Martha said. "Falling in love is supposed to be for us womenfolk only — you'd better help the poor man out of his embarrassment."

So the next time they met, she said, "You know, you really frightened me last spring."

He scratched his head under his hat.

"I didn't want to frighten you, Anna," he said. "Do I still?"

She smiled and shook her head.

"No — hardly at all."

A few days later, as Anna's family sat down to supper, Joska knocked on the kitchen door.

"May I have a word with Anna?" he asked István.

"Make it short," the father replied as his sons stirred uneasily.

Anna and Joska walked to the end of the beaten path that ran along the house. The evening was still light and the chickens were noisily disputing over their supper.

"Anna," said Joska "I know that you're a serious girl, not like the others, and that's what I like about you. But I have to serve in the army for three years before we can marry. Will you wait for me?"

"Of course," she said. "Oh, Joska!"

She looked around and leaned over to kiss him. He held her tight, and again she felt his warm breath, and his strong chest against her, and it seemed right. When they walked back to the house, the long wait before they could marry seemed as unimportant as the squabbling of the chicks.

The following week, Alex and Martha became engaged, and Anna reminded her father that long ago he had promised that she could go into service in Budapest upon her brother's marriage. In this way, she could be nearer to Joska's barracks and earn money for her dowry. Through a neighbor who had worked in Budapest, she got the name of an employment agency, which placed her as a maid in the household of Frederic and Elizabeth Ignatius.

PART III ~ ELIZABETH

"They don't let me lead a life of action"

Chapter 7.
Under the Eaves (1886)

It was terribly difficult to get up in the winter. Clara and Hilda were already up while Elizabeth crept deeper into the warmth of the eiderdown comforter.

"Lisa! you're going to be late to lessons and it will be the third time this week!" Hilda reminded her. "Oww! this water is cold."

She poured it from a porcelain pitcher into a basin and splashed her face. Clara was struggling with her long ribbed stockings. Elizabeth considered putting her thumb into her mouth, but then she remembered that she was nearly six and a half.

The girls shared a large dormer under the eaves. In the green summer of this Moravian mountain town, it had the feeling of being up in the trees, and the birds built nests right under the central window. But in the winter the floorboards were cold, and their clothes emerged chilled from the wardrobe. No fire was lit in the wood-burning stove unless one of them was ill.

The children's governess came in, a tall woman with a straight mouth permanently set in the expression she wore when she held pins in it. Seeing Elizabeth huddled under her comforter, she ripped off the child's bedclothes.

"Up, lazy girl! This bad habit must be broken," she said sharply. She spoke German, the language of educated households in the Austro-Hungarian Empire.

Elizabeth sat up, with her feet dangling, refusing to look at Fräulein Elsa, who was bringing clothes from the wardrobe.

"Put on your merino dress, we are going to the dentist this

morning, and you will have your lessons after lunch."

"But this afternoon I was going ice skating!"

"Well, you found your voice after all! You could say good morning then."

Elizabeth frowned.

"Hurry and get dressed, child."

The girl threw the dress on the floor.

"I will not have lessons instead of skating. My tutor is ugly and dimwitted and so are you!"

Clara and Hilda gasped.

"Very well, child. If that is how you behave, you will stay here alone all day where you can't insult anyone. Come, Clara, Hilda, I'll comb your hair in my room."

On her way out she swept Elizabeth's comforter under her arm. Left alone, the girl huddled on her bed, wavering between indignation and tears. She got her large porcelain doll and hugged her.

"You see, Emmy, for you it's easy to be good because you don't have to do all sorts of things, like buttoning all these buttons and having the maids tug at my hair and being polite and never being allowed to do what I really want. If I could get into the kitchen and help Augusta or embroider with Mamma or hang around the factory, I'd be dressed! But after all those buttons, what do I do? Sit in the day nursery trying to make letter after letter with a scratchy pen!"

Those eternal lessons were the bane of her existence. She was a bright child and usually grasped quickly what her tutor taught her. However, that didn't help. He simply asked her to repeat the lines she had written another fifty times.

"Penmanship, I wish to remind you, Elizabeth, is no less important than grammar, spelling, nay, meaning itself!"

In this way, he stretched out the lesson until lunch time and the more Elizabeth fidgeted, the more he emphasized the need to sit straight and tall. If there was one thing, he told her that was more important than penmanship, it was to eradicate willfulness from children.

Now the girl was beginning to shiver.

She dressed the doll first, hoping to catch a cold herself, but then she dressed, too. She could hear a maid open the dining room window under her. That meant that breakfast was over. She thought of her father neatly slicing off the top of his egg without offering it to her, as he did every day. Self-pity overwhelmed her and she burst into tears.

She cried for a long time. Then the door opened and her mother looked in, sad and serious.

"Elizabeth! Will you apologize to Fräulein and be a good girl again?"

Elizabeth shook her head. Her mother left quietly.

She looked out of the window for a while. There were carriages and carts going up the road. The horses' breath rose in warm clouds from their mouths. The coachmen were so bundled up, you could hardly see them. When she got tired of watching, she played with Clara's toys, the ones she was not allowed to touch. It would have been fun if only she hadn't been so hungry.

At noon, the door creaked open. Clara reached in, put a buttered roll down, and withdrew. It was wonderful to eat, but her sister's kindness made her feel guilty, and she put away Clara's toys with buttery fingers.

After that, time did not move at all. She tried a loud, screaming temper tantrum, which exhausted her and brought no one. When the afternoon coffee noises downstairs had quieted down, she was sitting by the window watching nothing at all, when she heard firm steps on the stairs. Papa! He opened the door and she threw herself into his arms.

After she had cried herself out, he took her hand.

"Why? why is my good, bright, pretty girl rude to people?" he asked.

"Because...because they don't let me — lead a life of action!"

She saw him suppress a smile.

"And what does my little girl want to do?" he asked.

"Bake. Ice skate. Lots of things — ordering people around, like Augusta does. Rearranging all the furniture."

"I see. And what is this about calling your tutor dimwitted?"

"He is, Papa. I mean I'm smarter than he is. And if he tells me one more time about the little archduke he used to teach, who never made ink blotches when he wrote his exercises, I'm going to scream. I hate that little archduke!"

Her father smiled broadly now.

"I know, Hilda and Clara also heard about the archduke, who seems to get more perfect every year. But I don't really think that you are smarter than your tutor, even though you are very smart. There's still a lot you can learn from him, isn't there?"

"I guess there is," she said as she twisted a curl of hair. "I haven't finished the multiplication tables."

"Different people are just smart in different ways," he said thoughtfully. "If you want to lead a life of action, your actions affect other people. So it is especially important to learn to be good and kind. Otherwise, you'll just be bossy. Like Napoleon. You see?"

She nodded.

"Now, I can't make you into a young general, and you still have to have lessons. But if you will concentrate on being good and kind all winter, I'll help you to know the world — not in books, in real life."

She looked up expectantly.

"If you keep to our bargain, next spring I'll take you with me when I go to Vienna for business. But everywhere we go, there are other people, lots of them, and you mustn't set yourself above them. And now, wash your face, play quietly, and when we call you for supper, come down and apologize."

She washed her face, hardly feeling her hunger. She wanted to be good and kind and gentle forever. But she also felt a little triumphant. Being willful had its points — neither Clara nor Hilda had ever gone on a business trip with Papa.

Chapter 8.
Longing and Panic (1890)

Elizabeth's trip to Vienna and Budapest alone with her father became a celebrated event in her family, but she missed her mother too much to want to go again.

Each day, after breakfast at their hotel, Emile would take the little girl with him to visit textile manufacturers and traders who sent fabrics to his factory in Moravia to be dyed. Elizabeth sat quietly in her velvet coat and hat, her gloved hands folded in her lap, while the men talked, fingered fabrics, and wrote down numbers in heavy notebooks. Most of the time she was bored, although she didn't complain.

She enjoyed looking at the books of fabric swatches that assistants flung on the tables, but she didn't dare to handle them. On one of the visits, the owner of a thread manufacture handed her a sample book of colored threads. The heavy cardboard with curlicued printing on the cover opened up like a menu into three sections. On each of them, thin stripes of shiny thread succeeded each other from top to bottom in subtle gradations of color that enchanted her — a dark blue, a slightly lighter blue, then one even lighter, until the thread had no more color than a pale spring sky. How could there be so many blues and reds and yellows! She bent over the sampler, following each line with her fingers, while her father and his friend talked business. When they finished, she reluctantly put the sampler on the table and got up to shake hands, as she had been taught.

"Keep it, my dear, it's for you," the owner said. Elizabeth was almost too thrilled to thank him.

Her father smiled as Elizabeth hugged her treasure to her chest.

"Maybe you'll want to work with fabrics or threads when you grow up?" he suggested.

"I want to paint colors, Papa," she said.

After dinner at their hotel dining room, where Elizabeth ate with her feet dangling from her chair, her father would ask the chambermaid to help Elizabeth get undressed. The maid was a hefty Viennese girl, who spoke a German dialect that Elizabeth had trouble understanding. She helped Elizabeth bathe and hung up her clothes quickly, anxious to get back to her work.

"So you'll say your prayers, ja?" she asked as she left.

Although Elizabeth knew that her family was Jewish, there were no prayers said in her home.

"Don't worry about that," her father said. "The people here are Catholics, they talk to their God before they go to sleep."

Then Emile would comb his mustache and put some cologne on his handkerchief before kissing her good night. He told her that he was going to the opera with friends or to the theater, and she tried hard to stay up waiting for him. But after a lonely time listening to the street and hotel noises, she would fall asleep, thinking that her mother had a much better way of soothing her to rest.

On the trip back, Elizabeth asked her father whether they had really been abroad. All of the people they met spoke German, some spoke Hungarian as well, but only a few spoke Czech.

"Yes and no," he said. "Hungary, Austria, and Bohemia, where we went to take the train, are different countries, but they all belong to the Austro-Hungarian Empire. So almost everyone speaks German, but they also speak their own language."

"Should my tutor teach me Hungarian?" Elizabeth asked.

"I'm not sure," he said. "But French would be useful if you enjoy traveling."

Within a year, Elizabeth acquired a new teacher, a Frenchwoman called Madame Theriot, whom she liked much better than the tutor who kept praising the little archduke's penmanship. Madame was thin, dark, and severe, but she took Elizabeth seriously and allowed her to read many of the books in her father's library except for some French novels considered unsuitable for children.

As she grew older, Elizabeth felt closer to robust Hilda, her oldest sister, than to timid Clara. It was Hilda who dragged her little sister on long rambles through woods and fields as soon as her hated homework and higgedly-piggedly stitching were finished. Clara was unwilling to climb over fences, cross streams by hopping from rock to rock, and get her clothes dirty. She stayed home or sat by her mother, who would take her shopping or let her help on complicated embroidery projects. Although Elizabeth had no patience for such delicate work, she grew jealous of her mother's attention to Clara.

One morning when she was eleven, Elizabeth looked out of the classroom and saw Clara in the yard, staring into a large vat of blue dye that had been set out by the factory workers to cool. It was a clear spring day and the shiny blue dye reflected the sky and clouds. Elizabeth saw Clara bend over and dip a finger into the liquid. Seeing her sister on tiptoe, her bottom up and her skirts in the air, was irresistible to Elizabeth's mischievous impulse. She crept up quietly and, with superhuman strength, grabbed Clara's waist, then lifted her and shoved her into the dye.

"Oww!" Clara shouted as she fell.

At once, Elizabeth was horrified by what she had done. The dye in the vat was shallow enough for Clara to turn and pull herself up, but she emerged coughing and spluttering, bright blue from head to waist. The workmen hearing the splash came running and lifted Clara out of the vat. Their exclamations brought her mother and Madame Theriot running into the yard.

"My two socks aren't even the same shade of blue!" Clara cried as she opened her blue eyelashes.

Elizabeth threw her arms around Clara and got blue all over her own dress and apron.

"Did you fall?" Louise asked Clara, as she pulled off her clothes.

"No, Mamma, I pushed her," Elizabeth said. "I thought it would be funny. I'm terribly sorry."

"Child, child," her mother said, at a loss for words.

"I think that she should scrub Clara's clothes and hers too, Madame, until the dye comes out," Madame Theriot said sternly. "If the vat had been warmer, Clara could have been badly hurt."

Elizabeth scrubbed and scrubbed, but the clothes were ruined. When Clara offered to help her, Elizabeth began to appreciate her middle sister's kind heart and forgiving nature. But as a further punishment, her parents decided that Elizabeth would stay home that summer instead of going to the seaside with her mother and sisters.

At eleven, Elizabeth was expected to start reading the classics. It was extraordinary, she thought, that the grown-ups, who had a fit if a child peeked at a so-called sexy book like "Nana," would let her read inflammatory works like plays by Schiller and Shakespeare, poetry by Goethe and Heine, and historical novels such as those of Sir Walter Scott. While there were no "mistresses" or "stock brokers" in those books ("sin" for Elizabeth always involved such people), the love stories portrayed were vivid and powerful. Her own response to the characters' emotions was intoxicating. Lying in the tall August grass, she experienced all the noble self-denials, the intense yearnings, and the inner conflicts of the characters. Still, it was lonely to be just with Papa and the servants, and she thrilled to hear the wheels of the carriage bringing the vacationers home.

"Mamma! Hilda!"

How wonderful it was to throw herself into her mother's soft embrace! Louise was all pink from her month at the seaside. It was only after admiring her mother's new hat and parasol that Elizabeth noticed the change in her oldest sister. Hilda looked as nearly fashionable as her large athletic frame allowed.

"It was the most wonderful vacation anyone ever had in the history of the world!" Hilda exclaimed.

Elizabeth's father, still holding the carriage door, exchanged a meaningful glance with his wife, who said that it was lovely, but that she had missed the rest of the family too much to agree.

"Clara? What has happened to Hilda?" Elizabeth asked, when the girls brushed their hair in the room they no longer shared with their oldest sister.

"She's fallen in love," said the fifteen-year-old, inspecting her nails. "That's what happens when you are old enough. Then you get married and you have lots of children and silverware."

Clara seemed awfully cool about this, but Elizabeth was embarrassed by Hilda's transports. It was difficult to study with Hilda interrupting to read poems that Hugo had sent or slamming doors because he had not written for a day.

But when Hugo came to visit in September, Elizabeth's childish cynicism gave way to enthusiasm. He was a slight, oval-faced young man with almond-shaped eyes. His clothes were kept in artistic disorder by his personal manservant, who created a sensation in the kitchen with his stories of serving in noble and city households.

The servants in the Schwalb household were wives and daughters of the factory workers, and they went home to their own houses at night. Only Augusta, who came from the Tatra mountains, stayed in the house, and none of the girls would dream of asking her to do anything personal. Hugo's manservant seemed chummy with his master but never lifted a finger unless it was for him. The girls were impressed.

For two weeks, the household was topsy-turvy. Louise and Emile arranged excursions for the girls, Hugo, and for their friends, and gave a dinner party, after which they rolled up the rugs and everyone danced to the tune of piano waltzes long past Elizabeth's bedtime.

During the day, since the young couple was on no account ever to be left alone, Elizabeth was excused from studying to chaperone them on their walks. The lovers' conversation was kind of dull ("Do you love elderberries?" "How wonderful — I've always loved elderberries"…), but she felt the electricity of passionate words or caresses they would have liked to exchange if she hadn't been there.

One night a string trio serenading Hilda at Hugo's request woke Elizabeth. Softly she opened her window, knowing that her sister was standing on the balcony of her unlit room. The intense melody of an early Beethoven trio floated up in the cool autumn night. Then Hilda threw some flowers to thank the players. Their cousin, the violinist, ducked.

"You're supposed to shake the water off the stems first!" he cried.

The last evening of his stay, Hugo, who had explained to the girls' father that he was an aesthete and lived for beauty alone, asked permission to play a Liszt piano étude by candlelight. As the room filled with passionate chords, Elizabeth, curled up in an armchair, felt an intensity of longing for the future that would bring romantic feelings and their fulfillment to her.

When the piece was finished, Clara made a move to turn on the gaslight, but Hugo raised his hand to indicate that she shouldn't disturb the magic of the moment.

The next morning came gray and rainy as Hugo claimed his carriage and left with his manservant. Elizabeth felt almost as despondent as her sister as she stared at the books she had neglected for two weeks. There had been an excitement in the air that had made her feel intensely alive. So this was love! Music and moonlight and a kind of clutching at the stomach every time the beloved's slightly nasal voice was heard! Elizabeth was too loyal to her sister to fall in love with Hugo, but she continued to dream of Ivanhoe, who she hoped would appear someday just as Hugo had.

Ivanhoe did not appear, but Uncle Ignacz did. He was the round older brother of their mother who had been asked by Emile to make appropriate inquiries concerning Hugo's connections. When he came to make his report, his nieces did not welcome the marzipan candies he brought with their usual enthusiasm. They were very tense. Uncle Ignacz sighed, popped a marzipan fruit in his mouth and followed his brother-in-law into his study.

The two men were closeted for a long time. Augusta went in and out with trays of coffee, liqueurs, and mineral water. Finally, the verdict made its way from the study to the kitchen to the stable, where Elizabeth overheard the terrible words "debts" and "fortune hunter." Then she waited while Hilda and her mother went into the study and half an hour later, she saw Hilda running from the house, her hands over her face to cover her tears.

When dusk fell without Hilda reappearing, Elizabeth wandered down to the quiet pond at the bottom of the garden where she could think undisturbed. She was indignant at her parents' cruelty in interfering with the course of true love. But, much as she grieved for her beloved sister, her true distress was at some obscure threat she felt to her own new-found emotions. She felt that the real world, in which Hilda and Hugo and her parents moved, was still separated from her by a transparent curtain, like the surface of the pond in which the reflections of the trees could be clearly perceived but not grasped. She had begun to feel the longings that belonged to adults, but their realization could only come in the future. Hilda's experience made her fear that they could never be fulfilled except in dreams. She was filled with impatience for adulthood and panic at the prospect. But out of the depth of her nature came an impulse to make a promise to herself.

"When I am older, I will disguise myself as a man, like Rosalind in 'As You Like It,' and I will go out into the world to choose my own husband. And I won't let my family interfere."

CHAPTER 9.
The Art Student (1898)

"Miss Schwalb, are you paying any attention to this class today?"

Elizabeth, startled, looked up at Thorleif Uwaldsen, who taught her life drawing class at the Vienna Art Academy. She threw an anxious glance at the tall, square-faced man with red hair. The students feared the moody, critical Norwegian. But he was smiling at her and she decided to be honest.

"I'm so sorry, Professor Uwaldsen," Elizabeth said. "I know it's awful of me, but I am bored to death with drawing William Tell and his son from the front, back, and sides. Will you give us a new subject soon?"

He corrected a few strokes of the skillful drawings that covered her easel.

"Hmm. You would be a more interesting subject, with your ivory smock, shiny auburn hair, and gray eyes, under the gray-white light," he said, still looking at her easel. "Of course, I would do you in oils, in a very different style."

Was he suggesting that she should sit for her portrait?

"I've never seen your work" she said timidly.

"You haven't been to the Secession Exhibit?" Uwaldsen asked. "I have a few works in it. But don't talk about them here, they're not in the Academic manner," he said, his tone showing contempt for the naturalistic style he was teaching. "Oh well, it makes no difference, sooner or later I'll get fired anyway."

His face grew dark.

"In the meanwhile, please remember that we are here for a

serious purpose," he said and walked away.

Elizabeth was confused. First he encouraged her, then he reproached her. She didn't need to be reminded to be serious about art. She was very proud to be an art student, and although she worked quickly, she paid close attention to her work. Then his suggestion that he might paint her made her blush. He really was very attractive when he smiled.

After her classes, Elizabeth called up Clara on the newly installed office telephone to tell her not to expect her for lunch. Poor Clara! Since the time Elizabeth went to stay with her as a student, she often wondered how her sister could bear the punctuality and stuffiness of her married life. Her husband, Adalbert, a prosperous Viennese attorney, had his secretary call home when he left his office so that the elevator could be sent down and the soup steaming on the table when he arrived. Elizabeth was distressed to hear the little lies and subterfuges to which Clara resorted to protect her children and servants from his ever-impending wrath if the household departed from its clockwork regularity. Now, as she walked to the Secession Exhibit, which was anathema to the proper Viennese middle class, Elizabeth was pleased to think how upset her brother-in-law would be if he knew how she used her freedom to come and go during the day.

Being an art student in Vienna could be a respectable occupation. The academy taught painters to complete large and pleasing landscapes, portraits, or historical scenes, which wealthy patrons would buy for their homes. But many of Elizabeth's fellow students rebelled against becoming fashionable painters. They wanted to wake up Vienna to the plight of the poor, to the passionate feelings that were suppressed in middle-class families. They proclaimed boldly that the nineteenth century was not only ending but falling apart to make way for a new and better world.

Elizabeth had listened to her friends without quite understanding what the fuss was all about. But when she went to the Secession Exhibit, she was shocked. Morbid, erotic images on every wall crowded into her mind, paintings of naked women with snake-like hair and expiring lips. Elizabeth's whole view of reality was shaken by these intimations of lust and agony. She shuddered — did Uwaldsen see her as he saw the women he painted, naked, with her hair undone? The thought was frightening and fascinating.

At the next class, Uwaldsen walked over to her.

"Well?" he asked gruffly. "Did you find it revolting? Inartistic?"

"Not exactly," she replied. "But I would be grateful if you would explain to me what you were doing."

He jumped at the opportunity and the following Sunday, he escorted her around the exhibit.

"Every line, every stroke is designed to heighten the expression of the feeling I want to convey until the viewer can share my anguish as his own," he said. "Art isn't about beauty. It's about feelings, despair, loneliness."

She started to understand how his designs and colors were meant, in ways that were new and powerful, to evoke realities such as death and physical passion. Still, the erotic vibrations coming from the paintings disturbed her. Even a quiet painting of a young woman at night by the water talked to her of longing and desire.

Uwaldsen took her to a cafe for sausages and beer. She smiled at him under her broad-brimmed hat. Sitting in the dark cafe with Uwaldsen, Elizabeth felt wonderfully bohemian. Finally, I'm really an art student, she thought.

"So what do you know about life, about love?" he asked.

"I've read about love," she said. "And I could feel the passion in Goethe's 'The Sorrows of Young Werther.' I cried and cried when he died."

"But it's all very noble and exalting, isn't it?" Uwaldsen said. "And they exchange a kiss, at most. In real life, people get hopelessly and desperately drawn to each other, and the result is terrible."

"Tell me about real life," she said, leaning back.

"I was born in a little town in the north of Norway, where it's dark and cold most of the time. And people's emotions are frozen too," he said. "My father is a clergyman, very obsessed with sin and redemption, so I got very interested in sin. I went to Oslo and discovered a whole world of people who thought differently, like our great playwright Ibsen, who unmasks the hypocrisy of bourgeois life. And I discovered my own talent."

"That doesn't sound sinful," Elizabeth said.

"No, but I drank a lot and still do. And I married a woman of the streets to redeem her, but I wasn't a good husband to her. I'm too moody. So we separated, and when I can, I send her some money. But I don't feel good about that."

He explained that so long as there was so much injustice and repression in society, passions between men and women were destructive, and that loneliness was the fate of everyone who recognized their feelings honestly.

"I wish I could save you from your despair," she said.

"You would be wasting your time," he said. "Anyway, I should take you home soon, your family will be worried."

Again, he was allowing her to draw near him and pushing her away. But she started to wonder whether she shouldn't be more critical of society's prevailing views, even of her own family. Maybe she was so bored with drawing William Tell because she wasn't exploring the great truths in life. The writers she admired had all shocked their contemporaries by their boldness.

Although Elizabeth enjoyed her student friends, she didn't share their bohemian way of life. Most of them were poor, far from their homes, and in revolt against their class. Living at Clara's, the condition her parents had imposed on her desire to study in Vienna, Elizabeth continued to lead the life of a young girl from a "good family." It was only when a friend of her brother-in-law's proposed to her that she became frightened at the thought of a lifetime of convention.

Elizabeth had met Professor Himmelweiss, who seemed very old — at least forty — at her sister's parties, and she discussed books and music with him. But it never occurred to her that he might be interested in her until one morning Clara said that he wanted to ask her hand in marriage.

"He can't be serious," Elizabeth said, her shoulders shaking with laughter. "He's twice my age!"

"Professor Himmelweiss is a great man," Clara said. "He has

written many books and people admire him."

"But such a very tiny great man!" Elizabeth said. "Can you imagine waltzing with an admirer who would grab you firmly around the ankles? And honestly, Clara, I think that if he got mad at me, he would bite me in the calf, like your dog Putzi."

"Nonsense," Clara said. "Putzi is an angel. He would never do such a thing."

Now both sisters were laughing.

"But don't you think it would be glorious to be a Frau Professor and leave your calling card everywhere and trail an adoring husband to the opera?" Clara asked.

Elizabeth leaned her chin on her knuckles.

"You make him sound like a ball on a chain."

She put her hand over her sister's.

"Are you happy being married, Clara?"

"Of course I am," she replied. "I love the job of running a household, and Adalbert is a very good man. At first, I was afraid of him because he seemed so gruff, but his bark is much worse than his bite. Oh no, here we go again with the dogs!"

When their laughter died down, Elizabeth grew thoughtful at the prospect of having to settle down. Even if she didn't accept this proposal, she would have others, and none of them would be from anyone like Uwaldsen.

"Seriously, Clara, you must tell Professor Himmelweis that I'm not ready to be married. I'm not even sure I want to get married at all."

"Is this one of your art student ideas?" Clara asked. "Never mind, I'll do what you want, Lisa, but you must write to our parents about this. I'm responsible for you, and I don't want them to think that I was at fault for standing in the way of a suitable match."

Elizabeth promised to write. She felt guilty because she had never told Clara about the time she spent with Uwaldsen. Also, she had stopped going to most of her classes at the academy, except for two — his and a sculpture class given by Katerina Talieff, a stout, maternal Russian woman.

At Katerina's studio, Elizabeth had discovered the joy of

working in clay. She admired her teacher's work, which portrayed homely models in classical poses, bringing out the beauty of everyday life without sentimentality or cant. Katerina portrayed mothers and children, washer women, nuns, old women knitting, instead of nudes or famous people.

Elizabeth confided to Katerina that she found Uwaldsen's paintings fascinating but unsettling.

"If you look at his women," Katerina said, "they're either Madonnas or prostitutes, with nothing in between. Open your eyes! I say to his kind. They're afraid of life, these men, they retreat into their inner turmoil."

"If a man truly loved you," Elizabeth asked, "wouldn't you be able to live as you want to?"

"Someday, maybe," Katerina said. "Suffragettes are talking about women voting, having their own property, lots of new freedoms. But I don't know any married women who are serious artists."

Elizabeth continued to see Uwaldsen in class and sometimes in the afternoons. On a cold winter day, they walked around a park where the trees were bare and black. Uwaldsen talked about their twisted shapes and skeletal aspect.

"Here," he said, "I have a gift for you."

He dug into his pocket and pulled out a notebook and a pencil of thick graphite.

"You should start sketching as you go, jotting down any shape that appeals to you. You don't have to wait for William Tell and his son."

She was overwhelmed. It was the first time he had treated her as a fellow artist.

When they reached her sister's house, he said goodbye to her under the sheltered porte-cochere, where carriages pulled up.

"And thanks ever so much for the notebook," she said, looking up at him.

With a sudden movement, he drew her to him and kissed her hard on her mouth. He drew back, tipped his hat, and left quickly. She felt an electric current vibrate through her whole body, her lips still savoring his kiss.

And yet a few nights later, away from Uwaldsen, she had a momentary glimpse into their incompatibility. With Clara, she took her nephews to a performance of Shakespeare's "Midsummer Night's Dream." Sitting behind these well-bred boys in their sailor suits, she was carried back to her own childhood by the fantasy of the play and by Mendelssohn's incidental music. She saw, as if she were coming home after a long absence, the clarity, the harmony, even, she now realized, the innocent acceptance of pleasure with which she had been brought up. She remembered her parents' response to Professor Himmelweiss's proposal. "We would like you to make a sensible match, but one that you would enjoy," her father wrote to her.

One morning in Uwaldsen's class, some of the students congratulated him on a new painting that had been accepted for the yearly exhibit of new paintings at the academy. Elizabeth overheard two of the students whispering.

"It's quite different from his others, and no wonder," one of them said. "It's a portrait of his new mistress, the actress Leona Kauffman."

Elizabeth felt her breath stop.

"You mean the leading lady of the Burgtheater?" the second one asked.

"Yes, he's just become her 'official' lover, according to the gossip papers," the student replied.

Elizabeth ran off to see the picture. Uwaldsen had painted Leona Kauffman in the style he had described to Elizabeth, flat, ivory smock in gray-white light, rich auburn hair dissolving in darkness, the head of the actress bent back, her expression lost in sensual satisfaction.

She was terribly hurt. He had played with her and led her on only to forget her in the arms of a much more experienced woman, one who enjoyed the sexual freedom of a famous actress. She was humiliated by the realization that their affair had been a near impossibility. She was too young, and their worlds were too different. But what was strange about her reaction was that she could hold on to the reality of her pain. She had been in love with Uwaldsen, but after a while she could accept the sorrow of losing him. In spite of the fact that so little had happened between them, she felt older and stronger. He had reaffirmed her as an artist, and she could continue to pursue her work even if the bohemian life was not for her.

Chapter 10.
Elizabeth Goes to Budapest (1899)

Elizabeth was glad that she had taken the steamboat to Budapest instead of the new express train that her cousin Helene had raved about. If you lived in Budapest and went to Vienna every month or so, as Helene did, you were glad to get the journey over with. But if you were a tired art student who had just completed the spring examinations — and the obligatory all-night dancing that followed — nothing could be more pleasant than the slow passing of the shores and of the occasional barges. Elizabeth leaned back, untied her straw hat, and let her writing pad slip from her lap.

Her letter was not easy to write. She wanted to tell her parents that she had decided not to marry. The only choice Elizabeth saw was between a self-destructive passion or marriage to one of the conventional young men who courted her in Clara's living room. She felt proud as well as fearful about this prospect, which was linked in her mind with her determination to become a famous sculptress. She was thinking of spending a year in Paris, alone, working in her own studio or in one of the studios that might accept her as a pupil. She was fearful, however, that her parents would object and refuse to help her. She wasn't quite ready to face a future of poverty.

Cousin Helene, round and rosy under her enormous hat, greeted her on a quay full of geraniums.

"But you look worn out, my pigeon! What's the matter with Clara's cook? Give your bag to my coachman, and we will go to Margaret's Island while he takes it home. You must immediately have a drink of mineral water and at least three Gerbaud pastries. They will do you no end of good."

She put her arm through Elizabeth's, and they plunged into the cheerful crowd thronging the river banks and the public gardens on the island in the Danube.

"I'm so glad to be here!" exclaimed Elizabeth. "Does everyone enjoy life as much as the people around us?"

"Your cousin Theodore doesn't," Helene said. "For the past six weeks, he has hardly left his newspaper. A suffrage bill is being debated in Parliament, and from the fuss everyone is making, you would think that the world is coming to an end. I'm afraid that I have to drag you to a political rally tonight when I'd much rather take you to the opera. But tell me about your sisters and your dear parents."

It was so easy to talk to Helene, who did her share in making the all-powerful pastries disappear, that Elizabeth just chatted away. People came and went on the graveled walks and the sun glittered on the water. She realized how tense she had been all winter, as she relaxed in this garden restaurant where the only question seemed to be whether or not to end their meal with an ice. Talking to Cousin Helene reassured her concerning Clara, who was happy in her way with her tyrant Adalbert, and Hilda, who had grown to esteem and like Dr. Zoruba, the husband she had married without passion.

"And I think that your wanting to be a sculptress is wonderful! But don't worry too much about marrying, my pigeon," said Helene comfortably. "In our family, we manage to enjoy everything, even family life. And now, we must dress for dinner and then we will raise funds for the unfortunates who do not dress or dine."

By the time they climbed to their seats just behind the platform where Cousin Theodore, as a prominent newspaper editor, had a place of honor, Elizabeth was exhausted by her long day. In defiance of the authorities, the speeches were given in the language of the ethnic groups being represented. This helped ethnic solidarity, but it didn't do much for Elizabeth, who took out her sketch pad and started to jot down the eloquent gestures of a Ruthene orator. She could understand the Slav and German speakers, but when the next Hungarian orator mounted the platform, out came the sketch pad again. He was young, blond, and tall, and as Elizabeth drew, she marveled at the firm straight nose, the thoughtful eyes over the high Hungarian cheekbones, and the long, expressive hands.

I wish I could do a bronze of him, she thought after the rally, as she and her cousin waited for Theodore to finish talking to the people he knew on the platform. Helene noticed the direction of her glance.

"Frederic, come here, so I can introduce you to my little cousin Elizabeth. Elizabeth, this is Frederic Ignatius, one of the bright lights of the Hungarian Bar."

"I was hoping that you would introduce me. But, excuse me for saying this, young lady, you shouldn't draw people at a political rally," Frederic said in German. "Some of these speakers are nervous at the thought of the police having their pictures."

"I'm so sorry, that never occurred to me. I'm an art student, and I was just sketching for my own amusement. Here, here's yours," Elizabeth said, embarrassed. She ripped up the other pages.

"Thank you," Frederic said. "You draw well! No unnecessary strokes. But isn't there something immoral about art? People are fighting for justice and risking their reputations, and if you're a painter, it's all just grist to your mill, isn't it?"

He spoke as if her opinion really mattered.

"I've never thought of it that way," Elizabeth said. "I always thought that politics were immoral and art pure."

"You're not going to start that now," interrupted Helene. "This child is falling from fatigue. Frederic, you may call on us tomorrow."

Frederic came the next afternoon, but he was quiet and distracted. The police had arrested several of the speakers from the previous night, and Frederic left soon to try to get them released. However, he asked Elizabeth to go to the Hungarian National Art Museum with him on Sunday. She agreed gladly. She found his quiet demeanor a challenge and wanted to rekindle the interest in her he had shown.

On Sunday, when she got out of her uncle's carriage before the massive building of the Museum, she saw that he was holding a bouquet of violets. He kissed her hand and she pinned the flowers to her hat.

"Were you successful in releasing your friends?" she asked.

"Yes, thanks to your Uncle Theodore," he said. "But I'm not going to bore you with politics today. I hope you will explain some of these paintings to me."

They climbed the steps to the Museum that, he told her, had been recently erected for the celebration of a thousand years of Christianity in Hungary. The exhibit featured works in the academic tradition of naturalistic, almost photographic, depiction of conventional scenes.

"My teachers in Vienna have taught me to find this kind of painting somewhat dull," Elizabeth said, a little apologetically. "Moralizing, story telling. Are there no modern painters in Hungary?"

Frederic confessed that he liked the "story-telling" paintings.

"But then, I didn't even know what a painting was until I came to Budapest to study law," he said. "I have some friends who paint in a more Impressionistic way. Would your family let you visit them next Sunday? They are only a railroad trip away."

She was excited at the idea. She would have to ask her parents' permission to spend a little more time in Hungary before going home, but the new telegraph offices that speeded communication would enable her to do so.

The Sunday that they spent in the country was warm and dry. Elizabeth loved the flat landscape of farms and grazing animals that the train passed and the cool, wooded hills on which the painters' colony occupied a dilapidated castle. The painters knew and liked Frederic and welcomed the visitor from Moravia. Conversation was in German, made easier by cool white wine and fresh bread and bacon. Elizabeth admired the paintings she saw, but even the most experimental of them didn't have the disturbing power of Uwaldsen's or of other Secession paintings. The painters, all men, were older than her fellow students at the academy in Vienna. Some of them had families to support, and much of the conversation dealt with their poverty.

"Even the fashionable claptrap you and Frederic saw in Budapest didn't sell enough to make any Hungarian artists self-supporting," one of the artists said. In the castle, they lived at the expense of a fellow artist who had inherited the estate.

On the train back, Elizabeth and Frederic felt so comfortable with each other that she found it hard to believe she had only known him for a few days.

"I worry about being a poor artist too," she confided. "I think that Parisians are more appreciative of art than the public your friends described, but then there are so many more artists to compete with."

"Paris!" Frederic said. "You're brave. But I would hate to have you go so far from me."

She gulped. So he did care!

"Where does he come from?" the girl asked her cousin, knowing what her parents would ask after her enthusiastic description of Frederic.

"From the arms of his proud mother, a poor widow in a provincial town. In other words, from nowhere," Helene said. "But since he came to the capital, every woman in Budapest wants to take him under her wing because he has a brilliant future. If only he didn't have so many ideas! He's an innocent like you. You should get along well."

Elizabeth understood better what her aunt meant by Frederic's ideas when he invited her to a public lecture by a well-known teacher at the law school. The professor spoke at great length about how laws were made. They were not made in heaven or derived from a venerable, wisdom-filled past, the professor asserted, but they were passed by interest groups that acted to protect the groups' own interests. Even though the lecture was given in German, Elizabeth found it almost as boring as the speeches in foreign languages she had listened to.

On this lovely summer day, the lecture was not well attended, and Elizabeth was surprised to be met by demonstrators when she and Frederic left the hall. Placards called the speaker anti-clerical and unpatriotic. Some of the signs were anti-Semitic — "Jew hey,

hey, Go away." Some of the demonstrators wore clerical garb while others sported colorful hussar uniforms with gold braids, spurred boots, and embroidered scabbards at their waists.

Frederic took Elizabeth's arm with a grim expression as they walked away from the lecture hall. One of the demonstrators blocked their way.

"Don't you dare," Frederic hissed.

"Hiding behind skirts, eh?" the man said as he drew back. "Since you know that no Hungarian patriot molests women."

"You should be ashamed," Elizabeth said forcefully in German, although she hadn't quite understood the exchange. Frederic pulled her, and they ran to catch the nearest trolley. They could hear fist fights breaking out behind them as they caught their breath.

"I'm so sorry. Were you frightened?" Frederic asked.

"No," she said, "I thought it was exciting. But why the anger?"

"I said you were brave, didn't I?" he said. "I'll tell you more when we get to Buda, to the Gellért Hill, where this trolley is taking us. That wasn't where I meant to take you, but there's a great view of the city and we can talk."

They leaned over the parapet to admire the new bridges over the river, the Houses of Parliament, and the broad avenues of Pest.

"You see, this speech is so controversial because we are still a feudal country," Frederic explained. "Parliament consists of the owners of large estates and of representatives of the Catholic Church, which is also a large landholder. They claim to represent a God-given order and oppose any assertion of workers' or of peasants' rights. This speaker's realism unmasks their hypocrisy."

"What a shame that those colorful Hungarian costumes hide such an unenlightened attitude," Elizabeth remarked.

As they watched the sun set over the river, she started to see the city with Frederic's eye, noticing the factories and dreary tenements in the distance.

They decided to walk down to her aunt's home across the river.

"What about the 1867 compromise with Austria that my Bohemian brother-in-law calls a pact with the devil?" Elizabeth asked, thinking of the fierce little doctor gesticulating while Hilda calmly moved coffee pot and cups out of his reach. Dr. Zoruba was referring to the "Dual Monarchy," under which Hungary got special rights in the Austro-Hungarian Empire, including a parliament, self-administration, and industrial development.

"I think I would like your brother-in-law," Frederic said. "Well, you know, when you deal with the devil, you get the usual rewards — material prosperity, limited, of course, to a thin layer on top, cooperation in suppressing all nationalities except Hungarians, and in the end, you lose your soul."

They stopped to cross a wide avenue full of carriages, and he took her arm again.

"I love explaining to you. I'm getting carried away," he said.

"I like it," she said. "Go on. So what are you doing about all this?"

"My friends and I organize workers' meetings in support of manhood suffrage. It's dangerous, because the police accuse us of organizing unions, which are outlawed. We're also thinking of starting a journal to educate the general public about the conditions of the poor."

They had reached her cousin's house. He took out his watch.

"I've made you terribly late for dinner," he said, as neither of them made a move to part.

"What exciting work," she sighed. "My friends in art classes want to use art to change the world, but you attack injustice directly."

They were both silent for a while, realizing how close she had moved towards him with her remark.

"I've always dreamed of a wife who would be a friend and a companion, someone like you," he said. "Would you be willing to work with me, if ..if.." his voice broke.

"I've dreamed of you too," she said. "You're better than my dreams."

He seized both her hands.

"Marry me, Elizabeth," he said. "It would be wonderful if you would share my life and my ideals, but that's not why. Marry me because I love you more than I can say."

"I will," she said, "even if I have to learn Hungarian, that impossible language."

"My Erszébet," he said, using her name in Hungarian. He blew her a kiss and left.

She ran upstairs to change.

My God, I'm engaged! she said to her reflection in the mirror as she washed her face. She took out her pins and redid her hair. To a stranger, a foreigner, and I'm so happy!

Then she stopped and remembered that her parents would have to consent to the marriage.

I'll get Helene and Theodore to help me, she decided. Although wild horses wouldn't stop me. She didn't think that any wild horses would be involved, although there would probably be the obligatory year of engagement. But what about her determination not to marry and to pursue a career as a sculptor? Because Frederic was offering her a chance to work, a career as his wife, suddenly marriage didn't seem to be so conventional to her. But had she been serious about her ambition if it disappeared so fast? Which one was her true self — the Elizabeth who loved art school or the Elizabeth who wanted to start a new life with Frederic?

In the flurry of congratulations that greeted her news, her picture of a Paris studio, high and light filled over an old courtyard, faded gently, her regret barely perceptible.

PART IV ~ THE MAIDSERVANT'S BOOK

"I hope that you will continue to be my friend"

CHAPTER 11.
City and Country (1902)

Elizabeth met Joska in a linen closet in the pantry adjoining the kitchen. When she opened the door to take out a towel, she stifled a scream at the sight of the soldier squeezing himself against the shelves.

"Joska Vas, at your service, Honored Madam," he said, turning beet red. "I'm engaged to Anna here."

Instinctively, he raised his right hand to salute her, dislodging a shower of napkins.

"How do you do," Elizabeth said, taking a few steps backward. Anna, trembling at the thought of losing her first job after a month because Joska had unexpectedly gotten a weekday afternoon off from the service, stared at Elizabeth from the kitchen doorway. Piri, the other maid, watched with an ironic smile, while the old cook stood impassively at her stove.

"Well," Elizabeth said. She put her hand on her mouth and quickly left the kitchen. Anna could see that her eyes were crinkling up in laughter.

"Mary, Mother of God!" Joska said, shaking himself. "I never expected to see her. What's your mistress doing in the kitchen anyway?"

"She comes and goes all the time," said Piri. "She's not like the other ladies. Anna should have told you."

"You'd better go now, Joska," said Anna. "I might not lose my place after all."

"I hope you don't, my girl, we can use the money," Joska said. "But then again you may as well be hung for sheep as lamb. I mean, to get fired for a few innocent kisses...."

He opened his arms and walked towards Anna, a suggestive smile on his face. Anna and Piri shoved him out of the kitchen.

"Leave the girl alone, you troublemaker!" Piri said.

Joska left, promising to meet Anna on her next day off. He was wonderful, but there were three more years before they could marry. If only he weren't so impatient....

Nothing more was said about Joska's visit, and in her heart Anna thanked her young mistress. She liked her modest, low-paying job, and she worshipped Elizabeth. To her, the young woman glittered, like a star over the flat lands. In the evenings, she would see her go out on her husband's arm, displaying a cameo over her low-cut gown or a high-necked gauze dress, with feathers or pearls interwoven in her hair. When Anna served coffee after dinner parties, she saw Frederic's friends make a circle around the young woman, whose Hungarian was still imperfect but who could lighten the conversation with a remark that made the grave men chuckle. Anna, a good housekeeper herself, marveled at the jellies, the delicate sauces, the fluffy pastries that Elizabeth had learned at home in Moravia, and that even the dour cook was willing to add to her repertoire. When the masterpiece was in the oven, when every pot, pan, and whisk had been used, the young mistress would cheerfully say goodbye and go to edit an article or speech for her husband, leaving Piri to remark, "Ladies and gentlemen sure leave a mess after them."

Piri's occasional sarcasm concerning those above her on the social scale seemed strange to Anna. Life in the village was so immutable that social differences were no more open to question than the weather or the capacities of the soil. All Anna cared about was earning her dowry and learning new skills for her future role. She didn't intend to move into Joska's house as a poor little bride, especially since his family was Catholic and felt very superior to anyone of the Baptist Chapel. By the time she went home, she would have seen a bit of the great big world beyond Kisbánya, and she should be able to hold her own against in-laws or others.

But she had trouble holding her own against Joska's desire. Country girls like Anna had heard about sex from an early age from adults who were concerned with the mating and birthing of farm animals. And Anna knew that many a bride "went up to the altar with the midwife in tow," as the villagers said, but her own pastor frowned on premarital sex. One afternoon, unable to bear the conflict between her conscience and her love, she dropped her mending and started to cry in the deserted kitchen. She was startled when Elizabeth came in and saw her crying. The young mistress, who always moved quickly, placed her hand on the windowsill as if to anchor herself, her lace cuffs falling over her hand.

"Has someone in this household been unkind to you?" Elizabeth asked. "I won't have it, you know."

Anna continued to sob but didn't answer. Elizabeth waited, then reached out gently to touch her shoulder. Her gesture unlocked a fresh flood of tears and Anna's desperate need to tell her trouble to another woman.

"No, it's nothing like that, Honored Madam. It's Joska. We are engaged but ..." Anna said in a low voice.

"What about him?"

"He wants proofs of love," Anna said.

"How can you prove love?" Elizabeth asked. "Love is ... ." She smiled and blushed.

Elizabeth had been married less than a year, Anna knew, and she suddenly saw her as a contemporary.

"You see, Madam, our strips of land are next to each other, and if we marry, they would be joined," Anna explained. "That's how we met, among the weeds," and her face brightened a little. "But we must have children to work the land, otherwise there's no point to marrying. At least, that's what Joska says."

"And what do you think?" Elizabeth asked.

"Of course I want to bear him children," Anna said. "It's just that to test me that way and to reject me if I fail ... . And the Bible says it's wrong."

"As if you were a farm animal, bought to breed!" Elizabeth exclaimed indignantly.

66

"Joska is a good man," Anna said, a little shocked. "But my Bible is everything to me."

She felt she had said far too much and had no business having this kind of conversation with her mistress. But it was too late to stop Elizabeth.

"I know. A doctor's certificate. Dr. Lang will examine you and give you a certificate that you can bear children."

Anna was embarrassed at the thought of being examined by a man to whom she had served after-dinner coffee. But what Elizabeth said about self-respect appealed to her.

Elizabeth went with Anna to Dr. Lang's office and explained her problem to him. The doctor was an elderly man, short and pudgy, with a white mustache. His office had a lot of glass cabinets all around and a weird, chemical smell. Anna was scared. Would he make her faint with chloroform, as she had heard the cook and Piri say?

Dr. Lang smiled at her reassuringly.

"Now, you know that these things are in God's hands, so I can only use the little wisdom He gave us. But you were right to come. Have you ever seen a doctor before?"

"No," Anna said.

Dr. Lang made Anna sit down and answer a lot of questions. He wanted to know her age, her parents' age and how her mother died, what illnesses she had as a child, and whether she had any pains or aches anywhere. Then he told her to go behind a screen and to take off her apron, blouse, and skirt, but to keep as much of her underwear as she wanted. She came back in her shift and underskirt, blushing.

"It's okay," the doctor said, "I see people without clothes all the time, but I'm only looking at what's under their skin."

"How can you do that, Sir Doctor?" Anna asked.

"With these," he pointed to some metal instruments on his table.

He made her breathe while he put a cold stethoscope on her chest and back. He looked in her ears with a sharp tube and poked around her stomach. Then he took her temperature under her arm with a glass tube. Anna was glad of that, since in her family they found out whether someone had a fever by touching their forehead with their lips. Finally, he held her wrist for a long time while he looked at his stopwatch on the desk.

"I think you are a healthy young woman and that, God willing, you can bear lots of children, both boys and girls. I'm going to write that down for you."

He looked up at Elizabeth, and Anna thought that he winked.

She thrust the doctor's certificate at Joska next time he came to visit, on a Sunday afternoon, as she sat embroidering by the gray light of the kitchen window.

"What? not even a stamp or a red seal, like by commission?" he teased her.

"Don't fuss," she said. "He examined me from top to bottom, it was quite terrible."

He leaned back in his chair and unbuttoned his jacket.

"Anna, Anna," he said. "I always knew that you were not like other girls."

Frederic Ignatius, tall and elegant, came into the kitchen.

"Could I have some tinder to light my cigar, please, Anna?"

He bent over the coal that the young girl held for him in metal tongs.

"Where is everyone this afternoon?" Frederic asked.

"Piri and the cook went to the Agricultural Exposition," Anna said.

"You should go," Frederic said. "There are harvesters and reapers from abroad, which are just magnificent. Aren't you a farmer when you're not a soldier?"

Frederic was looking at Joska, who shook his head.

"I can't use machinery on a three-acre plot, Sir Attorney, and as for buying chemical fertilizer, which I hear is a big thing at the exposition, that would be like taking the food right out of our mouths."

Frederic explained that he had a study group that met every week to gather statistics about social conditions and asked if Joska would be willing to come and talk to them about his work.

Anna looked expectantly at Joska, but he shifted uneasily from one foot to the other.

"Thank you sir, but no thank you. If word gets around in my district that I talked to city gentlemen about farming, I will be known as an agitator, and no one will hire me for work on the big estates. And if you can't work on the big harvests, you may as well emigrate to America."

"But that's just the kind of thing that city people should know about," Frederic said. "How can they help you if they don't know about your problems?"

"I wouldn't help them, frankly," Joska said. "I met men in the army, factory workers, who talked about smashing the machinery of the owners, and I was disgusted. I can't respect people who don't respect property."

Frederic didn't press Joska further. After he left, Joska turned to Anna and put his arm around her.

"I know that these folks have been kind to you, babe, but it is best not to tell anyone too much about what we have and what we don't."

He drew her into the neatly stocked pantry, where they kissed until her braids swept a jar of vanilla sugar crashing down on the floor, surrounding the lovers with fragrant dust.

Chapter 12.
Diphtheria (1904)

When Elizabeth came home from the hospital with baby Kate to an apartment filled with flowers, she could recognize everything except herself. Her energy was gone, her interests faded. Soon, little Kate became a stranger too. Since neither nursing nor wet nurses were fashionable anymore, a governess gave Kate her bottles. In her starched baby clothes, she was presented to her parents at afternoon coffee or before her morning walk in her pram.

Elizabeth couldn't understand the lassitude she felt. She stayed in bed for several weeks, occasionally crying for no apparent reason. Frederic, whose office was at the other end of the apartment, came to sit at her bedside several times a day, talking to her about their friends, politics, his work. She heard him as if he was on the other side of a waterfall.

Her first few years of married life had fulfilled her expectations of active and rewarding involvement in Frederic's political and social life. She not only helped with his work on publicizing the current problems of Hungary, her adopted country, but also with his law practice. Together, they entertained the commercial and landed clients who enabled the young couple to spend time on their political interests. She also learned to revive Frederic's courage with her own enthusiasm when he grew discouraged by political resistance to his efforts.

When she first moved to Budapest, Elizabeth enrolled in a sculpture studio with Frederic's friend, Marie. However, she soon found that her busy schedule made her neglect her art, and when she became pregnant, she gave it up altogether. She was disappointed. It was her first experience of obstacles to her ambition that were internal rather than external. Now, her delivery of Kate led to this new state of mind that made not only art but most of her life seem meaningless.

Elizabeth had heard of women who suffered from "neurasthenia," the term used for mysterious, lasting depression. It was considered a disease of the will, and such women were subjected to treatments by tonics, long stays at resorts, and bed rest. She didn't know why she felt as she did, but her active nature rejected the prospect of being relegated to invalid status. Slowly, Elizabeth started to get up for several hours each day, resuming her role in the household. She was stronger now and could go through the motions of everyday life, but she felt as if there was a hole somewhere in her reactions.

When Kate was three months old, Elizabeth found out that her old friend from student days in Vienna, Jean-Richard Ponselle, was coming to Budapest for the opening of a new play. She decided to give a dinner party in his honor, and the prospect brought back some of her old enthusiasm.

Anna had always worked closely with Elizabeth on her parties. She, too, enjoyed the preparations, the excitement, the triumph of a successful evening. From time to time, the cook or Piri grumbled that she was Madam's favorite, but Anna was so even-tempered, so willing to help them with extra tasks, that their grudges melted away. Anna could get up at six, which was late by village standards, lug the coal for the stoves from the basement, start the fires, and heat water on the kitchen stove. She would keep working until late at night, dusting the rooms after breakfast, making the beds with Piri, prepping before and washing up after every meal.

Anna was stimulated by the comings and goings in the household, where outsiders shared many tasks. Coal, milk, meat, and produce were delivered daily. A seamstress came once a week to mend or sew, a laundress to wash. These visitors brought news and gossip. Anna's home during her adolescence had been so sad and silent that she loved being part of the world at last. The Ignatius's world was one of artists, politicians, and professional people, Jews and Gentiles, who talked with pride of being middle-class and modern.

"Modern art, a style for youth, for a young century," Elizabeth said, unpacking a crate labeled "Fragile." "Isn't she lovely?" Elizabeth asked Anna, who was bringing in a basket of flowers.

It was a porcelain statuette of a young woman with her head thrown back. She stood as if poised for flight, one foot off the ground, her blue dress floating behind her. The lines of her muscular body were clearly apparent under the delicate modeling of the fabric, and her uplifted arm exposed one white breast. With a pang, Elizabeth wondered whether she could have made the statuette if she had become a sculptress instead of marrying Frederic.

Anna shook her head, smiling.

"You'd better ask my opinion of a new gosling, Madam. I know more about it."

Anna took off her kerchief and playfully crossed it over the statuette's exposed bosom. "There. Now she can appear before the Honored Sir Attorney and your cousin with the roving eye."

"Has Theodore been teasing you?" Elizabeth asked.

"Oh, only to say that I'm beginning to be a marriageable girl," Anna replied.

"You are," Elizabeth said, noticing that Anna looked suddenly grown-up with her long braids twisted around her head.

"Your cousin means no harm, Honored Madam. Not like some others," she said to Elizabeth, who was trying to fit roses into a circular flower holder without obscuring the statuette. "You need some shears, Honored Madam, and watch out for those thorns."

She went out and returned with the clippers.

"Who would harm you?" Elizabeth asked.

As Anna started to fold stiff damask napkins, she explained.

"Joska's uncle, the tavern keeper, says our wedding must be celebrated at his tavern. He's fat and bossy and he looks at me in a way that isn't right."

"Would you like to be married here?" Elizabeth asked.

The sound of a crying baby interrupted them.

"What is the matter with Kate?" Elizabeth said impatiently.

"She's been so fussy all day."

Anna could see that Elizabeth would have preferred to stay.

"Now, if I had a baby, I would never want to be away from it," she thought. It was the first time she had found fault with her mistress. "Of course, ladies and gentlemen are different, but a baby is a baby, and as for that governess, she's just a stuck-up old maid."

She was touched by Elizabeth's offer to have her wedding celebrated at her house, but of course she couldn't accept. If she was to live in her village, she wanted her village to come to her wedding.

That night, as Elizabeth and Frederic led their guests into the dining room, only the occasional glint of candlelight off the pale gold-rimmed Limoges plates competed with the circle of light in which the young woman in porcelain lifted her face to the future.

"How lovely!" exclaimed Jean-Richard Ponselle, the guest of honor, a short, robust Frenchman with bushy eyebrows.

"Well, I think it's an absolute horror!" cousin Helene exclaimed. "If she were nude, well, there are plenty of nudes in the Vatican, but this clinging dress, which reveals every line, this lack of prettiness, or femininity...I don't think that any respectable courtesan would appear in this attire."

"You're absolutely right, my dear cousin," Elizabeth said. "I'm sure that the ladies you have in mind are sorry to see the bustle, the stays, and the crinoline go. But I must tell you that I am thrilled with it."

Cousin Theodore adjusted his gold-rimmed glasses to examine the figurine.

"As a technical matter, my dear, it has merits. For a woman, well, my taste runs to ampler figures. But where does all this decadence lead us?"

"Ah!" said a guest, "Your famous crayfish bisque, Elizabeth."

Anna circled the table with the rich pink soup, exhaling the essence of nearly a hundred crayfish that she and Elizabeth had crushed earlier. With half an ear, Anna heard Ponselle compare the figurine on the table to the young women playing tennis.

Frederic talked about new ideas, social experimentation, and political vitality. Anna thought of the lively discussions that took place every Wednesday night in his study. "Socialism, most likely," Joska had said when she described the meetings to him.

Ponselle praised the new buildings of Budapest, which had grown fast since the millennium celebration of 1896. Elizabeth pointed to Leopold Langer, a comfortable, portly man at the other end of the table.

"You're looking at the architect of one of our glories, the Modern Theater, where your new play will be performed, Jean-Richard."

"I designed it as a jewel box to show off my wife," Leopold said.

Leopold's wife, a pale, red-headed woman sitting next to Professor Agosti, a Wednesday night regular, seemed to pay no attention to her husband.

Goodness, Irene Langer, whose face is on the posters! Anna thought.

When the soup course was over, Piri served fish while Anna helped the cook arrange the roast pheasant under glass. At the table, the conversation had turned to France. The guests at the table cherished memories of the tolerance, the gaiety, the splendor of the City of Light. Anna was tired and sweaty from serving eight courses, but she could tell that the guests enjoyed themselves, and she and Elizabeth exchanged a quick smile.

As she served dessert, Anna heard Professor Agosti say to Irene Langer, with real bitterness, "How can a Frenchman understand the incredible backwardness of this country, the total rigidity of its institutions?"

Coffee and Tokay dessert wine were served in the living room. Anna cleared the dinner dishes, washed her share, and went to bed.

When Elizabeth and Frederic finally reached their bedroom after everyone left, he lit a cigarette while she sat down at her mirror to undo her hair.

"That was a wonderful party," he said. "I hope you were able to enjoy it, even while you were making sure it went well."

Elizabeth sighed.

"All that talk about Paris reminded me of my lost dreams of

going there to be a sculptor."

"What's this?" Frederic got up and stood behind her, his hands on her shoulders. "You never told me."

"I'm never sorry that I married you," she said as their eyes met in the mirror. "But I wish I had done more work of my own before I got so involved in our politics and social life."

"I'm so sorry," he said. "You did create Kate, and she is beautiful, although a lot fatter than the statuette Hilda sent you."

She frowned.

"I don't feel as if I have much to do with her anymore. When we were together in the hospital, I loved her with all my heart. But now she is just a pink bundle hovered over by nurse."

"I'm very proud of her," Frederic said.

He started to unbutton the long row of hooks on the back of her dress. "Listen. Why don't we spend some time in Paris together after my trial is ended?"

She hesitated. Her regrets for her artistic ambitions were a kind of private dream she wasn't ready to share with him even though she had no idea how to realize them. But he was reaching out to her in her confusion, and she didn't want to reject him.

"Frederic!" She threw her head back against him. "Let's go to Sicily. The almond blossoms are in flower."

She was right about the almond blossoms. When they reached their hotel in Taormina, late at night, he called her out to the balcony to see the flowers floating like clouds in the moonlight over the black lava. It was too beautiful to sleep, and husband and wife fell into each other's arms under the white mosquito cover of their bed.

Frederic stroked her slowly, kissing her and murmuring endearments. At first, Elizabeth felt numb, but he continued until she felt growing warmth and excitement. She didn't need to pretend to enjoy his lovemaking.

"Welcome back from wherever you were," he said afterwards.

"Where was I?" she asked.

"I don't know, distant, tired perhaps?"

"Well, that's over now," she said as she kissed him.

Her sense that everything was meaningless wasn't quite over, but she felt during their holiday that life was slowly coming back to her. She saw that Frederic had fought and won to re-conquer their love, and the effort she made to return his affection and enjoy their holiday made her feel better. She couldn't really understand why she had been so down after Kate's birth, but she found a way to resist the pull of depression.

There was a sleepy intensity about Sicily that suited their mood perfectly. Absorbed in each other, they explored the traces of the conquerors, their monuments, their hatreds, and the poverty that survived them all. The vitality of Mediterranean life sparkled in every child's face, in the endless processions, in the strong-faced men who did not bow, and in the vegetation scrambling up the ledges over the blue sea. They were in Catania when a little boy with a donkey reached them with Doctor Kreisler's telegram.

"Kate gravely ill with diphtheria, return at once," it said.

The boat trip to Naples seemed endless. There was no express. The train from Rome stopped at every village. Frederic was very quiet. Elizabeth kept biting her lips to fight back tears of remorse and anticipated grief. At Venice, a letter from Cousin Helene awaited them at the Hotel Danieli.

> My dear children: You don't know how close we came to losing that heaven-sent angel. You are lucky to have that girl Anna working for you. Apparently, when Kate fell ill, your governess did not call the doctor and then lost her head. On her day off, your Anna came to see me. She had to wait all day, poor girl, because we had gone to the country. She asked me to intervene because by now Fraulein refused to admit her mistake. I called Dr. Kreisler at once. I sent your governess away, not without a scene. That poor child had to be watched day and night for fear of her choking. I think that Anna did not sleep for five nights in a row. Now Kate is out of danger.

Elizabeth, still in her traveling coat, opened the shutters into the Grand Canal. In the green water, the wake of a gondola troubled the shimmering reflection of the palaces. It was inconceivable to her that the experience of life, so joyful, so beautiful, should nearly have been denied to that innocent little creature in Budapest.

"Thank God for Anna," she said.

Chapter 13.
The Maidservant's Book (1905)

On her return from Italy, Elizabeth could hardly wait to see Kate again. Absence and love had blurred her image of the child's face, but when she saw the pink baby in Anna's arms, she realized that even a month brings changes in an infant. Kate sat up firmly, smiled toothlessly, and snuggled in Anna's neck when her mother reached out to her. Elizabeth dropped her arms, slightly disappointed, and Kate immediately peeked out to say "gaa."

"How intelligent she is!" they all laughed, and Elizabeth hugged Anna together with her burden. "And thank you so much for what you did!"

"Anyone would have done the same, Honored Madam," Anna said. "And that poor old thing just lost her head."

Although Anna had disliked Kate's governess, she felt sorry for her when she lost her job.

"No family, no village of her own," she said to Elizabeth, "just a succession of children belonging to others."

Elizabeth had become soured on governesses after this experience, and with Anna's help, she took care of Kate by herself until she could find a really satisfactory nanny. Anna promised to send her a girl from her village to replace her after her own marriage.

After her trip, Elizabeth felt such an upsurge of energy that nothing was too much for her. She again took part in Frederic's political activities, which she had abandoned during her pregnancy. It was at a study group meeting that she first heard about the discussion between Frederic and Joska concerning the fearfulness and land hunger of peasants.

"I'm relating this conversation to you because it illustrates one of our most fundamental problems," Frederic said. "There's no unity of interest between the poor of the cities and the rural poor."

Elizabeth looked around the book-filled study, where the silk-shaded lamps brought out here a gold-rimmed pince-nez, there the reddish glint of a beard and mustache. These men — and one woman, Marie Lensky, a shy sculptor with close-cropped hair — had the stimulating familiarity of people she saw regularly but could never quite predict.

"Bah," George Lender said, throwing his prematurely bald forehead forward from the semi-darkness of the sofa where he sat, "your friend — excuse me, Elizabeth — doesn't count. How many peasant proprietors are there in Hungary? A few thousand, dividing maybe five percent of the land into tiny, unprofitable plots. The millions of landless rural poor are proletarians, exactly like the city workers!"

"But do the rural poor want land, or do they want justice?" Frederic asked. "Joska Vas disapproved of men in his regiment wanting to smash machines, because they didn't respect property, he said."

The dispute swirled around Elizabeth. She had not realized that Anna and Joska were not typical of country people. She was also learning more and more about the deep divisions in her adopted country.

"The moment you redistribute land, you create a class of reactionary, middle-class peasants," said Sigmund Berry, who belonged to the left wing of their group.

"I can't understand," Professor Agosti's dry voice broke through, "why we must get bogged down in these discussions. Isn't our main purpose to expose the hard facts of our country's problems that the government wants to ignore?"

"I think the time has come for us to act," Frederic said. "The new suffrage bill would give the vote to men who can read and write, and we should support it."

He recommended that the group should start a series of evening classes on the model of the British and American experiments to make working class people more literate and educated.

Everyone agreed enthusiastically. Here, at last, was a concrete suggestion. The members agreed that besides literacy, workers should have evening courses on economics, physics, and chemistry. Each member agreed to recruit volunteer teachers, at first in Budapest, and in major provincial cities later.

"Could I give a class on painting?" Elizabeth asked, before she had any idea of what she meant.

Marie encouraged her.

"How about Hungarian culture? New and old, popular and classical."

"Including folklore, like the songs Bartok and Kodaly are collecting," Elizabeth said.

"That's a lot of work, Elizabeth," Agosti cautioned. "But the workers may enjoy it."

"Will my audience know what a painting is?" Elizabeth asked.

The group members assured her that at first the lectures would get the elite only — workers who read and write, artisans, printers, who probably attend political meetings.

"They will have had three or four years of formal schooling only but a good deal of curiosity — don't talk down to them," Lender said.

She threw herself into preparing her lectures. Early next morning, she turned the library upside down to assemble the reproductions she planned to use.

Why is it, Elizabeth asked herself, that I ever wanted to be an artist? I like making things happen in the real world. I must have deluded myself about having an artistic soul just because I have deft hands.

The first two lectures didn't go very well. The workers were all men, polite but quietly self-assured. They kept their hats on, under which Elizabeth caught glimpses of their sharp faces and thick mustaches.

Elizabeth passed books with reproductions through the audience. They admired the books, some appreciated the binding and printing, while others passed them without comment.

Elizabeth talked about perspective, color, and line. She could catch stifled yawns. The only part of the discussion that seemed to engage her audience was the subject of one painting, the legendary Hungarian king Mathias and his Italian wife Beatrice. Some of the workers said the queen was a foreign hussy, who introduced the wrong influences into Hungary.

"But she brought us noodles from her old country!" one of the men exclaimed.

"Yes, but she didn't know to put sugar and poppy seed on them to make them taste good," another said.

The audience laughed but drifted out soon after.

During her next lecture, the audience seemed smaller but equally bored. As Elizabeth went on, a sense of hopelessness grew on her. At least, last time they commented on Queen Beatrice and her spaghetti! Despairing, she turned to the audience.

"What would you like to know about paintings?" she asked.

"Well, you could bring some to show us," someone suggested. "Something big, with bright colors."

"Like the statues of saints in our churches, only flat," someone else suggested. "Not too difficult to carry."

"What I'd really like to know," a man with a deep voice spoke up, "is how it's done. I mean, how come Mary looks like a woman, or a sad mother? I can do wonders with wood, but I can't make people."

"Those are wonderful suggestions," Elizabeth said. "My friend Marie is married to a painter. Let me see if he'll come and talk to us."

At the beginning of the next lecture, a tall thin man introduced himself as Count Palffy, a representative of the Ministry of Culture. He thanked Elizabeth for her help in making the audience appreciate their country's great cultural heritage. A murmur ran through the audience. Elizabeth felt that it was an unfriendly one.

Tibor Kiss, her invited speaker, had brought an easel and charcoals, and made sketches of volunteers from the audience. He was a hit. None of them had ever been drawn, none had met an actual painter. The audience liked him even more when he talked about stretching canvas, mixing paint and varnish.

"But excuse me for asking, Sir Artist Painter," said a burly audience member, "what sort of a living do you make with that fiddle faddle?"

"A beggarly one. Last year, 350 paintings were bought in Hungary, mostly the work of foreign painters. I sold two."

Count Palffy got up and, as the representative of the Ministry of Education, remarked that he considered that statement subversive. Everyone knew, he said, that Hungary was a cultured, progressive nation, where no one made a beggarly income as the artist painter said. The audience got excited. They knew plenty about starvation; they didn't need some little bureaucrat to tell them what was going on. The official withdrew after threatening to get the police to close down the hall. The angry voices and raised fists subsided. It was considered a good show, and the rest of Elizabeth's lectures were filled with curious working men who hoped to scare off another person of authority.

To Frederic and Elizabeth's disappointment, the new suffrage bill, which might have expanded the electorate from five to fifteen percent of the public, failed in Parliament. Soon after that, Elizabeth woke sadly to the fact that Anna had to go home to publish her engagement.

On a misty fall day, Joska stood in his civilian clothes in the hallway leading to the back stairs, while the superintendent carried out Anna's trunk from her room. A crate with Elizabeth's wedding present propped open the heavy door leading to the cellar. Large printed letters proclaimed it to be *Enameled Cookware, Best Quality (Red) of the brand Mazda, winner of the Silver Medal at the Fair of 1905.*

Anna sat in Elizabeth's small sitting room. She had returned her serving maid's apron and wore her voluminous country skirt. Elizabeth sat at her desk, Anna's maid's book open before her. She glanced at the title page, which contained Anna's name, age, and address in her laborious, neat handwriting. Under these was a printed excerpt from the Servants' Law. She read:

Paragraph 3140 of the Servants' Law provides that contracts between masters and domestic servants are

covered by the Anti-Strike Act of 1892 under which
such contracts are public obligations, enforceable by
the master with the assistance of the police. Under no
circumstances may the servant fail to perform his or her
promised duties, except in the case of non-payment of
wages persisting for more than one year.

Paragraph 3145 of the said law prescribes the duty
of the servant to perform faithfully and conscientiously
whatever duties are assigned by the master.

Paragraph 3146 provides that the master may fire the
servant without the customary fourteen days' notice if the
servant's behavior gives rise to an accusation or suspicion
of theft, disobedience, venereal disease or immorality of
any kind.

The law continued over the back of the page. The only
obligation listed for the master was the payment of the agreed
wage at the end of the contract period if the service had been
satisfactory, and the obligation to enter the contract in the maid's
book for the purposes of further employers.

Elizabeth had heard of the Anti-Strike law that had been
passed to oppose any possibility of strikes by poor farm workers
and was brutally enforced by the police. She had no idea it applied
to domestic workers. She hated to obey the law Frederic was
fighting, but she couldn't omit her recommendation from the book
because without it, Anna could never find work again. She sighed
and wrote.

"Anna Nagy performed her duties in my employ
conscientiously, efficiently, and skillfully. She was respected by all
members of the household for her hard work, her good temper,
her sound judgment, and her high moral qualities. She leaves my
employ to my regret, after ample notice, in order to be married."

"I hope that in the future, you will serve your own household
only," she said as she handed the book to Anna. "As for my own
feelings..." she threw her arms around Anna as her voice choked,
"you have been a good friend to me, and I hope that you will
continue to be my friend."

"Oh, Honored Madam," Anna said, reaching for the apron she wasn't wearing to dab her eyes, "May God keep you."

Elizabeth walked Anna to the back door and shook hands with Joska. The cellar stairs, blackened by coal dust, engulfed the young couple. Elizabeth saw the heavy door slam. She felt the chilly words of the Servants' Law gripping her, wedging into her personal feeling of loss. She wished she hadn't read them.

PART V ~ WARTIME

"You fight your war and I'll fight mine"

CHAPTER 14.
War (1914)

Anna was walking home from her father's house to her own in the neighboring village where she had lived since her marriage. The dirt road ran between wheat fields. Most of them had been harvested, and the wheat sat in neat stacks under the cloudless July sky. Only a few fields still waved their golden hair in the light breeze, revealing the poppies and cornflowers interspersed in them.

Anna was trying to get home as soon as she could because she had left her baby with her mother-in-law, and it was past baby Esther's meal time. She was slowed down, however, by her little boy, Stevie, who trailed reluctantly behind her. He caught up with her only to tell her how annoyed he was.

"Why did you take me away from Grandfather's just as I was about to find it?" he asked.

"What were you about to find, my little turtledove?" she asked, without slowing her steps or the pace of her reflections. She was extremely annoyed at her in-laws, not for the first time. During her visit, her father had praised a noodle dish she had brought him once, and she wanted to make it again for him. However, her noodle cutter, a gift from Elizabeth, was at her in-laws' as were many others of her possessions. She had asked for it back several times, and each time she was given an evasive answer. She now suspected that the machine was broken or had been lent to someone else, possibly Joska's innkeeper uncle.

Stevie again caught up with her and tugged at her skirt.

"The treasure, Mother, what else would I look for?" he asked indignantly.

"What treasure would that be, my little one?" she asked as she stuck a corn flower she had picked into his hat.

"The hidden one, of course. I even found the tunnel the fairies dug for it, and I wrecked it in part when we had to leave just to get home to baby Esther…"

He ran off, distracted by a butterfly. Anna returned to her reflections. That noodle cutter, there was a real treasure now. All the village cut their noodles on the table with a knife, and they always came out in uneven widths. With the cutter, you just folded the leaves like a tablecloth, put them in the central compartment, and chop, chop, chop, the blade sliced it neat and even in seconds. Her mother-in-law's constant borrowing, paid back by occasional, sloppy babysitting, was just one of her many grievances against Joska's family. What was even worse was their attempt to pull the young household down to their level. Thanks to Joska's hard work and Anna's skill as a manager, they were beginning to prosper. His father and mother were poor people who feared and envied everyone who seemed to succeed, except for the innkeeper, who could do no wrong. Really, Anna thought, the only thing they've ever done right was to give birth to her Joska. In this conflict, however, he gave her little support. His obligation was to be a good son. He tried not to get involved in family quarrels, which he believed were created by womenfolk.

Stevie now gave up chasing the butterfly in the fields and rejoined his mother on the road. He asked her in a fairly calm way when he could resume his tunnel-wrecking activities. Anna finally figured out what he meant.

"Do you mean the tunnel that your uncle dug to provide drainage from the summer kitchen?"

Stevie turned red, sat down in the dust, and in anticipation of a scolding, opened his mouth wide to throw the biggest temper tantrum he could, just as they heard the loud drumroll of their town crier. This was a particularly insistent and long drumroll. A few seconds later, a faint echo of a drumroll reached them from Anna's village, and before it was over, the church bells started to peal like mad.

"Oh my God, a fire!" Anna cried out as she picked up the

child and started to run for home. When she reached the village square, the crier had just finished. It couldn't have been a fire because the atmosphere was one of subdued excitement.

"What happened?" Anna asked.

"It's a message from the emperor," a man said. "The Serbs have provoked us into war."

"Have they?" Anna had no idea who the Serbs were.

"The men are being called up," a young woman said. "And me just married two weeks ago!" She started to cry. Another man shamed her into silence.

"Is that all you can think of when your country needs you? Stop acting like a dumb peasant, girl, and stand up like a real Hungarian blessed by our Lord God!"

He had unconsciously echoed the stirring words of the Hungarian national hymn, "God bless the Magyar," and this was picked up by a few people who burst into fervent song, soon joined by the whole assembly. It was a solemn moment. The rich emotion of the words and music, the transcendent feeling of their love for their country, and their pride in the emperor's call to them — who usually counted for nothing — carried them to an exalted plane far from everyday life. They felt a sense of togetherness and of selflessness.

The singing was interrupted by the sound of a bugle that made everyone turn toward the main street. A small band of reservists, hurriedly assembled, was marching down to the square. As the crowd parted to their smart military step, Anna saw Joska among them. Everyone burst into frantic cheers and applause. Anna's neighbor reached over and, grabbing the cornflower from Stevie's hat, threw it at the band of heroes. Their corporal waved at the crowd.

"We'll show them what kind of men we are!"

The crowd's mood changed from solemn to vociferous. Fists were shaken, chests swelled, and someone shouted: "Let's drink to that!" A great surge carried people to the tavern.

Anna grabbed Stevie and hurried home. Going to the tavern in the middle of the day instead of returning to work usually ended in brawls. She wondered whether war was also like that. Neither she nor anyone else in the village had any living memory of war. But one thing was certain. Joska had arrived in the square as if he were already in a different world.

She found him at home.

"Could you polish my boots?" he asked. "I don't want to disgrace my regiment. They say we may leave tomorrow."

She threw her arms around him.

"You can't leave me, Joska, my dear heart, you can't!"

"Where is Father going?" asked Stevie.

Their evident distress pulled Joska back from the bachelor world to which his mind had already raced. He took Anna gently by the shoulders and explained that he was going away for a short time.

"Do you think that the Emperor would call us away from the harvest if our country was not in grave danger? And you, Stevie, you'll act a little man while I'm on the front and help your mother!"

His words only increased her apprehension.

"And how are we to manage the harvest and all?"

Joska's parents and innkeeper uncle rushed into the house. His mother, a tall thin woman, handed baby Esther, who was howling, to Anna, while Joska's beaming uncle started to arrange their future.

"Now Anna of course will come and stay with me while you're at the front, Joska. My cook is leaving, and with everything Anna has learned in service, she will have no trouble earning her room and board. You can bring the children, Sister, their keep is cheap, and as for the land, we'll all work it together and share the proceeds."

Anna's mouth fell open in dismay and fury. Esther started to cry again because her sucking was interrupted. Joska looked at his uncle uncertainly.

"You can't leave your wife here all alone," the latter said. "We have to help out — after all, family is family."

The hypocrite, Anna thought. Several times already he had asked her to cook at the inn, and she had refused. Now he saw the opportunity to get her to work for nothing.

"I can manage the land," she said. "I've been working it all along, and before I was married I managed my father's household alone."

"But that was before," Joska said, looking at the children.

"I'm not going," Stevie said. "This grandpa beats me!"

Joska's father protested. Sure he beat him, but he used to beat Joska too, and see what a handsome soldier he turned into! Stevie became quiet. He very much wanted to be a soldier. Anna felt that everyone was against her, and she was desperately searching for arguments. The innkeeper reached over to pat her behind with his fat, lingering hand.

"Come on, honey, you'll have a good life with me and not a thing to worry about."

As she shrank back in disgust, the dog Bodri sat up and bared his teeth at the innkeeper. Anna drew courage from the dog's loyalty.

"My father is coming to stay with me. My brother's wife is expecting again and has asked me to relieve her of his care," she lied. "He can harvest our plot, and I can even work on the big harvests with Stevie. And of course Father brings his flock with him."

Joska rallied to Anna's support.

"Let my wife have her way, Uncle. I know you meant well."

In her heart, Anna was sharpening knives. Never again will I ask them to mind the baby — better to leave her to Bodri's care than to get mixed up with these people! You fight your war, Joska, and I'll fight mine!

Chapter 15.
Pacifism (1914)

When the first sound of an explosion reached Elizabeth, she rushed to the larder, thinking that a poorly canned jar had burst. But all was quiet in the little room where Anna and Joska had once kissed. The whole apartment was quiet in the late July afternoon. For the past month, the children had been away, vacationing with Elizabeth's parents in Moravia. Elizabeth lingered in the cool storeroom. She was tired of standing on the hot balcony where she had been straining to see Frederic address a Socialist rally to protest Austria-Hungary's declaration of war on Serbia. It was only a few minutes before a new explosion rattled the windows. Elizabeth, who had never heard gunfire, now realized what was happening.

"Frederic!" she thought and ran back to the balcony. The square in which the rally had gathered intent listeners was now a scene of confused movement. Two wide streets led to it, as well as a bridge over the river. She could see that the horses and bright helmets of the police were coming from two directions, allowing a single escape route over the bridge. Panicked people in the square, however, could only see white puffs of smoke and were pushing each other towards the firing police. She shouted at them: "To the river! To the river!" but her voice could not be heard. She saw people falling, and fear and helplessness gripped her as she watched the crowd spilling out of the square.

From below, she heard loud pounding on the building's entrance door. It might be locked, and Frederic wouldn't be able to get in! She rushed downstairs and pushed the doorman aside.

"Madam!" he protested. "The police! The demonstrators! They'll ruin the carpets!"

She struggled with the heavy bolt as the noise outside increased. As soon as she succeeded in loosening the bolt, people surged past her into the house, pushing her and the doorman aside. Frederic was not among them.

"It's terrible out there," a man said, breathing hard.

The superintendent, an arrogant man in uniform, appeared. "Eject this riffraff," he said to the doorman. Elizabeth was outraged.

"Come upstairs with me," she said, "My husband is a parliamentary deputy, and our apartment can't be searched."

She swept up the stairs, followed by the strangers, leaving the superintendent and doorman muttering.

The newcomers, ill at ease, sat or stood in the elegant living room. Elizabeth's maid brought lemonade in crystal glasses on a silver tray. They took their drinks without thanking her.

"I was crossing the square to buy a yard of ribbon," one woman exclaimed. "I never thought that a mounted cop would nearly trample me! Just for a yard of ribbon!"

The others sat impassively, unwilling to discuss their presence at the rally now that it had ended. Elizabeth expressed her fears for Frederic. To her surprise, several people snickered.

"Don't worry, Madam, His Honor will be all right," a thin woman said. "The police don't fire on gentlefolk."

She tried to read their opaque faces. Some looked like industrial workers, coarse but alert. A peasant woman, who might have been attending the church on the square, sat dour and impassive, very different from her friend Anna. A little blond man dressed like an office clerk kept looking around furtively like an amateur spy.

"Are these the people for whom Frederic is fighting, for whom he may have been shot?" she wondered.

The telephone rang. It was Frederic. He was unhurt and trying to arrange for the release of some of the demonstrators. When she told him about the people in the apartment, he said that he thought the streets were safe now. They went at once. Only the little blond man lingered.

"You have done me a great service, Madam," he said. "I hope to be able to repay you some day. Delicious lemonade you make, Madam."

He slipped her a greasy card and disappeared. She nicknamed him Delicious Lemonade and started to laugh at his theatrical manner. Then she burst into tears.

Frederic came home late at night, haggard and dejected.

"You were right to open that door, but I'm so glad you didn't come with me. It was horrible."

She brought his supper into his study, but he couldn't eat.

"This war is a great excuse to frighten people away from socialism, and the government is using it. What is most discouraging is that most people think that we are traitors to oppose the war."

"When it doesn't really concern us," Elizabeth said. "I'm sorry the Archduke was assassinated in Serbia, but why should we help Austria keep her empire? "

"I hate all the saber-waving, spur-clanking militarism that's led up to this," he said. "When I took one of the wounded protesters to the emergency room, the surgeon said 'Never fear, my lad, I'll fix you up, so that you can be ready to die for the Fatherland.'"

Elizabeth told him about the people who had stayed with her and how uncertain she had felt about them.

He was calmer and started to eat.

"The worst part of going to war is that it brings into play so many unknown quantities. But some things are clear. Every effort we made to make Hungary independent of Austria is now doomed."

She wondered whether after the war, which no one expected to last long…. He interrupted her.

"Darling, if you had been listening to me during the past year, you wouldn't expect a short war. All the European powers have treaties to come to each other's aid and huge arms buildups, so we can expect a long battle."

She put her hand on his arm.

"You're right. I haven't been listening to you much lately. I hate the whole subject."

He kissed her palm, too worried to quarrel.

"Never mind. Now other people's politics have overtaken us, and I don't know when we'll ever be free of them."

"We should bring the children home from Moravia right away, shouldn't we?" she asked. He suggested that she should travel alone while he would go to Berlin to make a last attempt to persuade the German Socialists to honor their pledge to vote against the Kaiser's war budget. He didn't sound hopeful.

The train to Moravia was jammed with vacationers trying to get home. At every station, soldiers were boarding freight trains and each stop was the scene of singing, of eager youths and proud women. As Elizabeth approached her native land, the enthusiasm lessened. Elizabeth felt more at home in that atmosphere, but relief only came when she breathed the cool mountain air of her childhood and saw her home that, on each visit, seemed a little older, a little smaller.

"Your children are at Hilda's," her father explained as he helped her out of the cab. "Tell me, since you are married to a politician, how dare these foolish diplomats trouble your parents' old age with all this commotion?"

"I'm not sure this is what they wanted, but enough saber rattling can result in more hostilities than they bargained for," she said, kissing his pink cheeks between his curly white whiskers. Elizabeth's mother smiled a wan, gentle smile from the couch where she was required to rest most of the day.

"I've enjoyed the visit of your two little devils," she said, coughing.

Augusta, the housekeeper, brought coffee in the familiar large rose cups, and she too, like the house, seemed more faded, less formidable.

Andrew and Kate came home and ran to embrace her.

"Mother, you came just in time. Uncle Ian showed us the most fantastic mineral collection, and the day after tomorrow he is taking us to a quarry! Would you like some diamonds?" Andrew asked, "or do you prefer amethysts?"

Elizabeth couldn't bear to tear them away from their vacation.

When she could slip from Hungarian back to her native tongue, Elizabeth felt as if she were discarding an uncomfortable corset. Now she wondered if she would ever again sit for dinner at that round table, bathed in the pink light of the opaline chandelier.

Her children sat gloomily in their compartment as the train moved through Moravia. They hated leaving the peace of the grandparents' old house, the freedom of the fields and woods, and the calm attention they received from their childless Aunt Hilda and Uncle Ian. Elizabeth could feel their resentment turning against her during the long journey back to everyday life, to busy parents, and to the gray threat of school on the horizon. She wasn't cheerful either. A fellow passenger shook her head as she unpacked her knitting.

"My, my, what frowning faces! It's bad enough that war has been declared, you need not act as if the world was coming to an end!"

But it was, Elizabeth felt.

CHAPTER 16.
Waiting (1915)

Winter came and bitter frost settled on the window panes. It stayed. Then slowly the ponds thawed, the roads turned to mud, and the first tendrils of the sweet peas reached for the sunlight. The earth heated up, spring went, and the burning sun held the world immobilized in the endless song of the crickets. Then the chestnuts fell, the leaves turned, and the wind rose during the night. The quiet time of indoor work returned to Anna, but Joska did not.

The first few months of his absence were the worst. Contrary to what she had told her in-laws, her brother Alex was not anxious to part with her father. Although the old man wanted to help his daughter, he couldn't. The reason was his flock. The sheep had always grazed on a large outlying estate that gave the family grazing rights for four months of labor. When old István could no longer do that kind of work, his son took over and got two-thirds of the soft, woolly skins.

Anna needed her father more and more. The tavern-keeper was circling her like a fox around a chicken coop. She was angry at her brother for not allowing her father to move in with her. When she tried to obtain the grazing rights for her father with her own labor, the estate steward laughed at her.

"That's man's work that your brother does. We don't give that to women. There's plenty of work that you can do, picking, gleaning, and hoeing."

"How many months would you want me to work for the grazing rights?"

He waved his hand.

"Forget it. Grazing rights are for household heads only."

She went home, discouraged. He might not consider her a householder, but the responsibilities were hers. Especially, she worried about the land. She did not want to do the hoeing and gleaning she usually did on the large estate because she had to harvest her own vegetables and potatoes, but the employer sent word that if she didn't work on this harvest, she couldn't work on the next one either. So she went with Esther slung on her back, a little bag of poppy seeds in her mouth to quiet her, and Stevie trailing behind. Then all day Sunday she had to pull her own potatoes, terrified of the first frost. She strung up the peppers and the onions, and Stevie clapped to see the kitchen all decorated with them. By the time she got ready to pickle the cucumbers, most had rotted.

Her greatest comfort during those early months came from the pink postcards coming from Joska. Their arrival was irregular, but the contents were reassuringly the same. He would ask about her health and tell her that his was good. He reported that the weather was cold and rainy, the food poor, and from time to time, he would mention meeting a fellow from his own village. He was on the Russian front. Galicia, he said, is ugly and flat. He never forgot to send his regards to all he knew and to commend her and her children to God's care. Anna sometimes wondered why he didn't speak of battles won or lost, but so long as he said he was well, the cards made her happy.

On a dreary, cold morning before Christmas, Master Andrew's daughter told Anna that captured Russian soldiers might be quartered in the village with the lone women to help with the farm work.

"It will be nice to have some men again," said the girl, "for the work and for the relaxation afterwards."

Anna shuddered at the thought. If she would not even let Joska, whom she loved, touch her before they married, surely she wouldn't let anyone else come near her now.

She went to see her brother, although they had not talked to each other since the fall. She offered to provide for her father, without asking for any share in the flock, and also to let her brother cultivate her rye field in return for half of its harvest. He agreed and promised to keep the bargain secret, since Joska had never authorized her to dispose of the land. He didn't mind helping his sister so long as his ever-increasing brood did not suffer, and old István blessed the reconciliation of brother and sister.

"For myself, I only want to keep enough sheepskin to have Esther and Stevie decently clad," he said. "If a shepherd's grandchildren can't have sheepskin coats on their backs with embroidered tulip edges all around, I don't know why I've worked all these many years."

The last months of winter were warm and peaceful. Her father chopped wood for the kitchen, and his presence added a sense of completeness to their family life. It reminded Anna of her girlhood days when she kept house for him after her mother's death. He started to teach religion to Stevie as he had taught her. She had less work to do. The pig had been slaughtered, the sausages stuffed, and she would sit and mend while her father told the children stories from the New Testament. She knew that the earth was resting under its snow, and in the barn the animals were warm.

* * *

Elizabeth hadn't seen Anna since the outbreak of the war. She admired the little boy hiding behind her skirts. She brought cool drinks of raspberry syrup with seltzer for Anna and Stevie. Soon, Stevie lost his shyness.

"We took the train to Budapest!" he crowed. "And it belched like mad! and Esther had to stay at home with Grandfather!"

Kate and four-year-old Andrew came to drink the fizzy drinks with the guests. Andrew wore a blue and white sailor suit. Kate's long curls tumbled onto her wide white collar. At their mother's suggestion, they took Stevie away to play. He followed, dazzled by their childish elegance.

Anna had grown a little stouter, but her face was unlined and determined. Only her eyes showed worry.

"Joska?" Elizabeth asked.

"I haven't heard from him for six months, Honored Madam," Anna said.

"But you received no notice from the army either?" Elizabeth asked.

"No. It seems like a long time. He wrote so regularly."

"It is a long time."

"So I was wondering, " Anna continued, "The Honored Sir Attorney Frederic being a deputy, maybe he could inquire, because people like us, they don't tell us anything."

"Anna, don't worry," Elizabeth said. "There's so much confusion on the front, so many people in hospitals, so many letters lost. But I'll call Frederic right away."

Only then did tears come to Anna's eyes. She wiped them away quickly and bent down to pull out sheepskin hats and mittens from her satchel for Andrew and Kate that her father had made for them.

As she went to the hallway to call Frederic on the phone, Elizabeth imagined how Anna must have felt during the past six months, nursing her fears alone but refusing to give up her stubborn faith in life. After leaving a message for Frederic, Elizabeth turned the conversation away from the war.

"How are you doing? I was so glad to learn that your father finally came to stay."

"It's a real blessing to me, Madam," Anna said. "But I had to give my brother the right to half the profits of our rye field. Joska wouldn't have liked that."

"So you have to decide all this now?" Elizabeth asked.

"Even my father asks me what to do," Anna said with a sigh. "You know Madam, it's not that Joska and I had time for a lot of sweet talk before he left, but the love was there. Has your life changed, Madam?"

"We don't entertain much," Elizabeth said, "and I have more time for the children. Frederic attends Parliament, but the military run everything."

The two friends parted with Elizabeth promising to write as soon as she got any news. Stevie was torn between regret at leaving his new friends and their splendid toys and joy at the prospect of another train ride. Elizabeth wrote:

> My dear Anna, Frederic found out that Joska was
> last accounted for before the battle of Przemysl, in
> Poland. It was a big battle but his name didn't appear
> on the casualty lists or on the lists of those hospitalized
> afterwards. There is a chance that he was taken prisoner
> by the Russians. Unfortunately, the Austrians and
> Russians do not exchange lists of their prisoners. Frederic
> says that the only people who might be able to find out
> are at the newly formed Red Cross in Geneva. I will write
> to them. It was wonderful to have your visit and my heart
> is with you in hoping that we will soon have good news.

* * *

Late in February, Anna caught cold. It was a worrisome time
of winter, as the meat from the pig slaughtered at Christmas started
to run out and the abundance of summer produce was still a long
way off. Scarcities from the war were also beginning to make
provisioning more difficult. One day, the store had no thread, the
next day, wicks could only be had at black market prices. After
several days of walking around with a feverish feeling, she fainted
one morning as she was getting out of bed.

When she regained consciousness, she heard Esther crying.
Her father was sitting at the table, his head between his hands. She
tried to get up, but she fainted again. Much later she was aware of
a woman standing at the sink. Anna's bed had been straightened,
and she could hear both children playing in a corner quietly. Her
head throbbed. The effort of trying to guess who the woman was
proved too much. She dozed off.

For another day she slept and woke in a fever, thinking that
she should get up, that Joska might come, then thinking that she
was in Budapest and wondering what Elizabeth had done with
some wallpaper she had picked out. After some time, the healing
woman from the village woke her up with leeches, which she put
all over her body. They were black and disgusting, but her fever

subsided. The next morning her head was clear, and she kissed both children. She asked her father who had scrubbed the room so clean. He answered a little peevishly:

"Why, the neighbor. Your sister-in-law couldn't come over to help."

"That wasn't Master Andrew's daughter that I heard."

"No, it was Marcie, from the other side."

"Oh, she's reappeared, that fine hussy?"

"She sure makes good noodle soup," the old shepherd said.

Anna got dressed and did a few chores around the house; then her legs gave way, and she had to go back to bed. Marcie came by just as Stevie arrived home from school. She was a large, full-bosomed woman. From under her clean kerchief, black strands revealed her heavy, shiny hair. She had brought a gift, a toy engine made of metal. The boy stared open-mouthed at the first factory-made toy he ever owned.

"How about a thank-you, young man? Before you feel the back of my hand?" asked his mother. "Marcie, how could you?" she said, forgetting every prejudice she ever had against her neighbor.

"Oh, I get around," she replied. "Sometimes these things fall into my hands as payment. Let me build you a smoke fire. The healing woman prescribed it for you."

She put dry corncobs in an iron basin, and when they were smoking she sat Anna on a chair over it and covered her with a sheet.

"You've certainly grown into a fine figure of a woman since you left the house next door as a skinny little girl," Anna said.

Marcie laughed complacently.

"Yes, the men don't seem to turn into stone when they look at me. Neither do I, I might add, when I look at them."

Anna asked her what she had done all the years since her parents farmed her out as a little gooseherd. Marcie had worked at everything poor girls did: She herded geese, then turkeys, then she dragged the babies around whose mothers were too busy to tend them. She graduated to serving maid on farms and in the neighboring towns.

"My work was good," she said. "I take to hard work like others to drink, but the men made me lose my jobs. I was always falling for some fellow, and employers don't like that. My blood is too lively, I guess."

"I heard you even tried a different life in town," Anna said, "but people are malicious."

"No, they were right. I worked in a whorehouse for a while, but I didn't like it. I'm not lazy like the girls who go there, and I like to pick and choose my men. So I got married to one of the customers, a nice little man, a great dancer, but he's in the army now. Anyway, he served his purpose. He got me out of there, and then I inherited the house from my poor old folks after I probably did my share in driving them to their grave. That's how come I was here when I saw that your father didn't know which way to turn."

Anna thanked her for her kindness. Marcie's visits became less frequent, but her songs could still be heard. She had frequent men visitors, and one evening a gypsy came to entertain a party that lasted all night. Marcie would disappear for a few days, sometimes coming back with a present for Esther or Stevie. Anna was jealous. She had neither Marcie's money nor her high spirits. Anna looked at herself in her mirror and thought that Joska would find an old woman waiting for him when he returned.

One day Marcie rushed in.

"Anna," she said, "if anyone asks, tell them I was here yesterday all afternoon. It's important."

She ran off. Anna shrugged — some jealousy between her suitors, she thought. She was surprised to see two county policemen filling up her doorway an hour later. Their dark faces were expressionless. Anna recalled that people who fell into their clutches preferred not to talk about what they did to them at the station.

"Hey," one of them said, "was that woman Marcie with you yesterday?"

Anna stared, uncertain what to say.

"She wasn't now, was she?" said the other one.

Anna found it difficult to lie. The policemen and the absent Marcie seemed to breathe a kind of shady atmosphere into the kitchen that froze her.

"I don't know what you're talking about, but Marcie is a good neighbor," she said.

They laughed.

"We'd love to have her as ours for a nice long time."

They left. Anna felt terrible. Marcie's house stood empty for a week. As soon as Anna heard singing next door, she rushed over.

"Marcie, what happened?"

"Nothing, actually. I got caught smuggling cigarettes, but they didn't put a finger on me. The price went up twice while I was hiding, so I decided to confess directly to the judge and to pay the fine. By the time he collected it, I had earned it back."

"I'm sorry I let you down," Anna said. "I thought it had something to do with men."

"Who needs men when city folk pay three pengöes for an egg? By the way, would you like me to sell yours?" Marcie asked.

She stood with her hands at her waist, her head cocked. Anna thought how much nicer Marcie's red cheeks and bright eyes were than the county policemen representing the law.

"It's a topsy-turvy world, I guess," she said.

"And we'd better take advantage of it while it lasts," Marcie said. "This war can't last forever and when the husbands are back, we'll have to dance to a different tune."

So Anna started to sell her produce through Marcie. Gradually, her health came back, together with her serenity. One day, as Esther was playing at her feet, she was adding up the profits. She was amazed at what a chicken, a bunch of beets or carrots fetched — four or five times the prewar prices.

"Mother, when I'm big enough, will you farm me out to herd the geese?" the child asked.

Anna shook her head.

"No, my turtledove, you stay with me. I don't want another woman bringing you up."

"But maybe I could herd the geese like in the story you told me."

"Don't you worry, my little one, we've found our golden goose."

And she wondered what Joska would think of her now.

CHAPTER 17.
A Separate Peace (1917)

What Elizabeth could not write to Anna, under the wartime censorship, was that she and Frederic now had a faint hope that Hungary would withdraw from Austria and its war before the Hapsburgs' defeat, which he saw as inevitable. Not long before she wrote to Anna, Elizabeth, passing by Frederic's study, saw that the door was still open, although all of the members of the study group had arrived.

"Come in, my dear," Agosti waved to her. "We're waiting for your husband. Do you know what could have detained him?"

There was a warmth in his voice that surprised her. She said that Frederic attended a session of Parliament in the afternoon but had planned to be home in time for the meeting. The gentlemen offered her the choice of the large velvet armchairs that surrounded the low table in the center of the study. Through the balcony doors, the lights of Buda glimmered across the river. No one observed the blackout. Suddenly, Frederic came in, hatless and flushed.

"I'm sorry I'm so late, but a very exciting thing has happened. Count Károlyi kept me after the session. He invited us to join a pacifist party he is forming. He has formally broken with his party, together with about twenty other deputies," Frederic explained, as the others looked amazed at the news. "He says that if we want independence from Austria, it's time to stop letting our men be killed for her."

Frederic bent to kiss his wife.

"Did he offer to support our program?" Sigmund Berry, the

103

socialist, asked.

"He wants us to join him in a broad program of social reform. On its face, the offer is irresistible. However...."

The count was a maverick in his own class: a descendant of one of the noblest and richest families in the land. He held liberal opinions and had opposed the war from the start. The general view was that the count could not rely on any broad-based support, and personally, the group distrusted him. At best, some said he was a naive idealist; at worst, an opportunist.

Agosti cut through the debate.

"We can't afford to consider what the count is like. We have two seats in Parliament, and he may be offering a real entry into power."

If Germany and Austria lost the war, Agosti explained, it would be those who had opposed it, like Count Károlyi, who would form the next government in the countries that were no longer under their rule. Agosti had faith in the sincerity of Károlyi's attitudes. His enthusiasm was contagious, and Elizabeth felt self-confidence radiating from the normally dry scholar.

A few days later she found the source. After years of friendship, which had started at one of Elizabeth's dinner parties, the actress Irene Langer and Professor Agosti had fallen in love. Irene, her red hair glowing against her lovely white suit, paced up and down Elizabeth's small sitting room with her lioness stride. She laughed and she cried.

"It's ridiculous, my dear, but he is the great love of my life — late, inconvenient, but there you are!" she opened her hands wide and shrugged.

This was not, she said, like her discreet, short-lived affairs, which had never interfered with her successful career or her prosperous, conventional marriage.

"I can't describe to you what it is to be loved like this. Edward, dear heart, knew nothing about women when he met me. To what I taught him, he joined the maturity of a man who for years channeled his passions into his intellectual endeavors. The result is that all-consuming 'coup de foudre' that everyone talks about but never meets."

Elizabeth couldn't help getting carried away by her friend's intensity. Agosti wanted Irene to get a divorce from Leopold Langer right away. Agosti was very insistent, and the actress responded to a man who was not intimidated by her beauty and success.

"Irene — just move in with us until your divorce!" Elizabeth said. "You can't go back to your husband after this."

"Elizabeth, you're wonderful!" Irene answered. "Oh my God, I'm late for rehearsal."

She ran off, soon to be replaced by her two maids bringing six trunks of her hats, shoes, and dresses. Only one of the maids moved in with her, but Irene's smelling salts, odd hours, and telephone calls took over their whole apartment.

Frederic was horrified.

"Langer is a good, decent man who loves her," he said to Elizabeth. "How can she desert him and her children after all these years? Suppose this is a momentary infatuation between herself and Edward Agosti. Can't they learn to forget each other if they think of their other obligations?"

Elizabeth was ready to scream. Did he think that passion could be set aside like a troublesome appointment? Irene's stay led to many arguments between her and Frederic. They were ended by Leopold Langer, who offered Irene a prompt and generous divorce settlement. Of course, she lost the right to see her children, but since the law was entirely on his side, she had no choice.

Frederic put his arm around Elizabeth's shoulder as they watched the carriage that took a radiant Agosti and a somber Irene to the civil registry where they were to be married.

"You see, I think that a passion such as theirs, which tries to fuse two people into one, creates a lot of unhappiness. You and I are different: I am slow and leaden, while you are quicksilver. But I love you across that gap."

She leaned her cheek against his. The artist in her saw her friend's ideal of perfect love as an achievement, however transitory. But she also valued Frederic's tolerant affection. He had helped her balance her commitment to passionate impulses with her enjoyment of the real world, which she knew did not yield to emotion.

"Does the world yield to reason, I wonder?" she asked, when their new pacifist party became discouraged as months went by, and the French and British did not answer messages dissociating Károlyi's party from Hapsburg Austria and the German Kaiser.

"Someone should go to Switzerland and try to meet the French or British representative on neutral territory," Frederic said. "But we've already risked prosecution for treason by contacting the enemy."

"Why don't I go?" Elizabeth offered. "My friend Jean-Richard's new play is opening soon in Zürich. His invitation would give me a good excuse. Also, I want to go to Geneva to the Red Cross. Anna saved Kate's life. I would like to help find out what happened to her husband."

Count Károlyi got her a special visa. She left, promising to bring back all the chocolates she could for Kate and Andrew.

Chapter 18.
The Amethyst Pin (1917)

Austria was desolate. From the train window, Elizabeth could see fields overrun by weeds, shabby children, and houses that had not been whitewashed since the outbreak of the war. But Switzerland looked as serene as ever. The stationmaster at Buchs was white-haired and grandfatherly, and geraniums smiled at the station windows. The custom guards did not smile. They inspected her papers with keen interest. Only when her visa was judged satisfactory did they bow and address her as "Gnädige Frau." She felt that she was only an appendage to her passport.

Jean-Richard had come to meet her at the Swiss frontier for the last leg of her trip. They ran to catch the train to Zürich and laughed like schoolchildren as they threw themselves panting against the velvet seats of the first-class compartment.

"I can't believe that you are here," he said. "A visitor from Mars could not be more exciting than you, coming from" — he lowered his voice — "the other side."

"I'd like to know who can put us on different sides," Elizabeth said.

Jean-Richard and his sister Madeleine had to go into exile in Switzerland. His opposition to the war had endangered them in France, and they were living in Geneva when Jean-Richard was not directing his play in Zürich. Jean-Richard had matured since she last saw him at her party in Budapest. His figure had filled out, his blue eyes were bright and sparkling, and his graying hair drew a wild halo around his ruddy face. Other passengers looked at him, then glanced back with recognition.

"So," she said, "you have become famous!"

"I'm controversial," he said modestly. "Also, I spend more than I earn, so I have to keep on writing."

"What is your new play about?"

"The war, what else?"

He explained that he had wanted to dramatize the war-weariness and cynicism of the men he had visited in the trenches. His hero was a wine-grower during the Thirty Years War, who keeps rebuilding his house as armies come and go but finally gives up and becomes a wandering looter and beggar.

"The kings and bishops end the war and divide up his land, but it's no good to them because he won't cultivate it anymore. Maybe he'll come back if they rearrange things to suit him."

"It sounds rather grim," Elizabeth remarked.

He laughed.

"So you will have come all this way to see a play you probably won't like?"

"Actually, I had some other reasons for coming as well."

She explained her mission concerning Joska but didn't mention the message to the Allies that she was carrying. Frederic had warned her that there were spies in Switzerland watching foreigners. Jean-Richard said his sister Madeleine was working for the Prisoners of War Agency of the Red Cross and might help her locate Joska.

"She is also neglecting me for the first time in my life. You know, Madeleine has been sister, mother, and companion to me since our parents died. "

"This war has changed everything, hasn't it?"

"The men in the trenches say that afterwards everything will be different, better. They'll never be able to do this to us again, they say."

The mountains had turned purple when he escorted her to the dining room where pink silk shades cast a trembling glow on each table.

As Jean-Richard refilled her glass, Elizabeth realized that this was the first time since her marriage that she had dined alone with a man. There was a strange contrast between the somber content of their conversation and her exhilaration at being away from her everyday family ties. When they were both students, they had made a pact to become "true friends" and only rarely had a flirtatious tone crept into their relationship. But as they talked about matters of deep concern to both of them, she wondered if this kind of conversation was not more dangerous than an open flirtation.

The days she spent in Zürich passed quickly. In the mornings, she was alone, blissfully alone. She walked a great deal, admiring the prosperous city and choosing presents for Kate, Andrew, and Frederic from the elegant store displays. She enjoyed discovering the quiet old streets left from a more modest past when Zürich was just another German Protestant town of skilled townsmen. Because Switzerland was neutral in the middle of a Europe at war, poorly dressed refugees speaking a variety of languages mingled with the more prosperous Swiss. But in the little side streets, she could hear the sounds of peace: the hammering of cobblers, the whining of the wood saw, the rhythms of the printing press.

Elizabeth took a train to Berne to transmit Károlyi's note to the Allies asking for a separate peace for Hungary through the American Consulate, since the United States still preserved a precarious neutrality. A distinguished-looking gentleman from Philadelphia received her kindly.

"I wish I understood the complications of Balkan politics, my dear lady," he said. "But if this note can further the interests of peace and democracy as you say, it will reach the French safely."

She refrained from explaining that Hungary was not the Balkans, and she thanked him for his discretion.

A few days later, the American ambassador forwarded a coldly worded reply from the French military attaché.

"Hungary has supported Austria and its brutal warfare on our allies Serbia and Russia. She will have to pay the price of aggression to the victorious Allies. The Hapsburg Emperor, not Count Károlyi, represents Hungary."

It was outrageous for France and its allies to treat her country as a unified enemy when so many Hungarians wanted freedom from the Hapsburgs. Could she have done more? Would she have endangered Frederic as a traitor if she had gone directly to the

French and pleaded with the military attaché to consider Károlyi's request? Officially, she was an enemy, and his note treated her as one.

In the meantime, she attended rehearsals of Jean-Richard's play. As he had predicted, she did not like the play. It was powerful but too allegorical for her taste. She enjoyed the company of the actors, however. They were hard-working, extroverted, and excited by the technical innovations of the play. At the Grüner Heinrich restaurant, they all spoke too loudly and sang drinking songs as if they were operatic choruses.

After the tumultuous opening night, which turned into a frenzied peace demonstration, Elizabeth took the train to Geneva to visit Jean-Richard's sister Madeleine and the Red Cross offices where she worked. There was no one to meet her at the station, although Jean-Richard had promised to write to Madeleine ahead of time.

Elizabeth took a taxi to the suburb where the Ponselles lived. The road wound upwards from the lake opening a widening vista of terraced brown vineyards over the blue lake. The taxi stopped before a modest stucco villa. Madeleine, pale and sharp-faced, came to open the door. She must have just come home from work, because she still wore a hat, although an apron had been thrown over her gray city suit.

"Elizabeth! Please excuse me for not meeting you. I worked terribly late and came home to find the cook gone because she didn't get paid. But I can't skip dinner. We're always feeding waifs at this house, and I didn't want to disappoint them."

She took Elizabeth's suitcase up the stairs.

"How was the play? Wonderful, wasn't it?" and turning around, her pinched face was lit up by a smile Elizabeth guessed to be reserved for her brother. "It's the first opening of his I've ever missed."

When Elizabeth came downstairs, Madeleine was peeling potatoes. Elizabeth reached for a kitchen knife and joined her at the wooden table, admiring the sunset on the lake, which glowed red and gold on the snow-capped mountains.

"I would gladly trade all this beauty for the dusty main street of any French town," Madeleine said.

As she cooked, she told Elizabeth that she had started a special inquiry for Joska as the Red Cross did for every prisoner of war it took under their protection, but her hopes of a response were slim. Russia was in the throes of a wave of strikes, and her Russian friends in Geneva felt that another 1905 revolution was beginning.

"Many of the Austrian and Hungarian prisoners were sent to Siberia and communications are impossible. However, tomorrow you could look through the unsorted Hungarian mail and see if anyone mentions your friend's husband. If you could help us by translating some letters, we'd be grateful."

Elizabeth was discouraged. She had come to share Anna's faith in Joska's survival, but now the thought of that Russian immensity where he might have disappeared overwhelmed her. Even if Joska was still alive, would he survive his captivity?

The guests began to drift in: a Belgian poet, tall and pale, a Russian with fierce eyes, accompanied by a young Russian woman, and an Austrian deserter, who announced proudly that he was being followed by five different spies of his government.

"But four of them watch each other, so that makes us even."

The guests described the distrust and dissension in their small community of exiles, isolated in Switzerland's wealth and security, and she felt sorry for these idle, idealistic young people. They drank and talked while Madeleine, quietly efficient, brought soup, meat, potatoes, and the wine of the region. Elizabeth felt like a student again, surrounded by people for whom intellectual discussion was daily fare.

They questioned her concerning Jean-Richard's new play, and the Belgian praised the beautiful actress who had the lead. Elizabeth saw Madeleine's face darken with jealousy. To change the conversation, she told the guests about her search for Joska.

"Is there really going to be a revolution in Russia?" she asked. "And what will happen to him then?"

"Let me find him for you," the Russian said. Everyone stared. "I would give anything to get back now. This is our chance, I have no doubt of it. But I need money for my train fare, as well as for bribes for getting visas. If you would help me," he turned to Elizabeth, "Once I get home, I will leave no stone unturned to locate this man."

"In Siberia?" she asked incredulously.

"That's where most of my friends live," he said with a laugh. "At the Czar's expense. If there's a revolution, they will be returning in droves."

She hesitated.

"I brought only enough money for the trip."

He fixed his dark eyes on an amethyst pin she was wearing. It was a present from Frederic, on Kate's birth.

"Well, his name is Vas, Joska, a very common name. His wife is Anna, and his children are Esther and Stevie. He is from a village called Kisbánya, and he has one cow, a black spotted one and one goat, whose name I think is Rosie. He whistles beautifully."

Everyone was laughing except for Madeleine. The Austrian said "You don't need to tell him the names of the ducks and the chicks because they have been roasted long ago."

The guests stayed for a long time, smoking Turkish cigarettes from Jean-Richard's study. While they were clearing dishes, Elizabeth asked Madeleine in a low voice.

"Would you vouch for this man?"

Their hostess shook her head slowly.

"I don't know. People with ideals are mostly faithful to their ideals. But you never know."

The next morning, Madeleine took Elizabeth to the offices of the Prisoners of War Agency. In a high-ceilinged library, rows of desks had been installed. Some forty men and women sat at them with typewriters or file boxes. The room was so full that the aisles barely allowed them to pass. The clicking of typewriters and the low buzz of conversations between workers maintained a steady hum.

"These are unsorted Hungarian letters," Madeleine said to Elizabeth. She explained that each letter should be translated into French and each name filed on index cards, phonetically as well as correctly spelled.

"Handwriting! If I could tell you the tragic misinformation that has been caused by misspelled names of people and places! If you need any help, let me know."

Elizabeth smiled as she remembered the tutor she had so hated as a child, who valued handwriting above grammar, "nay, meaning itself." Her mood grew somber as she started to read. The inquiries came from wives, sweethearts, and parents, revealing their anxiety. "Tell me that he is well...." "He is a strong, sturdy boy. How could he get diphtheria?" "You must find him.... He always wrote regularly."

The responses, which she found in another file, came from prison and hospital officials. They were cold and brief. "Deceased on such and such"; "Buried on such date"; "Transferred"; "No record of." A slow trickle of letters, Madeleine told her, had started from the soldiers themselves to the agency if they had heard of it. Very few of these came from the Eastern Front, too far from Geneva's reach.

Although Joska's name did not appear, Elizabeth became so absorbed in her work that she almost forgot him. She finished her batch of letters and asked Madeleine if there were any from Moravia. Homesickness swept over her as she read the names of towns she had known. A letter from a Czech soldier in a Polish hospital caught her attention.

"We nearly had a riot for a few days. A bunch of Hungarian wounded prisoners of war came in, from the battle of Przemysl. They were in fairly good shape. Feelings ran high because our regiment had been mixed in with Hungarian soldiers before we were captured to keep us 'loyal,' quote unquote, to the Hapsburgs, and we hated them all. We Czechs were hurling insults at the Hungarians, threatening them with our crutches. Actually, they were strangers to us from around Kisbánya. Ours had been from Balaton. Anyway, they were moved to Siberia before we had a chance to strangle them."

Elizabeth finished her work and went to find a jeweler to sell her pin. This was all she had — a vague allusion in a letter, a stranger's promise to find a man he didn't know. It seemed a thin thread in a stormy world.

She took the train across Switzerland to return to Hungary. In Zürich, as she changed trains, newsboys announced that

President Wilson had asked Congress to declare war on Germany. Elizabeth bought all the papers she could. Wilson didn't just want to punish Germany for its aggression. He declared that America would wage war for liberty and peace and to make the world safe for democracy. Elizabeth remembered how much she had liked the American envoy and how little he knew about her part of the world. She was encouraged by the news but worried about whether the American president could achieve his aims.

"Keep your doors locked"

CHAPTER 19.
The Curling Iron (1918)

'You again? Didn't I tell you to stay inside?"

Esther wanted to tell her mother something, but Anna's tone made her stick her finger in her mouth and stand uncertainly, shifting from one bare foot to the other. In the October sunshine, Anna and Stevie were harvesting the grapes from the vine that covered the trellis running along the house.

"The postman is wanting to talk to you at the gate," Esther finally said without removing her finger from her mouth.

"For heaven's sake, why don't you say so? Keep picking, Stevie," Anna said as she hurried to the gate. The postman, a small dark man with a drooping mustache, held a letter in his hand but did not hand it to Anna.

"Good day, Mrs. Vas," he said. "It's been a pleasure to serve you.

She returned his greeting, puzzled.

"Is there a letter from Joska?"

"Well, seeing that it's from Budapest and it may be important to you, I brought it out, but it may be a while before I bring another."

"Won't you come in for a glass of wine, Mr. Antal?" she said, seeing that he showed no inclination to hand over the letter.

"Thank you," he replied. Anna recognized Elizabeth's handwriting on the envelope.

"The world has come to an end, Mrs. Vas, and the Postal Service with it," Antal said. "The Emperor has abdicated. There is no more Emperor of Austria-Hungary."

Anna stared and refilled his glass without taking her eyes off him.

"How can he? I mean, the emperor is the emperor, whether he likes it or not."

"That's what happened. It's because of the war, that's why. The enemy won, and they took his crown."

"They took Saint István's crown?"

"And that's just part of it. The postmen aren't getting paid anymore."

Anna felt the bright day darken — no crown, no mail. But she was used to mobilizing her resources for the most immediate threat to her family's well-being.

"If my dependent's allowance comes or a letter from Joska, will you deliver them? I'll make it worth your while," she said.

"I think you'd better hide your livestock and the wine too," he said, as he poured another glass. "Soldiers are coming back from the front, and you know about them."

Stevie, who had come in quietly, jumped on his words.

"Does that mean Father will be back?"

Anna reached for the letter from Elizabeth, and the postman stood up. Only when he had left did she realize that normally the town crier would have announced the end of the empire. His silence added to the ominousness of the situation. She read:

Dear Anna, good news at last. We have positive evidence that your dear Joska is alive. This morning, a soldier just back from Russia appeared at my door. He was sent by the Russian I met in Switzerland. My visitor had been a fellow prisoner of Joska's and saw him four months ago in Siberia in fairly good health except that one foot had been amputated. From his description, I don't doubt that he saw your husband. I rewarded the man but did not suggest that he should visit you. I didn't like him. I wrote at once to my friend Madeleine at the Red Cross in Geneva to see if she could help Joska get back from that wilderness.

So much for the news of most immediate interest

to us. I don't know what other news you get in the
country. Here, all is in turmoil. I would have thought
that the church bells across the square which we so often
enjoyed together would have announced peace, but the
government doesn't even admit that we lost the war. The
war is over, but I don't know whether we have peace. The
Dual Monarchy is dissolved, but we don't seem to have a
new government. Keep your doors locked, my dear Anna,
and kiss your children for me.

At first, Anna sat very still. Joska had been gone so long that
he was almost a ghost to her. But when she told her children, they
started to shout and scream.

"Father will be back! He's all right! When? When will he
come?"

They danced out of the kitchen onto the pathway, and they
hugged and kissed and overturned the vat of grape juice. Anna
smiled and kissed them, hardly aware of the grape juice running
red along the path.

"My poor dear man, what hasn't he been through!" Anna
said. Although normally she kept stubbornly to herself, she took
the children by the hand and went to her in-laws. Joska's father
beamed.

"Siberia! A hero! Whoever from the village has ever been so
far!"

Anna's mother-in-law, who had become quite resigned to her
son's death, burst into loud wails.

"A foot cut off — how will he hoe? The swine! Who knows
what else they did to my son? Will you be able to have more
children?"

Anna was annoyed. She wasn't a young bride, and she didn't
hold on to their land during Joska's absence to divide it between a
lot of new brats, as her in-laws did for every piece of bread.

"Come on, children, my father will be back from the fields,"
she said.

On their way home, they saw three soldiers trudging along
the road in a kind of a daze. Stevie nudged his mother, and she

noticed that one of them carried a small gun under his arm. Anna remembered that during Joska's military service, he had never taken a weapon home with him. Discipline required returning them to the arsenal.

Her father smiled at her news.

"Bless you daughter, you won't be needing me anymore."

The next day, the old shepherd took to his bed with chest pains as if he had been straining to keep well all this time. Anna sent for the medicine woman. She told Anna that she had been unable to replenish her supplies at the pharmacy, and she now resorted to herbs and homemade remedies. The town was like a blind man holding his breath, she said. The stores were locked, the county courts closed.

On the way to her fields, Anna noticed unusual activity in the village square, as if the hum of the village was filling in the silence of the country's government. Villagers who had never spoken up were now declaiming against a growing list of evils: high prices, compulsory labor contracts, vaccination, every form of authority. Old memories of the Revolution of 1848 sprang to life.

"They freed the serfs and gave them land, but what about the rest of us who aren't even serfs?" one man asked.

Anna was frightened as the tone grew more and more heated. She heard the crowd decide to storm Count Almássy's castle and seize his lands. Her brother-in-law, the tavern keeper, now spoke up. His oily voice flew smoothly over the hubbub.

"And what makes you think that the count isn't there?" he asked.

"He's gone, they're all gone!" they replied. "They left with the emperor."

"Don't be fools," the innkeeper said. "The emperor may leave, he's a foreigner anyway, but the count is sitting up there with his dogs and guns. And how will you go about seizing the land?"

His question troubled them. Even the most illiterate was aware that land ownership involved registries and deeds. Someone suggested burning down the county register where the records were kept.

"Why don't you seize what's easy to grab?" the tavern keeper asked. "Do you think that those locked stores in the market town are being guarded? Aren't most of the owners Jews, anyway?"

Anna hurried away as an expedition of demobilized soldiers and villagers got under way. When she had served supper to her father and put the rest of the food on the table for herself and the children, she noticed Stevie's empty place.

"He hasn't been home all afternoon," Esther said.

Anna locked up the livestock and went to the houses of the boys Stevie knew. She could hear her heart pounding in the quiet streets. She had to knock for a long time at each door before it opened. Finally an old woman told her that Stevie had probably gone to the market town with her grandson. Anna walked home quickly, pulling her kerchief tight around herself. Her good little reliable Stevie!

Anna lay on her cot, listening to her father's labored breathing and to Esther's peaceful one. The church bell had just tolled one when she heard a knock on the door. She jumped up and opened it to a dazed little boy. With one arm, she drew him against herself, then she pushed him away to slap him.

"And don't wake everybody up, you good-for-nothing!"

He sat down at the table and handed her a long iron implement.

"Here, this is all I could get. Can I have something to eat?"

"A curling iron," Anna said. "What on earth am I going to do with it?" she asked angrily. "You're going to take it back tomorrow. And if you think that curling my hair or Esther's will turn us into fancy ladies, like those speech-makers on the square promise, you've got a lot to learn, my boy."

"I can't take it back," Stevie said. "I'd get arrested."

"You'll just have to wait till things settle down, and then you'll return it. No son of mine is going to turn into a common thief."

He munched his bread abstractedly.

"I didn't go to take anything," he said. "I went to listen to them talk about freedom and all that stuff. But you wouldn't understand."

There was tension between Anna and Stevie for the next few weeks, but she was distracted by her father's illness. When

November set in with its cold rain, her older brother came to bring firewood. Brother and sister quietly discussed the division of their father's land. The old shepherd paid no attention.

In the late evening, her father spoke to Anna.

"Do you have any message for your mother?"

Anna wept.

A few days later, two men dressed in city clothes knocked on the door.

"Is there a man in this household?"

They explained that they were from the National Council, registering people for the coming elections. There was to be universal manhood suffrage and a secret ballot because Hungary was now a republic. Wondering what part Frederic and Elizabeth had played in bringing this about, Anna told them that her father was too sick to vote.

"I'm the man in the house," Stevie said, glancing at his mother with a mixture of fear and defiance.

"You've got the right spirit, son," one of the canvassers said, "but for voting, you have to be twenty-four."

Anna went back to work, thinking of Stevie's look. The next evening, she cleared the supper dishes, lit a candle, and called Stevie to her.

"I think that you should take over the accounts for this household. You've had more arithmetic in your school than I ever did in my three grades."

As her father dozed in the flickering candlelight, she explained what each product of their land and farm was worth, how sales were made, and taxes were assessed. Stevie nodded and bent over the notebooks, biting his tongue as he copied an entry.

CHAPTER 20.
The Chrysanthemum Revolution (1918)

As Elizabeth had written to Anna, the military defeat of Austria-Hungary brought no tolling of the church bells ushering in peace. Day after day, Frederic would come home from legislative sessions in Parliament, exasperated by the government's attitude.

"It's all very well for President Wilson to say what peace will be like, but right now, this country is governed by the same people who got us into the war, lost it, and refuse to admit it."

She remembered the elation with which her family reacted to Wilson's Fourteen Points earlier that year. The text, in translation, was smuggled in, since government censorship wouldn't let the newspapers carry a message from the American President "addressed to the people and democratic leaders of Central Europe." Fourteen-year-old Kate, her long braids brushing Frederic's shoulder, read with him, while her brother Andrew ate the bread and jam she had abandoned on her plate.

"Open covenants openly arrived at. What are covenants, Daddy? Freedom of the seas, who cares? What were my classmates so excited about?"

"Wait, Kate, wait," Frederic said. "We'll get to the part about us soon. Wilson wants to end the abuses that got us into this mess. For example, governments made secret treaties — covenants — and people had to go to war even if they didn't want to."

"Andrew!" Elizabeth reached over to snatch Kate's breakfast from him. "You've had enough."

"Why is the American president talking about us?" Andrew

asked. "Does he mention me?"

"No, Andrew, but he promises to divide Austria-Hungary according to the nationalities that lived under Austrian rule," Frederic explained. Normally, he would have joked with Andrew, but he was serious. "Austria went to war because it was afraid of Serbs, Czechs, and Bosnians revolting against the emperor, and rightly so, because they were oppressed."

"So Hungary would finally be free from Austria?" Kate asked.

"The trouble is," Elizabeth interjected, "that Hungary also rules over ethnic minorities — Slovaks, Croats, Ruthenians, Serbians — who want to go their own way. If they did, Hungary would be much smaller."

"But free," Kate said.

The months that followed showed that the Hungarian government was more afraid of losing power and territory than of losing the war. When minority soldiers mutinied against Hungarian officers too closely identified with the Austrian crown, the Hungarian Prime Minister thundered: "We'll take those curs down with us, if it's the last thing we do!" And mutinies on the dwindling front were brutally suppressed.

Elizabeth remembered the letter from a Czech prisoner of war that had led her to Joska's trail. "They were moved before we had a chance to strangle them," the writer said, referring to Hungarians prisoners of war from Anna's village captured by the Russians. Ethnic resentments were not cooled by common defeat.

Life became more and more abnormal. Throughout the war, Elizabeth's family didn't experience shortages. Budapest even enjoyed a temporary prosperity from money made by those selling supplies and high-priced wheat to the military. But now, uncertainty began to take its toll. Frederic's clients didn't want to start any legal actions because they were waiting until the government fell "or restored order." Elizabeth found it hard to manage her household on their savings because the value of the currency was falling daily.

A heavily censored letter from Moravia from her sister Hilda told Elizabeth that their mother was gravely ill. Elizabeth scraped together the money for a railroad ticket, but at the Austrian border, the passengers were ordered to get off. The army had requisitioned the train to evacuate wounded soldiers from the Italian front. Elizabeth sat on her suitcase among harried, noisy families. Many were traveling to hospitals to visit their wounded or to relatives in the country, where food was still available. When she asked the conductor whether another train would be available, he shrugged.

She had not seen her mother since the start of the war, and she desperately wanted to bid her farewell. She was able to get a train through Austria to the Czech border, but got stuck again. While she waited for her connection, a telegram from Frederic asked her to return. He was afraid she might be cut off for a long time because the Austrian railroad workers were about to go on strike to demand the emperor's resignation. From what Hilda wrote, it might have been too late to see her mother alive. With a heavy heart, Elizabeth returned to Budapest.

As the early glow of October faded into rainy cold days, a sense of defeat finally started to permeate Budapest. The sight of bedraggled soldiers, gaunt and disabled, brought home to the city what government censorship could no longer conceal. The war was over, lost completely.

The anger and rebelliousness of the soldiers were infectious. Day after day, larger crowds stood in front of the National Council's headquarters at the Hotel Astoria, in silent defiance of the king's government. Count Károlyi, who headed Frederic's political party, was elected head of the council. Postal workers, teachers, policemen joined the National Council. Schools opened and closed sporadically, phones and trains stopped running.

"Why doesn't Count Károlyi, as head of the council, declare a republic?" Elizabeth asked Frederic as he was about to go to a meeting of the bar association, where he hoped to persuade the lawyers to support the council. "The Austrian National Councils forced the emperor to resign, why can't we?"

"Revolution means war — and haven't we had enough of that?" he said as he buttoned his coat. "The king has appointed a Hungarian prime minister with orders to shoot rebels. Even though he lost his empire, the king wants to hold on to part of the Dual Monarchy — the Hungarian crown. I have no idea when I'll get back tonight, don't wait up."

Later that morning, Elizabeth saw a crowd gathering in the square where the antiwar demonstrations had taken place four years earlier. Kate joined her on the balcony to listen to the speaker, a small freckled socialist, who was slowly whipping his audience into a frenzy. Through the rain and wind, his words came in fragments.

"To what have you come home?" the speaker asked. "To your families, who barely survived on the pittance they got while you suffered in the muddy trenches, to see the comfortable life of the profiteers who sold inadequate rifles and rotted wheat to the army, to the politicians who can't even negotiate a peace treaty for our country? Does anyone care about you?"

As darkness fell, more and more people crowded into the square.

"Look, Mother, the women students from the university!" Kate cried.

The speaker went on to more and more approbation from the people in the square.

"To the castle!" someone shouted.

The cry was taken up and drowned the speech. Someone hoisted a Hungarian flag, and the crowd, singing the Hungarian national anthem, poured out of the square towards the empty castle across the river, symbol of the king's authority.

Elizabeth remembered what Frederic had said about the king's orders to shoot demonstrators. After the crowd emptied the square, Elizabeth and Kate went inside, but when she called both children to dinner, Kate was no longer in the apartment. She must have left through the back stairs.

Elizabeth panicked. When they left, the demonstrators were peaceful, but how would the guards at the castle react? And some of the demobilized soldiers had rifles.

"Stay here," Elizabeth said to Andrew.

She threw on her raincoat and walked to the Hotel Astoria, hoping to find Frederic. The wet streets were dark and empty. Just before she reached the hotel, a barrage of gunfire broke the silence. She rushed in and pushed through the crowded lobby until she found Frederic. People were bringing in the wounded on stretchers.

"Kate's gone!" she shouted. "She's joined the demonstrators."

"Oh my God," Frederic cried. "I'll try to intercept her. We can't find a doctor," he shouted to his wife. "Could you get one?"

He dashed out into the night, against the flow of retreating demonstrators. Elizabeth went to the Municipal Hospital. The doorkeeper wouldn't open up for her, but finally brought a message from the director that if the mob got hurt, it was their own fault. She ran to her own doctor, who said that he would go to the Astoria after picking up supplies from a pharmacist he knew.

When Elizabeth finally reached home, Kate, wet and excited, opened the door.

"Kate, how could you?" Elizabeth asked, too relieved and exhausted to be angry.

"How could I not?" Kate said. "It was the most exciting night of my life, all these people wanting the same things I wanted."

"But the chaos, the danger, the soldiers...."

"Wouldn't you have gone at my age?"

Kate pressed her mother for approval. Elizabeth would never have defied authority in that way, but then her girlhood world was completely different. Before she could answer, Frederic arrived and hugged Kate.

"I'm proud of you, but don't disappear again without telling us."

Frederic had met a demonstrator who had recognized Kate and told him she was safe, but he wanted to make sure. He told his family that he was going back to the hotel.

"We'll stick it out now," Frederic said. "We owe it to the people who were killed this afternoon. Thank you for calling Doctor Kreisler, darling. By tomorrow, it will all be resolved, one way or another."

While Andrew went to bed and Kate fell asleep on the couch, Elizabeth paced the silent apartment. A five-hundred-year-old empire, tottering within, defeated abroad, was still capable of taking her husband's life in one night.

The gray dawn was the worst. Her strength ebbed away, her doubts gnawed at her. When she saw the first glint of light, she went out to the balcony. The square was empty and peaceful. The sun rose brightly, and by seven the newsboys were shouting the prime minister's resignation in favor of Károlyi, the first president of the new Hungarian Republic.

* * *

Frederic came home for breakfast, wearing a white chrysanthemum in his buttonhole. November first was the Feast of the Dead and vendors usually sold the white flowers to mourners going to cemeteries, but now the flowers became the symbol of the successful revolution.

The family had barely finished its meal when the doorbell started to ring. Friends and relatives, wearing the white boutonnieres, came for news from Frederic, since communications had still not been restored. Kate and Andrew went off to find their friends. In the late afternoon, the apartment finally quieted down. Frederic took a nap before going to an evening session at the Astoria. Count Károlyi had to name his cabinet and issue orders to restore government.

Elizabeth picked up the flowers strewn about the apartment. Even though the Feast of the Dead was a Catholic holiday, it reminded her of not being able to visit her mother's grave, and of the incompleteness of her mourning.

She took out the letter in which her brother-in-law Ian described her mother's last illness and death. Grief and guilt and loss overwhelmed her, obliterating everything around her. "Mamma is too good!" she had burst out once, when her father praised, to the unruly girl she had been, the sweetness and self-effacement of his wife. Now that phrase burned her. She felt that she had taken as a reproach to herself what had simply been her mother's nature: gentleness, modesty, lack of self-confidence in some ways but a persistence in kindness rooted in determination, even stubbornness.

Although she had been awed by her younger daughter, Louisa Schwalb had never ceased to love or accept her. Her mother had never been, her daughters had agreed, "modern," and Elizabeth felt keenly, in the midst of the dislocated, brutal modern world, the pain of losing the kindness and tolerance her mother had radiated. The very clarity with which she saw her mother's qualities hurt her. Death fixed her image on a canvas, instead of the warm, changing impressions made by the living. Elizabeth's youthful rebelliousness now seemed tame compared to Kate's. She had moved closer to her own old age and death.

Chapter 21.
Homecoming (1919)

"Wife," Joska said, "I've come home."

Anna stood up from the kitchen stool and stared at the crippled soldier standing in the doorway. He leaned on his cane and waited as if he had said the words he had long prepared and didn't know what to do next. The next moment she was at the door, sobbing and clasping her arms around him, her head on his shoulder. He hugged her with his free arm, but he didn't kiss her. She moved away.

"Come and sit down and eat and drink. The merciful Lord be praised who brought you home."

He limped to a chair, his wooden foot pounding the earthen floor, and sat down heavily. Then, as she embraced him again, he kissed her, but mechanically, with a reserve that seemed to imprison him like the dust that covered his clothes and shoes. She moved about quickly, getting bread, onion, sausage, and a cool pitcher of wine from the cellar for him. Then she started to laugh.

"Aren't you even going to ask about the children?"

He nodded. She told him that Stevie and Esther were both in school and that he could only be proud of his good, hard-working children.

"So how old are they now?" he asked.

"Six and nine," she said. Her heart tightened at the impassivity with which he ate. After a while, he looked up.

"The harvest?" he asked.

"It was a good one. And Joska, I was able to buy the plot on which we met, do you remember?"

Again, no reaction. How cheerful and jovial he used to be!
Dutifully, she continued her news: her father's death, the rye field
she inherited, the prospects of getting more land now that they had
a republic, the small repairs she had made to the house. He listened
but didn't respond much.

"I heard that you were a prisoner in Siberia. Did you take a
train home?" she asked.

"A train, trains, finally a boat" he replied. "Your friend in
Budapest sent a boat to pick me up. I think I'd like to rest now."

For the next two days he slept, getting up only for meals.
He greeted the children the same way he had greeted her, with
an effort, and they were disappointed. On the third day, he got
up early and went back to work. When there was a job that he
couldn't do because of his lame leg, he asked Anna or Stevie to
help, showing no surprise at their skill in the men's jobs such as
chopping wood or patching the roof.

After a few days, while Joska locked up the livestock for the
evening, Stevie spoke to his mother.

"I liked the farm work better when Father was gone."

Anna smoothed down his hair.

"This way, you have less to do and more time for your school
work. Big changes are coming and it's important for you to be
educated."

Joska didn't talk about his war experiences or his
imprisonment. When he went to the tavern, which he did more
often than he had before, he sat with a group of ex-soldiers who
drank morosely and silently. At the other end of the room, noisy
drinkers reminisced, argued, and talked politics, but Joska did not
join them. After drinking, he made love to Anna, but he was rough
and somewhat brutal. One evening, she refused because she said
that she didn't want any more children. He raised his cane and hit
her on her head and shoulders. Anna clenched her teeth and let
him do what he wanted.

The day after, Anna sat at the kitchen table staring at a piece
of paper as the winter evening fell. Joska was at the tavern and
the children had gone to visit her brother. Anna had finally figured
out that Elizabeth, through the Red Cross, had sent Joska money

that enabled him to get back through Russia and the Black Sea. But she couldn't bring herself to write her a thank-you letter. She didn't feel grateful to Elizabeth. The room was getting cold. How happy those years now seemed when she had struggled alone to keep the household going! She had worked hard but done as she pleased. Even when she tried to abdicate as much responsibility as she could to Stevie, there was harmony and warmth in the house. It occurred to Anna that since Joska's return, Esther had not acted mischievously once. She felt that the child was keeping a tight rein on her spirit. Yes, Joska had changed. She couldn't imagine him whistling a song now.

Anna started to resent Elizabeth. Why had she intervened? Wouldn't it have been better to leave Joska's fate to God, who may not have wanted to bring him back from Siberia?

Anna got ready for bed, still thinking about Elizabeth. It was different when she had worked in Budapest, she thought. Even though they were maid and mistress, they were both young and giddy and they had felt sisterly. But over the years of separation, Elizabeth had just been lady bountiful, doing good deeds from a distance. Anna did not feel young or giddy anymore, that was certain. She was stouter and harder than she had been as a young wife. And if her fate was to get blows and pregnancies from a drinking husband, she thought she would soon be old, like so many village women her age.

As she tossed in bed, unable to sleep, she recalled the first real conversation she had had with Elizabeth, about Joska wanting her to prove her fertility before their marriage.

"As if you were a farm animal, bought to breed!" Elizabeth had exclaimed. Anna could see her now, standing in the kitchen pantry, one hand wide open, the other poised on the counter as if caught in motion. No, she was not going to give in now, Anna thought. She had her God-given dignity and Joska would have to respect it.

Anna didn't write to Elizabeth, but next time Joska tried to hit her, she raised her strong forearm to ward off the blow. She stared hard at him. He looked away to avoid her eyes and dropped his arm with a shrug. Anna was still angry. In this way, they established a truce between them and he stopped demanding sex.

The winter passed. It was a bitter cold one. The wartime shortages had not disappeared. Anna could see that many of the fields had not been harvested, even though their owners had been demobilized. Many wives complained that their men were unwilling to return to work. At Joska's uncle's tavern, Anna heard some of the ex-soldiers organizing to demand what they claimed the government owed them. There were refugees too. In the stores, Anna competed for the scarce goods with ragged Hungarians streaming in from the villages now occupied by Rumanians or Serbs. Anna resented them when they bought the last available candle or the last pair of boy's shoes.

The mail came again and the speeches in the square had quieted down with the cold weather. Late in February, the drummer announced that the government had voted to redistribute all the large estates. Anna and Joska applied for two acres at the county seat, but nothing happened.

As spring was edging its way toward summer, a thin sharp-nosed man with cold eyes asked for Joska when he was out in the fields. He introduced himself as Eugene Kiss, Commissar of Agriculture for the district.

"We have some common acquaintance, you and I — Mrs. Ignatius, the bourgeoise in Budapest who gave me a gold coin but wouldn't tell me where to find you. Nice lady, typical of her class," he sneered.

Anna didn't care for him. The next time he came, he found her husband at home, and Anna was surprised to see that Joska seemed glad to see his former fellow prisoner. Kneading bread gave her an excuse to stay in the kitchen to listen to the men's conversation.

"What wouldn't we have given for this kind of bread in Siberia!" Eugene said. "That black Russian bread, even if you could get it, what a poor excuse for gluing wheat together."

They reminisced, Joska putting in a few words here and there. Eugene didn't seem to mind conducting most of the conversation by himself. Anna was pretty sure that he was just leading up to something else.

"So you've come back, you're sitting here on your behind, feeling sorry for yourself, and pretty soon, you're going to let the same thing happen to you again, right?"

When Joska looked at him amazed, he asked, "Don't you know anything? Do you know that we're at war again? That we have a Communist government trying to defend us from the Russians and the French?"

They had vaguely heard of young men reenlisting to protect border villages, but they were not sure why. Eugene explained that in March the French had given the Hungarian troops twenty-four hours to draw back from their armistice positions in order to give nearly a third of what was left of Hungary to the Rumanians, "to whom the capitalist pigs promised it in 1915!" he said, pounding the table. The Károlyi government ("you know, your fine friends in Budapest") had the ground cut out from under its feet.

"So we took over," Eugene said with pride, "because we could organize a red army of workers."

"And this is where you come in, friend Joska," he continued. "I want you to organize a soviet of the small landholders of this district."

Joska stared.

"That army has to be fed," Eugene said. "And, all of a sudden, food is not for sale. The small proprietors, like yourself, are slamming the doors in our faces. I came to you, Jozsi, because you're smart in spite of your peasant stubbornness. You've seen civil war too, and it isn't very pretty. That's what we'll end up with if these people don't come around."

"Why would people sell," Anna asked, "when each week their currency buys less and less?"

"Currency!" Eugene snorted. "Money isn't anything. It's just a capitalist tool. We will abolish money very soon."

Anna's mouth fell open.

"You're going to abolish money?"

Joska showed less surprise. In Russia, the prisoners had discussed Lenin's ideas.

"Why don't you go to the landless peasants first?" he asked. "You are giving them the large estates, aren't you?"

"No," said Eugene breezily, "we're not. We want to keep them together to make collective farms on a large scale. But let's get to the issues. You've been through a lot, Joska, and you know that the past isn't coming back. Nobody is going to give it back to you or to our country either. "

Anna saw that Joska was thinking hard. Something in this speech had gotten to him. But after a while, he shook his head.

"I'm not going to talk to the others. I know what your ideas are, and somehow, they always stuck in my throat. And I don't care what happens to you or to your red army or to me."

Eugene got up.

"All right, sit here and rot. Too bad that the Budapest lady arranged for you instead of someone with a little more guts to be rescued by boat."

He left without a farewell.

"What an awful man!" Anna said

"He's not all bad," replied Joska. "He has his religion and he believes in it. He's a Communist."

Anna couldn't see what Eugene's views had to do with religion. If anything, she soon decided that they belonged to godless fanatics. The villagers were shocked when two young men from Budapest, "who had been Israelites," they said, burst into their church and interrupted the priest to lecture about the evils of religion. The youths were greeted with sullen silence. But afterwards, the grumbling about Communism as a "Jewish, Budapest invention" spread to every household.

Over the summer, the new government sent out more and more emissaries into the countryside to take over local administration. Agricultural workers were paid in kind, in coupons, and finally on the hated piece-work basis. Red army troops had to be stationed in the village to prevent sabotage. Joska and Anna watched the rising tempers around them and, like their neighbors, stopped driving to the market to sell their food. They ate well that summer instead of stinting their own table in favor of the market, and Anna and Esther spent hours every day canning fruits and vegetables. Joska put on weight. He seemed a little more relaxed but still stayed aloof.

Early in August, an elderly man stopped at their gate to buy some food. His straw hat, vest, and dusty spats showed that he came from the city. The children stared at him. Timidly, he offered several hundred pengöes for some fat, green pepper, and eggs.

Anna gave him a cool glass of water and a basketful of produce. Joska looked on without objecting, but as the man thanked them profusely, Joska asked him not to come back.

Anna felt the visitor's humiliation with a sick feeling. Is this what ladies and gentlemen were coming to? Could her proud mistress be going begging from farm to farm? Why hadn't Elizabeth turned to her? Probably because of her ungrateful silence. She felt her own dignity assaulted by the old man's lack of it.

As the afternoon wore on, she felt more and more disturbed. She was angry at Joska too. It was his behavior that had cut her off from Elizabeth and the tradition of loyalty and gratitude with which she had been brought up.

When he went to the tavern that evening, she packed a crate of fresh and canned vegetables and of smoked meats. The next morning, she got up while Joska was still sleeping, and she thrust a goose into a basket. She harnessed the market wagon and climbed onto the driver's seat just as Joska was coming out to the well to wash.

"Where are you going?" he asked amazed.

"I'm going to Budapest, to Mrs. Ignatius. If anyone asks you why, tell them that your friend Eugene asked us to feed his folks, and we were afraid to refuse."

Joska felt the ground sway under him. He couldn't believe that she would undertake this journey without his permission. For the first time, he felt that in their mutual silence, he had lost her. What was even worse, he realized the danger in which she was putting herself. It was useless to refer to Eugene's authority for violating the boycott. The Red Army had been defeated by the Rumanians, and the Communist Eugene had probably fled or been killed by now. The road to Budapest was a battleground between the advancing anti-communist forces of Admiral Horthy and the fleeing Communists.

Joska felt fear for the first time in years.

"Wife!" he cried "Turn that horse around, for God's sake."

She could no longer hear him. Esther and Stevie came running into the yard and were amazed to see their father with tears in his eyes. He put his arms around them and letting go of his cane, hugged them roughly against himself.

Chapter 22.
Anna Visits Elizabeth (1920)

When Anna reached the road to Budapest, the sun was already up. The full heat of the coming day could be guessed from the brightness of the sunshine. There were no carts on the road. She knew that the peasants were boycotting the Budapest market, but still, by eight in the morning, some people should be going somewhere. There were horse droppings on the road, but no one appeared on horse or on foot. When she passed a farm or a village, the shutters were closed and the doors locked. Her uneasiness mounted. She saw a dog lying dead by the side of the road, the blood coagulated by his throat. Anna whipped her horse while she wondered whether to hurry on or to turn around.

She decided to stop at the county seat, which was nearby, to visit a woman from her village. Margaret, a widow who earned her living by helping bereaved village families with death certificates, funeral arrangements, pensions, or insurance, made it her business to know what was happening.

She had almost reached the town when a troop of horsemen swooped down the road from behind and surrounded her cart. They were soldiers, talking quickly in a language she couldn't understand — Rumanians, she assumed. One of them jumped up on the seat beside her and grabbed the reins. He had black eyes and smelled of alcohol and sweat. Anna froze. She heard the others jump up onto the cart, her crate of food being pried open. Turning her head, she saw the food being hoisted down over the side. One soldier opened the basket and cried out in pain. Her goose had bitten his hand. He slammed the basket top on the cackling beast and jumped off the cart. They all mounted their horses again except her neighbor, who reached over and smiled, revealing blackened teeth and a breath of concentrated garlic. He lifted his eyebrows in a question, and Anna shook her head violently. The others yelled at him to hurry. He handed her back the reins, jumped off, and the Rumanian soldiers rode off in whirlwind of dust.

Anna sank back in her seat. Oh, Good Lord, she said aloud, thank you for protecting me. Then she thought with anguish of the food she had lost. She climbed back to refasten the goose's basket.

"Sure it's the Rumanians," Margaret said as she poured her a small glass of apricot brandy. "They've been through here like the seven plagues of Egypt. They'll take the hinges off your door together with the door. The only reason they didn't take your goose is that they're going to Budapest today, and even they know that you can't build a fire to roast a goose in front of the Royal Bastion."

Anna told her of the garlicky proposition the soldier made to her, and Margaret laughed.

"They're thieves rather than murdering bandits. Anyway, no one is dying these days anymore," she added mournfully. During the boycott, peasants were eating better than ever, and even feeding their old folks, who seemed to live on and on now.

Margaret persuaded Anna to spend the night with her. The next morning, people in the town started to come out of their houses.

"They've gone!" they said, of the Rumanians. "Let Budapest feed them now!"

Anna reached Elizabeth's apartment at noon.

"Anna! what a wonderful surprise" she said, somewhat flustered. "Come in!" she added, smoothing back her hair.

In spite of her cordial tone, Anna felt that something had changed. They did not embrace as they had done after long absences in the past, and Anna felt guilty about not having written for so long.

The apartment too looked different. In the past the white dust covers over the silk upholstery had only appeared when the family went on vacation. The curio cabinet was empty and the silver candlesticks and gilded clock were gone from the buffet.

Anna thanked Elizabeth for her help in making Joska's return easier, and Elizabeth raised her hands in protest as if it had been nothing. Again, Anna felt that her thanks were too late to be accepted, and she only talked about Joska quickly, describing his trouble walking and his ingenuity in continuing to do most of his work. She talked about her children more freely and enthusiastically, but Elizabeth seemed distracted.

After a few minutes, Elizabeth excused herself to make a telephone call. When she came back, Anna felt that she should leave. She handed Elizabeth the goose, asleep in its basket, and apologized that she was unable to give her the other foods she had prepared.

After she was alone again, Elizabeth sank back gloomily on the sofa. Anna's visit had brought home to Elizabeth how much her situation had changed. Earlier, she had often accepted presents from Anna, knowing that it gave her pleasure to give as well as to receive, but now the mention of Joska reminded her how she had lost her power to help others even in the small way in which she had influenced his fate. She was too worried about the uncertainty surrounding her to respond properly to her old friend's visit.

Just now, when she had called Frederic, he told her that behind the Rumanian advance, another reactionary group was waiting to take over the country, led by Admiral Horthy, who owed his fame to his suppression of a naval mutiny during the war by shooting every tenth sailor whether he had mutinied or not. Elizabeth shuddered at the thought.

Two weeks after the Rumanians entered Budapest, Admiral Horthy rode into the city on a white horse. The crowd cheered, welcoming the return of the prewar aristocracy in the gleaming uniforms of the Austro-Hungarian Empire. The admiral made a speech forgiving "Budapest, this sinful city" and promising that there would be no reprisals against patriotic Hungarians.

Frederic prepared to resume his private practice. Elizabeth's last maid, Rosie, returned, and the silver reappeared. Food remained scarce, and Elizabeth was discussing with Rosie how to

supply the household when the doorbell rang. The girl returned
to say that a strange little man wanted to see Mrs. Ignatius. His
card said "Gyula Mezei, Police Department, Investigative Branch,
Silverware."

Mezei greeted her formally and asked:

"May I presume to inquire whether you have knowledge of
your husband's present whereabouts?"

Elizabeth thought that he had gone to the former offices of the
Law Revision Commission to retrieve some books.

"He is in grave danger, Madam. I came to offer my humble
assistance in facilitating his escape from that peril, at a price,
I'm sorry to say, because I am a poor man, Madam. I have been
demoted from agent provocateur to silverware thefts, but I'm not
without gratitude for past favors rendered."

She was bewildered by his speech. He explained, elaborately
and circuitously, that detachments of former officers called the
"Hungarian Avengers," who had been roaming the countryside,
had reached Budapest. These men, he said, had been eliminating
communists and Jews by methods he did not care to describe to a
lady. A list of their targets in Budapest was given to the city police
by the authorities with the order not to interfere. Mezei had seen
Frederic's name on the list, and he offered to smuggle him out of
the country for five thousand crowns.

As he spoke, Elizabeth finally remembered that Mezei was one
of the people she had sheltered during a bloody demonstration
in 1914. His furtive and pretentious manner had impressed her,
and she had nicknamed him "Delicious Lemonade." Now she
understood why he had been so grateful — as a police agent, he
had been afraid of the workers rather than the police.

"You're just tying to extort money from us with a cooked-up
story," she said.

He shook his head sadly. She could see that he disliked the way
she had shattered his gentlemanly facade. He got up.

"Well, at least it will not be said that Mezei Gyula lacks
gratitude towards the ladies."

At the door, slightly embarrassed by her rudeness, she said —
"And anyway, the admiral said that there will be no reprisals."

He opened his eyes wide.

"Oh well, if he said that, there will be no reprisals. Farewell, Madam."

Soon after he left, Irene Agosti called Elizabeth. She had been out of town on a theatrical tour and planned to have lunch with her husband on her return, but her servants had not seen him since the previous day. His office did not answer, and she wondered whether Frederic knew where he was.

Elizabeth dropped the receiver when she saw Frederic standing in front of her, white, his pupils distended with shock.

"They've murdered him," he said. "Is it Irene?"

Elizabeth nodded. Several seconds went by and he reached for the receiver, but the actress, impatient, had hung up.

"She'll find out," he said. He covered his eyes with his hand. "Not everything, but enough."

He told her that Agosti's secretary was in the professor's office the previous evening when a detachment of Hungarian Avengers had burst into the office — just to ask a few questions about the Hungarian territories given to other nationalities when he served the National Council, they said. The jangling of their spurs, the revolvers glistening at their waists, and their empty, arrogant faces had bred terror in the young secretary. Agosti had looked around quickly, but he was surrounded.

"I expect to see you here tomorrow promptly at eight, and please remind me that I have a lunch date with my wife," he said pointedly to his secretary.

The Hungarian Avengers swept him down the stairs. In the morning, Agosti didn't appear. After calling his home, the secretary notified the police. At the police station, he said, they gave him a funny look, but they took down all the information. He returned to the office, waited, and was thinking of calling Frederic, as Agosti's closest friend, when the police called him to identify a body pulled out of the Danube.

"It was after that that he came to see me. And Elizabeth, don't ever tell Irene or anyone else" — he shuddered — "they put out his eyes before shooting him."

Elizabeth clenched her fists and put them together in front of her. She felt cold and tense, angry and afraid.

"Hungarian Avengers, that's what he said," she said to herself. "I didn't hear anything else. I'm not registering it. I'm not going to think about it."

She reached for the telephone and dialed.

"I would like to report a theft of silverware. Could you send Officer Mezei to handle it right away?"

"Elizabeth," her husband cried, "Have you gone crazy?"

Chapter 23.
Anna Visits Again (1920)

Frederic wrote:

I am only in Vienna but I feel as if an ocean is separating us. Mezei performed his promised duty conscientiously. Around three in the morning, we reached a desolate little village where we exchanged his truck for a cart. I was beginning to look like a stranger in my old clothes, full of hay, unshaven, my mind slightly clouded by the cherry brandy he shared with me to ward off the cold. He became lonely and invited me to climb onto the driver's seat next to him. We drove through the vast empty plain along the river banks with the stars shining in the sky over the open space. Mezei was in a confessional mood and told me the story of his career as an agent provocateur. It was his job to get as many of the socialist workingmen in trouble as he could. This job was perfect for him — he is as sincere in his envy of the rich as he is in his contempt for the poor. It shows what my state of my mind was that I could listen coolly to these tales of the downfall of the men with whom I worked before the war, as if Mezei's story took place in a foreign country that had nothing to do with me. Agosti's murder makes that hopeful past seem to belong to another world.

Everyone here thinks that Horthy's regime will not last more than three months. A lot depends on foreign recognition of his government, and hopefully, his excesses

will prevent France and Britain from supporting him.
I look upon our separation as very temporary. Kiss the
children for me....

Elizabeth sighed. She missed him terribly. But right now, even
to travel to Vienna, she would have to borrow money. She gave
Frederic what little money they had before he left. He hoped to
look for work at once and send her money, adding, "With your
resourcefulness, I know that you can manage till then."

She really didn't know where to begin. She was not trained
in any of the professions. She knew of some women who had hat
shops or fashion boutiques, but she had no capital to start one.
She couldn't quite picture herself working as a sales clerk or in a
factory for the pitiful wages those women got, although it might
come to that.

She was surprised to find how few friends she had left in
Budapest. People ignored her on the street, and several of her
acquaintances wrote to explain that they did not want to see her,
"as under the present political circumstances, she could surely
understand."

Her cousin Helene arranged for her to get some work
translating articles from French and Czech for a publisher.
One day, after she had come home very tired from delivering a
manuscript, Rosie ushered into the living room two officers from
the Hungarian Avengers.

They've come for me, she thought. My poor children.

But they turned to Kate, who was in the room with her.
"This must be the young woman we came to see. Are you Kate
Ignatius?"

When the girl nodded, the younger man, who had a dueling
scar across his forehead, said to Elizabeth, "We won't need you,
Mrs. Ignatius, we just want the girl to come with us to answer a
few questions about the Students' Radical Union."

"Where she seems to have spent quite some time," said the
other severely. He was older, with short, graying hair and the
monocle affected by Budapest gentry.

Kate took a step forward and raised her head proudly.

Elizabeth, fearful of what she might say, put a hand on her arm. The girl's beauty, as her hair fell back and her mouth half opened to speak in a contemptuous manner, gave her an idea.

"It's that boy!" she shouted. "That miserable, no-good boy!"

Kate looked at her mother, surprised.

"Do I have to be reminded of that disgraceful episode?" Elizabeth continued in a loud voice. "Does a mother's shame know no limits?"

She could see that Kate was about to contradict her. She slapped her as hard as she could. Kate started to cry. Elizabeth had now worked herself up to a hysterical pitch.

"Leave this room at once! Get out of my sight!"

Kate was protesting through her tears, but Elizabeth pushed her out.

Then she collapsed in a chair, her lace handkerchief over her eyes. The soldiers waited.

"Sit down, sit down," she waved at them. "You are gentlemen — you can understand what a family goes through when a girl of fifteen forgets herself."

She leaned forward confidentially.

"Please don't think that my husband and I were glad to hear that the child spent her afternoons at the Students Radical Union. But that fiction was a thousand times better than how she actually spent them. She had been seeing a boy all that time."

"Well, if she doesn't know much about the union, she'll be home so much the sooner," the younger one said, somewhat tentatively.

The older man shook his head and looked at Elizabeth admiringly.

"Would you like a glass of water? I'll ring for your maid."

She thanked him faintly.

"I hope that in a new Hungary of virtue and Christianity, the girl will repent and reform," he said.

He bowed and left, the other following reluctantly.

Elizabeth dared not move until she heard the door slam behind them. Then she waited, afraid that they might change their minds. When five minutes had elapsed, she went into Kate's room. Kate had washed her face and was combing her hair. She looked at her mother coldly.

"Don't you think that I have any backbone — any principles?" She glowered, her eyes darker than usual. "And to think that you could make up such a cheap, half-penny romance! Disgusting."

"But Kate, it isn't a matter of having principles — these men were not taking you to ask a few polite questions."

"What would they take me for if not for information?"

Elizabeth could not bring herself to repeat what she had heard of girls being raped repeatedly, of the pure sadism of the Avengers.

"They are ruthless and unscrupulous men," she said, leaning against the doorpost with fatigue.

"I think that what you did doesn't show many scruples either," the girl said.

The next week Rosie left, writing a note in which she told Elizabeth that she would not work for a family visited by the Avengers. Although she was glad to spare the expense of Rosie's wages, after doing the household tasks Elizabeth had less patience than ever with the dullness of translating articles. Frederic had not found work in Vienna. He wrote that the impoverished city was filled with Hungarians who competed for the scarce jobs to be had. He was beginning to dislike the atmosphere of false hopes, intrigues, and rumors of the colony of exiles, and he was thinking of trying his luck in Paris, where some of his friends had gone.

On a particularly dreary day, Elizabeth sought refuge from the rain in the Royal Art Gallery. The children were not yet home from school, and she did not look forward to seeing Kate. It amazed her to see how long the girl's resentment lasted. If Frederic were home, one of them would do something dramatic to break the spell, but Elizabeth did not feel up to it. She thought that seeing the old familiar masterpieces would restore her mind to some equanimity.

The paintings were like her friends — some no longer talked to her. The gorgeous rich Titians she used to love, the harmonious Raphaels stared past her. She sat down before Rembrandt's portrait of a young artist. He wore a dark hat, a dark cloak, and the background was dimmed in shadows. Even his eyes were shaded. Only one hand and the fine chin were lit. But through the gloom, she could feel his warm, thoughtful gaze.

It's the man's sorrow that shines, not the trappings designed to make us look invulnerable, she thought.

She wandered off in search of other Rembrandts, comforted by the humanity of his people and their acceptance of sadness. A woman with enormous blue eyes and gold hair greeted her.

"Elizabeth! How nice to find someone else who needs to escape this awful weather. Isn't it a bore?"

Countess Caja was Countess Károlyi's sister. Elizabeth knew that she had remained loyal to Count Károlyi and his wife when all her relations had deserted them, and she felt friendly towards her.

"Actually, I'm glad I came here. A painting started to talk to me."

"Really? You are lucky — they don't mean a thing to me, except that once in a while one can sell them to pay debts. It's a shame, considering that I am on the board of directors of this museum. Come with me, and maybe you can explain what the fuss is all about."

Elizabeth started to talk about the Rembrandts. They came before a painting that Elizabeth had used as an illustration in the course for working people she had given before the war. Some of her prepared lecture came back to her — she grew eloquent, and Caja clapped her hands together.

"I can't believe it, you actually made me interested in the lines and the colors. Could you do some more?"

Elizabeth promised to dig out her old lecture notes. Caja, full of enthusiasm, promised to bring some of her titled friends. The visit was repeated, and the board members liked the lecture so much that Elizabeth was asked to do a series for visiting dignitaries.

As she outlined the shapes in the air, Elizabeth's hand longed for a sketch book and a pencil. She really wanted to give a nature drawing class in her home, but she was afraid to try after all these years. Tentatively, she asked Caja's friends whether they wanted to try copying. They were enthusiastic. An afternoon spent before easels — hats off and much laughter at their own clumsy efforts — brought her a little closer to her goal.

Elizabeth now had a meager livelihood until Frederic could find a job, but she was terribly lonely. Her relationship with her students at the museum was friendly but distant. She could not get used to her sudden isolation. Frederic's next letter was a disappointment — he had been able to arrange a lecture tour to England but nothing permanent to permit their reunion.

Afternoons at the museum increased her sense of isolation. There was a subtle condescension among the women that hurt Elizabeth. Had they talked politics, they would have come to blows. At one point, she had to give a tour to British and French representatives who would decide what the peace treaty terms would be for Hungary.

"I hope that after this tour, you gentleman will be less inclined to believe left-wing slanders about the barbarian Admiral Horthy," one of the noblewomen said.

The visitors laughed. Elizabeth went home thinking about Agosti's murder and about resigning from the museum.

When she reached her landing, the smell of cooking greeted her in the hall. It was a rich perfume, a mixture of meat, spices, and of a cake baking in an oven. She thought that someone in the house must have visitors from the countryside. Opening the door, she realized that the odors came from her own kitchen. She was nearly run over as four overheated happy runners dashed past her. Kate, Andrew, Esther, and Stevie, dressed up in old clothes, were playing cops and robbers.

"Anna's here, Mother!" shouted Kate, as she nearly tripped in a long silk petticoat she wore with a man's hat and sunglasses. At the pantry door, her friend stood, a smile on her flushed face. Elizabeth didn't even take off her coat. She threw her arms around Anna and burst into tears.

"There, there," Anna patted her and reached for a handkerchief.

"No, no, I'm going to have a good cry and no one is going to stop me," Elizabeth laughed through her tears.

Anna waved the children away.

"You can go on playing, everything is all right. I'm here with your mother."

PART VII ~ EXILE

"I was perfectly happy"

Paris (1921)

1.

Well, I promised to write and describe everything to those of you (e.g. all of you) who have never lived in Paris, but really, I wish we had never left Budapest. I know, I know — it is because, finally, Papa got a job at the Archives Nationales in Paris, editing foreign laws ("Big deal!" I said, and Mother looked at me with that "No daughter of mine would say such a thing" look). It wouldn't occur to any of them to ask us children what we want. Andrew is still such a baby even at twelve, but I'm nearly seventeen — do they realize what that means? I don't wear braids anymore. In the evening, I put my hair up, although I am thinking of cutting it short, actually.

It's not that I don't care about Papa, but I was perfectly happy in Budapest even without him. Mother gave art classes and we managed, especially with Anna's help. And how I will miss my gymnasium! I was at the top of my class. I had lots of friends, beginning to flirt with boys, and now I have to fall behind one whole year and study like mad to catch up with the French curriculum, not to mention the French language....

Mother also told us that the apartment he found for us was "very French" and from the enthusiasm with which she described the surrounding neighborhood, we guessed that she meant cramped and uncomfortable. But when she let out that the bathtub was in the kitchen, Andrew and I got hysterical.

"An arm, a turnip, a leg, a carrot," Andrew scrubbed with an imaginary brush. Not that he cared whether he bathed or not, he added.

On the train, Mother had tried to explain Paris to us:

"It's on a very grand scale — more like Vienna than Budapest or even Prague. Where we have churches, they have cathedrals; where we have one museum, they have six or seven. But it's not what makes it exciting — it's the liveliness of the people, in the parks, in the stores...."

"They jump up and down all the time?" asked Andrew.

"No," she smiled. "I know I'm not doing a good job of explaining — their hands jump up and down, they talk with them... It's something about their minds: they are more curious, wittier than our sluggish compatriots... They are more civilized..." I'd like to know how people who put their bathtubs in the kitchen call themselves civilized.

2.

The morning after we arrived, I heard the entrance door slam before I was dressed and my father's steps in the hallway. In my robe, hairbrush in hand, I went to see what he was doing. There were two newspapers on the table, flowers, and a platter of fresh croissants. He was bending over the coffee maker.

"It's a wonderful machine. It can spit hot milk and coffee at you simultaneously," he said, as if he was affectionately describing an ill-tempered relative.

"Did you go to the bakery already?" I asked. I felt funny seeing my tall, elegant father in the dingy kitchen.

"I always do, since I've been here making my own breakfast. But it's much nicer to have you here to share it."

I went on brushing my hair, not quite approving. He smiled.

"My dear Kate, shouldn't you do whatever you are doing to your hair somewhere else?"

My mother's lively steps clicked behind me in the narrow hallway. Although she too wore her robe, her hair was already pinned up, and she wore shoes and stockings.

"Frederic! What a lovely surprise!" and she kissed him.

We ate our croissants in front of the open window. The noises of the narrow Paris street came up to us. There are more cars, more trolleys and buses than in Budapest, and a faint smell of gasoline rose over the thin, undernourished trees. Women were beating rugs on balconies. Under ours, a beggar woman stopped and sang in a cracked but powerful voice:

> *Sometimes he beats me,*
> *Sometimes he cheats me,*
> *But I love him anyway....*

"Throw that poor woman something," my mother said to Andrew, who was leaning over the railing, "although I find her idea of love depressing."

It interested me, however.

Like the gasoline, a whiff reached me of love as an irresistible force, a pain to be relished. I wondered if at home I would have been allowed to hear such songs.

3.

I am alone in the apartment with a stack of books. Father is at work; Mother went to see her old sculpture teacher who is a Russian émigré and she took Andrew with her. This morning I had my first tutorial. My tutor is a professor at a lycée, who agreed to coach me. Her fee is low but the gratitude she expects is enormous. She is dry as a stick, with short, jet black hair, and horrors! — her eyebrows are plucked. She calls me Mademoiselle and I call her Mademoiselle and we go back and forth like some kind of comic ballet: "Mais oui, Mademoiselle," "Mais non, Mademoiselle," etc.

Let me tell you about the curriculum. Ugh! I am not so worried about algebra, geometry, or Latin — I may even be ahead in Latin because we were taught by priests for whom it was a living language. But French literature, French history, French composition, and French rhetoric terrify me. Over half the curriculum consists of exalting the French language! I can see Mademoiselle wince every time I pronounce an "R" in my hard, Hungarian way. Even philosophy, one of my best subjects, consists of Descartes and Pascal.

"Do the French ever study Kant or Schopenhauer?" I ask.

"Mais oui, Mademoiselle, at the university."

I lean out into the street to procrastinate. We had a queer French lunch in a little neighborhood restaurant. Lukewarm artichokes, which I rather liked, then a soup made with (I swear) lettuce, then some unmentionable parts of beasts: brains, tripes, snouts. The restaurant has marble floors, long leather benches along the walls, and a cat in the window. Most of the customers know the ugly old waitress, and they discuss the menu as if all earthly happiness depended on whether to take the veal or the tripe. My parents think it's charming. My idea of charm is sweeping into Maxim's in a long glittering gown, with the waiters concealing their recognition of my celebrity....

4.

I think I made a friend today. My parents dragged me to a reception at Mme. de Coligny's.

"She was very, very nice to your father before we arrived," Mother said sternly as she pinned on her hat. I saw her relax when she came face-to-face with Liane de Coligny. Our hostess is very plain, short, swarthy, with a trace of mustache. But she has kind, liquid eyes. She seems curious and intelligent. She is half Italian; and after telling Mother how glad she was to meet her, she immediately asked her what she thought of D'Annunzio. There is much talk of the poet nowadays as he is about to be ousted from Fiume, which he had taken from Hungary with a small band of adventurers.

"I don't like him," Mother replied, "not because I place any personal claim to Fiume, but because I don't like symbolist poetry, theatrical gestures, and his superman pose. Just plain men will do."

"I agree," Liane said. "Men are wonderful, aren't they?"

I thought that was a funny remark, not quite what Mother had meant. In spite of the mustache, it made me think that Madame de Coligny had had her share of adventures. The salon was populated predominantly by males. The conversation delved into the claims to Northern Italy, and I drifted towards the tea table.

"Try these," a girl with a small head and slanted eyes suggested, pointing to little puffs filled with whipped cream. "My name is Odette. I hope you dislike politics."

On the spur of the moment, I decided that I did. I introduced my brother to Odette and to the cream puffs.

"Are all the people here politicians?" I asked, looking around.

"Many of them are. Liane encourages the foreigners to bring their children because it's her tactful way of feeding some who often go hungry."

Andrew stopped eating, embarrassed. Odette smiled:

"Never mind, that doesn't go for you. I can see that you're a pig rather than a waif. Anyway, my father is a politician. He's a socialist of the old school — small town schoolteacher, labor organizer, pacifist. He's an old dear but not very interesting. What is yours?"

"He's a lawyer, a social democrat," I said lamely. I wished I could discuss my parents as flippantly as my new acquaintance did hers.

"What do you find interesting?" I asked.

"Have you seen the Russian ballet yet?" she asked, raising her thin eyebrows. "You should — they are extraordinary. The colors, the richness, that exuberance...."

As she told us about the performance she had seen, my father came to introduce us to some acquaintances of his. Odette and I shook hands and exchanged addresses. I hope I'll see her again. She is a nervous, scrawny creature but full of life.

I was surprised to hear my father say on our way home that Madame de Coligny's was one of the very few French homes to which foreigners were ever invited.

"But the French are perfectly happy to share all this with us," he said, his hand sweeping the wide, lively boulevard on which we were walking.

"French interiors depress me," my mother said. "Too many drapes and screens and tapestries. In the salon we just visited, unless you stand right at the window, you wouldn't know that the quays of the Seine are right outside — the air and light are shut out."

My father put his hand under her elbow.

"Come and make a detour at this corner. I want to show you a little square."

He took us to a tiny square that was almost entirely occupied by an old tree spreading its gnarled branches. A bench had been built around it, and the houses looked down with the sad eyes of their windows. A dog walked by at a leisurely pace, a bird sang. Suddenly, it occurred to me how much shorter Odette wore her skirt than I did, and the afternoon was spoiled.

5.

"What am I to do with my leisure?" my mother asked in a half-serious, half-playful way.

We had been in Paris for nearly a month now and the dreaded reopening of schools was upon us. We had bought cold cuts and salads and were eating supper in our tiny living room. It got dark early now and the electric lights were on.

"The French don't make French salad the way we do," Andrew said, wrinkling up his nose at the mayonnaise of diced carrots, potatoes, and peas.

"If they did, they'd call it Hungarian salad, wouldn't they?" Father asked, smiling.

"Actually, they call it 'Salade Russe'" I said.

"What is this about your leisure, my dear?" Father turned to Mother. "You should enjoy it."

"I do, but I miss my responsibilities. I don't think we can do much entertaining here — she looked at the room — and I will not spend much time supervising the staff. I asked Marinette whether she would mind sweeping under the beds as well as around them and she asked me tartly whether I spend much time under them."

"Shades of the French Revolution," my father said. "She does look the way I imagine the women who sat knitting under the guillotine. Maybe we should have had one…"

I hope he means a real revolution, not a guillotine.

"I thought that Madame Talieff invited you to do sculpture in her studio," he said to my mother.

"She did and I look forward to that," Mother said, pouring tea. "But what I really miss is teaching my art classes. I was getting to love those sessions, although some of the pupils were truly hopeless. Children, do you remember young Countess Pulski? She had a limp, aristocratic hand and everything she drew drooped. Behind her back, we called her painting 'the drought'."

We laughed but I saw a shadow settle over my father's eyes.

"I guess I would have liked the thought of your teaching if you hadn't gotten paid for it," he said.

"But that was nice," my mother said, innocently.

"Not for me," he replied, with bitterness in his voice. "You know how proud I've always been of your talents and your many interests. But that a woman of our class should have to earn money with them sears my heart. It's only because I was not able to support you properly."

She looked at him sympathetically, but then she lowered her eyes and fussed with the teapot, a slight flush coming over her face. I'm sure it had never occurred to her that supporting us while he was exiled was a reflection on him. Andrew and I held our breath. This conversation, I thought, would never have taken place in front of us at home.

"Well, anyway, I was not thinking of giving art lessons here," my mother broke the silence in a conciliatory tone. "I can hardly compete with the Académie des Beaux Arts."

"I have a project for you," I said. "How about quizzing me on irregular verbs?"

"Are there any others?" Andrew sighed, leaning his hands on his fist and gazing despondently over the remains of the supper. I had completely forgotten that he too had to face the French schools. But while I had been having fits about it, he had quietly taken his daily French lessons and gone back to reading Jules Verne in Hungarian. That evening, he said to me, "If Mother earned some money, I could get a bike."

"And I could get a creamy white silk blouse with a wide collar..." I dreamed. "Aren't you scared of school, Andy?"

"I can get a soccer ball away from any French kid," he said calmly. And I bet he could.

6.

November. A light gray drizzle enveloped the gray buildings. I kept taking off my hat and scarf, hoping to develop a sore throat. Sometimes, after lunch, with the strange food still heavy in my stomach, I delayed in the square, dragging my feet to the bus stop, to the cold, formal, unrelenting discipline of class. On some days,

I couldn't understand French at all. I felt I am drowning at the bottom of a deep well, in a sea of strange faces....

Finally, one morning I woke up feverish and achy. I felt ashamed and foolish: a cold won't solve my problem for long. But it was wonderful to lie in bed in the middle of the morning. The street noises seemed miles away. Mother brought in a hot infusion and put her cool hand on my forehead. I smiled and dozed off.

When I opened my eyes, she was sitting in an armchair, with some sewing on her lap. Her gaze was far away, over the roofs that can be seen through the courtyard window. Her face, usually so mobile, was sad. When she saw me awake, she stirred herself, at once active and energetic. "Goodness, child, this infusion is completely cold. Let me make you a new one."

When she returned, I asked, "Were you thinking of home, before?"

"I was thinking of your father," she explained, somewhat reluctantly. "He is very sweet about his job and tries to take a real interest in it, but for a man of his talents..." She shook her head to indicate how little she thought it offered him.

"Wouldn't it be better if we went back to Budapest?"

"It's not a simple decision. If your father goes back, he has to face charges by the Horthy Government."

I sat up in bed. "Why? Because he belonged to a different political party?"

"They don't look at it that way. The charges are that he betrayed Austria/Hungary during the war by sending messages of peace to the French. What they really have against him is that he drafted the land reform bill and tried to repeal the anti-strike law."

Then she added, "He has asked me to go home next month to talk to a lawyer about all this. You will have to take care of him and of Andrew while I am gone."

I groaned and slid down between the covers. "Oh, Mother — that and French too?"

She smiled. "Frederic and Andrew still understand Hungarian. And don't worry so much about your grades! Be patient!"

The bell rang. She returned from the door with a little blue telegram addressed to me. I ripped it open: Odette was inviting me to the Russian ballet. She had an extra ticket for that very night.

"I guess you can't go," my mother said sadly. I could have cried.

Later, lying in bed, I tried to think about my father being tried for treason. I looked at a fold in the sheets and tried to focus on what it meant — disgrace, treason, death? I felt fearful and uncertain.

A scene came to my mind as if I had been there. A man is sitting in a stopped train in Austria, reading a newspaper. Suddenly, four or five men jump up onto the platform, rush into his compartment, and drag him off. There is no one in the station. He cries out but no soul turns to hear. They bundle him into a car and take off towards the Hungarian border. After a few minutes, a distant shot rings out. The sun keeps shining on the deserted station. The train takes off.

I took a sip of my bitter tea and stared at the ceiling. Yes, that is what could happen to my father. If he were adjudged to be a traitor, any patriotic Hungarian could be expected to be rewarded for executing the sentence. But we are not in Austria, I reminded myself, we are in Paris.

I became aware of noises across the courtyard. Someone started practicing the piano. A woman laughed. I sighed a sigh of relief. For the first time, I felt a small debt of gratitude to France.

7.

My parents spent more and more evenings at the small dining table in the living room, with papers spread out in front of them. Their conversation invaded the whole tiny apartment with its tension, even its silences. My father would lean back in his chair, his long fingers on his chin, deep in thought. My mother waited, pencil in hand, until he would suggest a name or a fact that would be useful in his defense. Often, they would laugh, enjoying the common recollection and the work together. "They do get on, don't they!" I would say to myself, as I sat curled up on the sofa, trying to concentrate on my Greek. I felt excluded by their harmony. Soon I would cough and pretend to have difficulty with my translation. They would stop and invite me over to the table, without the least sign of annoyance. I put my book in front of my father, my long hair grazing his shoulder, while he scanned Aeschylus by banging his pipe on the table, "It works out all right, you just have to stress the third syllable...."

"OK but it still doesn't make sense...."

"Look, Kate — 'with his gleaming knife, he smote him on the throat'...."

"Oh, I see — I thought that meant helmet and I wondered why he took it off."

My mother looked up. "Don't you want a cup of tea? Maybe we all need a break."

"Break! break!" shouts Andrew from the next room.

The following week, after we took my mother to the station, we walked home dejected. I asked Father, "Are you worried about this trial?"

"Right now, I'm worrying about whether to stand trial or not. If I do, I might get convicted, but if I don't, we'll never be able to go home again."

"You're not likely to be acquitted, are you?" asked Andrew, with surprising realism.

"If there is an ounce of fairness left in Hungarian justice, I should be acquitted of treason," he replied. "As for the land reform bill, I can't deny that I drafted it. I'm rather proud that I did. But whether there is any fairness in these trials is what I hope your mother will find out." He pulled out his pocket watch. "Would you like to see a moving picture? We could catch the next Mack Sennett showing if we hurry."

It wasn't Sennett. It was Chaplin, and we laughed till tears ran down our cheeks. It was only when we banged the door of the apartment that the fact that Mother wasn't there waiting for us hit us.

8.

After three nights of dining out, I promised Andrew and Father a home-cooked Hungarian meal. On Thursdays, we had the afternoon off from school. As soon as lunch was over, I took a basket and went down to the market. It wasn't, strictly speaking, a market as much as a market street, lined on both sides with food stores and crowded with carts of fruit and vegetable vendors on the sidewalks. From our avenue, the entry to the street was blocked by an enormous truck and a small car facing each other and unable to pass. The truck driver, from the majestic heights of his cab, was pouring insults onto "that little tadpole," which was refusing to back up. The car's driver, gesticulating with his cigarette, started to explain to fascinated bystanders how much room that "big, inflated ox" had if he really wanted to turn into the street. I wondered how even a small car could move between the carts as little boys darted between them, and the crowd grew, enjoying the dispute. I made my way to the butcher shop.

"Veal? Veal stew? I've got the freshest you can imagine. Could you find anything more rosy, more baby-like?"

The butcher made me slightly queasy. He was the kind of large, friendly ogre who could be selling human flesh.

"And how will you prepare this, little miss? With a nice white sauce? an old provincial dish, unfairly neglected."

I confessed that I had been thinking of a goulash. He shook his head in polite disapproval, but the lady behind me took my side.

"You are wrong, Monsieur Dugrand, nothing can be nicer than goulash in the Hungarian manner, with a little bit of onion and lots of paprika. But don't get the Spanish paprika, go up the Rue Talleyrand for the real thing."

I thanked her politely. Even I knew that any Hungarian dish involved lots of onion. Having destroyed her culinary authority, I went into the dry goods store with its neat rows of canned food and hanging dry sausages to buy Spanish paprika. When I came out, the truck was just backing up, the driver muttering in peaceful contempt about the idiots who built that intersection. I bought flour, salt, and eggs for dumplings. The vendor winked at me. "And don't go dancing the polka with those eggs in your basket."

On the way back, an old herb-seller woman persuaded me to buy a fragrant bouquet. For a few pennies, I had enough for a lifetime. I couldn't see how she made a living.

At home, I burned the onions. Mother's cookbook prescribed Hungarian paprika as indispensable, so I sent Andrew off to the

Rue Talleyrand. While he was gone, I made up an enormous batch of dough and beat it till my arms were ready to drop off. Next came the meat, a bit of water and tomato, and then my brother arrived, red-faced from running up the stairs.

"Thank you, Andrew. Can you also help me make the dumplings? Read the rest of the recipe while I stir in the paprika."

He read in a nasal tone to emphasize the patronizing manner of the recipe writer.

"Then we take a floured board and with sharp knife, we snip off tiny bits of dough into a large kettle of salted water, which we have previously brought to boil...."

"Why didn't it tell us about this earlier?" he exploded. I boiled the water, afraid that I had lost my assistant. But he stuck it out, and we scraped the dough bit by bit into the water.

"Listen, Kate," he said, "this is going much too slowly. By the time we throw the last dumpling in, the first one will have boiled to juices."

So we worked faster and faster, snipping off larger dumplings each time. By the time Father rang the bell, we were hurling veritable chunks of dough into the cauldron.

"Help!" I shouted. "The goulash is burning!"

We sat down to a dinner of scorched meat and lumpy dumplings.

"If only we had these as weapons against the Horthy Whites!" Andrew said.

We all drank the sour French table wine.

My father raised his glass.

"To my daughter and her first dinner. May she have many servants," he added.

9.

Uncreative in the artistic sense, my father would have been a wonderful collector if he had been rich. I discovered this when he took me to the Jeu de Paume Museum one Sunday afternoon. Andrew did not want to come. He had discovered a Spanish boy two flights above us who was as crazy about chess as he was. The two communicated in grunts and broken French. From time to time, one of them would curse himself in his own language for a bad move. Their obsession irritated me, and I was glad to leave them staring at their board.

Father and I got on the platform of a bus which was going down the Champs Élysées. The bus conductor was young. He had a mustache, and he hummed a song about cherries and strawberries. At each stop, he rang the bell to tell the driver that the bus was ready to leave, then went inside to collect the fares. When he was finished, he came back and started the song at the beginning. He never got past the second verse, maybe that's all he knew. It was pleasant and windy on the platform with just the three of us. Then a middle-aged couple, corseted and red-faced, climbed up heavily and shared the platform with us. At the Rond Point, two young couples jumped up and crowded us into corners. The young men were what the French call "Papa's boys," rakish but with the expectation of inheritances showing in their gold cufflinks and Borsalino hats. The girls looked cheap and gay, with tired eyes behind their make-up. I envied the freedom of young men to pick their partners from all classes of society. Even if I were a university student, I couldn't invite the young bus conductor to spend the afternoon with me. When we reached the Tuileries, he jumped off and reached up his hand to help me off. He smiled and said: "Au revoir, Mademoiselle," and I was pleased.

I had never seen Impressionist paintings before. Father said, "Step back, lower your eyelids, and let the air shimmer between you and the painting."

Gradually, I adjusted to the fuzzy outlines, the colors trailing off into other shades. A woman in a red dress crossed a field under the sun; London dissolved into mist. At first, I missed the clear outlines of the Old Masters; then I became excited at the naturalness of the scenes.

"They wanted to catch a particular moment," my father explained. He took me to see Monet's paintings of a cathedral at various times of the day. I confessed that I found them boring. But when we left the museum, I was seeing the trees of the park in a new way, more complex, more changeable. I was aware of light and of the composition of color. We bought ices and sat on the iron benches.

"When I came to Budapest, this kind of thing was a revelation to me," Father said. "I not only hadn't seen paintings, I hadn't seen anything."

He talked about his provincial youth, when he was about my age. I had known my paternal grandmother before she died and heard about the large country house where forty cousins could sit at an enormous table that was burned for firewood during the revolution. Andrew and I loved the stories of my father's early childhood, of his father who was a farm manager, of horses and dogs and country beggars. But now he told me of his gymnasium days, and I could sympathize with the seething ambition of a bright young man, hemmed in by his mother's widowhood, piety, and provincialism.

"When you struggle with the earth day after day, as country people do, the idea of looking at it as something beautiful doesn't occur to you. Besides, my home was very puritanical. Once, I asked my mother to admire a sunset, and she said she couldn't afford sunsets."

We laughed. I was determined, however, not to let the personal nature of this conversation be diluted by a discussion of art, so I risked a daring question: "When you were a young man in Budapest...did you have adventures?" He lit a cigarette. "You know, darling, I don't pretend to have been a saint, but I was a very idealistic young man, besides being somewhat timid at first. The kind of relationships that boys of my class had with girls of the lower class — and of course these were the only adventures you could have — quickly soured on me. Those affairs were so transitory, so unequal, that the girls just tried to get as much as they could out of one, poor things, and the men tried to give as little as they could. There was no trust, no friendship, nothing but hungry greed."

I tried to imagine the girls of those days. A magazine illustration came to my mind, of a pert, flirtatious face and a long dress exaggerating the wearer's figure.

"And so you waited for the great love of your life," I said, realizing that was what I was doing.

"I did worse than that," he replied. "I fell in love with a married woman. She was sweet and unhappy, and I passed some of the worst months of my life trying to persuade her to run away with me. Divorce in those days was a terrible scandal, and she couldn't face it, but I couldn't face lying and dissembling, so we broke up."

"Do I know her?" I asked.

"I don't think so," he said. "I've never seen her since, and I must tell you, I hardly thought of her until now."

That shocked me. I thought that love, especially guilty passion, was sacred, and that forgetfulness was impossible.

"I think that those painters also taught me to look at your mother," he continued. "When I was a student, I saw a painting by Renoir of a girl in evening dress, with bangs, staring out of an opera box. There was something so mischievous, so lively in her smile that I wished I could afford to buy the painting. Of course, I couldn't, and it went to Russia. But when I first saw your mother, I recognized that same wit and liveliness."

He looked at his watch, and we started to walk toward the bus stop. Carefully dressed French children rolled hoops along the crunchy gravel walks. I mused about my father's confidences. They were very interesting but not sufficiently romantic for my taste. He seemed to discuss relationships between men and women as if they were like other relationships between people.

I know that they are not.

10.

Mother writes from Budapest:

> My dears, you can't imagine what a strange feeling it is to be a foreigner in your own city. It makes me realize how deeply I have sunk roots into my adopted country and it's all your fault! Through you, Frederic, Kate, and Andrew, I have become Hungarian instead of Czech. Anyway, enough of philosophy — you probably want to know what I am doing instead of what I think. I think of you, by the way, on those rare occasions when dear Cousin

Helene and Uncle Theodore let me sit quietly at home in the evening, instead of dragging me to parties and plays. I would like to know more about your schools, new friends, piano lessons, etc. Have you found a place to ice skate yet? Children, please write longer letters!

On most days, I have been visiting a strange world of lawyers, officials, and bureaucrats, and meeting a category of people referred to by Helen and Theodore as "well-connected." That means that they are connected to the Horthy regime, but willing to meet me and to discuss our case. What an unpleasant bunch of people! Baron von Reddich will serve as an example. He has small eyes lost in a sea of fat and an oily voice. He told me that he was a fellow law-student of yours, Frederic, and that he has great admiration for your "intellectual processes" even though he doesn't agree with your ideas. I'm not sure what that means. I think that he would like to help you, but not too much: just enough to make him feel that, finally, he is as good as you are. Was he a baron already in law school? I would prefer not to accept any favors from such an unattractive man.

On Sunday, to escape, I took a train to Kisbánya, unannounced. It was wonderful to see Anna again, who scolded me roundly for not warning her of my visit. She would have killed a gosling, stretched the dough for strudel, etc., etc., which is exactly why I didn't warn her. She told me that her family did not get the plot they applied for during the land reform period, and Anna is very disappointed. Joseph, however, looks forward to having his son, who is tall and strong, back at the farm. Esther was there and she is a darling. She made crackling for me with her quick, plump little hands. I wish my Kate were as skillful in the kitchen! I came home contented and overfed.

I had better stop now. Tomorrow, I will see one of the potential defense lawyers you suggested, Frederic, and I will report. By the way, one of the well-connected is dear

Countess Pulski, my old pupil. She is as languid as ever
and could hardly raise her aristocratic pinky to ring the
bell for our coffee. However, she is anxious to pull some
strings for me. She asked me to take a gift to her sister in
Paris, some family heirloom she can't entrust to the mail.
Love, love, and more love to you….

11.

Mother's return from Budapest ended my glorious intimacy
with my father. Freed from trying out omelets and scorching meals,
I was able to knuckle down to my studies just before my midterms.
I passed everything, not gloriously, but barely. To think that I, Kate
Ignatius, got an 11 out of 20 in composition! It burned me. My
parents, however, said that I had done splendidly and bought me a
ticket to the Ballets Russes as a reward.

My head is still spinning from the excitement of
"Scheherazade." From the moment the curtain went up, I was
transported to a magical world of slave girls, of camels, of
powerful sultans, and crafty beauties. The sets, the costumes, the
music are splendid, excessive. Purple tops over pink pants; statues
dripping with diamonds and pearls; dancers reclining over gold silk
pillows and suddenly leaping about like flames. When the curtain
came down, I sat dazed. How could I go back to the monochrome
of everyday life? Even my parents' reaction to my enthusiastic
description seemed insipid. "I'm happy that you enjoyed it, dear,"
mother said. I slammed the door of the tiny bedroom. It wasn't
until I was able to talk to Odette over the telephone that I could
feel some of the magic coming back as she shared my excitement.

"You know this place that never existed, that Baghdad of
the Thousand and One Nights? That's my home, that is where I
belong. This school, this home, this schoolgirl's uniform — they
are just prison walls!"

She said, gravely, "You are a butterfly in a cocoon. Soon you
will spread your wings and soar. In the meanwhile, come for tea
next Thursday."

I felt better.

12.

Pablo, my brother's friend, is insane. I mean really insane.
Yesterday, I came home from the library, and I had just gone into
the kitchen to boil some water for tea, when Andrew called me
urgently:

"Kate, come quickly. Pablo has gone crazy!"

In the living room Pablo was jumping up and down, his hands
cupped, growling and cursing in Spanish. Andrew explained that
for once they had decided not to play chess, but some other game,
and the frustration of trying to communicate had gotten the boy
terribly upset. He was a comical but scary sight, obviously looking
for some object on which he could vent his rage. I said to Andrew,
"Why don't you run upstairs and get his mother?" when we saw
him rip open the package that mother had set out on the table to
take to Countess Pulski's sister.

"No!" I yelled "That's not ours!" while Andrew grabbed a
vase and dashed the cold water, flowers and all, at Pablo. Pablo
started to laugh. Andrew said, relieved "Honestly, Pablo, you
looked like a gorilla! a big crazy gorilla." And Pablo joined us,
"Gorilla! Gorilla! Banana, por favor!"

It wasn't till after I came back from the kitchen with tea for
all three of us that I remembered the package. It was ripped open,
dripping over the living room rug and full of 100 franc bills. My
brother and I looked at each other:

"That's an heirloom?"

We spent the evening drying and ironing money. It was funny
to see our bathroom tiles papered with 100-franc notes, and even
my parents couldn't resist suggesting inappropriate uses for all that
money. Finally, they were all counted, recounted, and back in a
neat package, except for a few that got torn and were replaced by
bills from Mother's emergency cash under the cigar box.

13.

I told my parents that I'm not going on to the baccalaureate. I
want to become a stage designer. I'm not sure I chose my moment
well. I came home all excited from having had a long discussion
with Odette about life and the future, and I found my parents

talking to Dr. Csolnoky, a colleague of my father's, about the impending trial. But that's the trouble with that apartment! The moment you open the door, you are practically in the lap of the adults talking in the living room.

"Mother, Father!" I said "Can I talk to you right away? It's really important."

"Dr. Csolnoky, this is my daughter, Kate," Father said, as if I had always wanted to meet the tall, graying guest.

"How do you do," I said, ungraciously.

"How is the young lady enjoying her stay in Paris?" he asked.

"I hate every minute of it," I replied.

I still had my coat on. Without looking at anyone, I walked out of the apartment. I walked fast, into the wind, down our street, and into the wide avenue. Here I had reached a major decision about my life and I couldn't even talk to my parents about it! I turned away from the direction of the Metro, which reminded me of my daily trip to school and walked towards the part of the avenue I had never explored. The sidewalk cafés had been enclosed by glass partitions, befogged by the heat. I could see rows of empty tables, six or seven deep. Soon the lights would go on, and everyone would find refuge in a warm, cozy home while I wandered on. I really wished never to go home. The cramped quarters, my parents' financial worries, the isolation of our family, all depressed me. If I could attach myself to the bright, glittering world of the stage by joining a company as a stage designer, I could escape.

And yet I knew that my parents would oppose my plan. A girl from a "good family" doesn't become a commercial artist. A painter, maybe, a musician — but the theater just isn't respectable. "At least, you must finish your studies," they will say. Why? I didn't want to be cultured. I wanted to be alive. Odette told me about an American girl she met in the park once. She was twenty, she lived in a little flat on the left bank, and she wrote a feature for her newspaper at home on the artists who worked in Paris. What an exciting life! Odette wanted to introduce us, but unfortunately she had forgotten to ask the young woman her name.

Walking had distracted me somewhat. The avenue was quiet,

residential. The large, varnished entrances to the apartment houses, through which a coach could be driven when these houses were built, alternated with quiet little pastry shops, milliners, and bookstores. The avenue ended at a park. I dreaded the wind on the open lawns, and I turned back. For a while, I stood before a café. I would have loved to sit down and order a hot chocolate. I felt in my pocket. Besides my bus allowance, I only had half a franc. I didn't know if that would be enough, and besides, I had never entered a restaurant alone. In a bakery, I bought a roll with a bar of chocolate in it. What a schoolgirlish treat!

On my way back, I passed a parked car with a red-headed woman in it. She sat very still, staring ahead. She had a proud, cold profile, emphasized by her hairdo, which was piled in an elaborate bun. I suppose she was waiting for the driver of the car, who might have gone into the house. I was sure that he was a man — a husband or lover perhaps. She paid no attention to me, and I continued to walk. I don't know why seeing that woman made me feel better. Somehow, her patience in waiting for whoever she expected made me realize that, inevitably, someday my own time would arrive. Nothing could prevent my becoming a woman, with my own life, my own preoccupations. I went home, ready to face my parents' reproaches for my ill-mannered behavior. But they disappointed me again. They were sitting where I had left them, only the guest was gone. My father's cigar glowed in the dark; they had forgotten to turn on the lights, absorbed in their discussion. I wondered how bad the news from Budapest was.

"My goodness," my mother said, "it must be very late. Shall we call Andrew and go to the Russian restaurant for supper?"

She didn't even notice how late I had come in. During dinner, they told us that Dr. Csolnoky had looked over the charges against Father and the evidence Mother had collected. Based on what he knew of similar trials that were taking place in Budapest, he was certain that Father would be convicted. He did not think that the contacts Mother made in Budapest were good enough to get the charges dropped. It was a somber meal and I put off talking to them about my new ambitions.

14.

As the winter wore on, we suffered from the damp Parisian cold, and what surprised us, we stayed cold. My overcoat was short at the sleeves and hem and tight under the elbows. Andrew's was scuffed and worn, as well as tight. But we could not afford new ones. So Mother had one of her coats altered for me. Although it was more attractive than mine had been, the material was lighter and I shivered until I got into the stuffy underground warmth of the Metro. Andrew refused to have my coat altered for himself. Indoors, we were cold too.

"Do you recall our big porcelain woodstoves?" Mother sighed, as we vainly fiddled with the knobs of the lukewarm radiators. Nostalgically, we tried to recall the exact colors of each stove, which filled the room with radiating warmth during the bitter Hungarian winters. For a few weeks, we even looked for a new apartment with heating, but anything we could afford would have taken us out of the neighborhood we had become attached to.

Mother took a job sewing sequins in one of the great dressmaking houses. Although she grew to like the French girls who worked there, the tedium of the work nearly drove her to distraction. I don't know what they paid her, but it seemed to make little difference to our finances. Father smoked fewer cigars and one Sunday, Mother said, "Maybe we should skip lunch — after all, Madame de Coligny serves such enormous teas."

Andrew and I exchanged glances. We remembered Odette saying that the lavish meal was Liane's way of helping refugees in need without hurting their pride. We were embarrassed.

When we arrived that Sunday afternoon, a group had gathered in heated debate around the small red sofa before the fireplace. A new guest was sprawled over it, one leg carelessly entwined in the gilded curlicues. He was a man of forty or forty-five with deep blue eyes, high cheekbones, and a gold beard.

"Odoetov," one of my parents' friend, explained. "He will be Lenin's ambassador to France when the Bolshevik government is recognized." Hearing his name, the Russian stopped in mid-sentence.

"My eloquence isn't so remarkable that it can't be interrupted" he said with a smile, "What is your opinion, Ignatius, of the young German republic?"

My father replied that he was worried about attacks on Weimar from the radical left and the radical right. Odoetov accepted the challenge and defended the Marxist Spartacus movement. There was a bluntness in his manner that fascinated me.

Odette came in and we withdrew to the embrasure of the living room window where we liked to talk.

"He's awfully attractive, isn't he?" I asked her, referring to the Russian.

"Farnham, the British socialist, is more my type," she said. "Underneath that angelic exterior, I suspect a deep sensuality, bordering on vice."

"Odette, you haven't any idea what you are talking about," I giggled, impressed.

"Anyway, who cares about whether the Wilsonian ideals have been fulfilled? We don't look at life the way anyone did before the war."

"You mean because we wear short skirts and vote?"

"No, I mean that we thrill to discontinuity, to the absence of form, harmony, structure. Only art expresses the post-war consciousness."

I saw my mother glancing towards us. I knew she would have enjoyed joining a conversation about art, but she just smiled at me and looked away.

"My poor mother," I said to Odette. "She wanted to be a sculptress when she was young, and now she is sewing sequins."

"Oh, well, everyone makes their own life," she shrugged. "Can you get away next Saturday? My cousin is having a dinner dance, and she gave me permission to bring you."

I was delighted by the prospect and babbled about it all the way home. The only shadow on my happiness was the sudden discovery that a Greek quiz had been scheduled for Monday, and I had forgotten to prepare for it.

I sat down in our living room while Andrew went to sleep on the couch which served as his bed. Through the half-open door, I could see my mother brushing her hair.

"He certainly isn't the gloomy type of Bolshevik," I heard her say, "I found him charming."

"This is a different breed from our little red fanatics of 1919," my father replied.

With half an ear, I heard them discuss various kind of communists and why Father objected to total economic planning. He said something about Hungarians and forged rubles, some story that he had heard from Odoetov, and they both laughed. My Greek was not progressing, when suddenly Mother's voice came clearly into the living room. "Frederic," she asked "do you think that Countess Pulski was sending forged money to her sister? I used one of the notes she sent — you remember? I replaced the torn ones and a woman at a store refused to accept it. She said she didn't like the feel of it - do you suppose it was because we ironed it?"

"It would certainly be typical of our great Hungarian aristocrats to swindle an émigré family out of two hundred francs," said my father, disturbed.

I slammed my book shut and asked Mother to wake me early. One really had no privacy in this place!

15.

Mother, Andrew, and I spent Christmas vacation at Aunt Clara's in Vienna. What warmth, what comfort, what a feeling of home! To open my eyes and peek over the eiderdown quilt at the beloved Biedermeier furniture of my room, to ring for my hot chocolate with whipped cream and Kaiser rolls, made me want to pinch myself — is this a dream or is our life in Paris just a bad novel that I read by mistake? I never got up before eleven, ready to face a chorus of derision by my cousins.

"Good day, your royal highness! How extraordinarily well you look, unscathed by revolution and inflation! What is your pleasure for today?"

"First, I would like to have my disagreeable male cousins thrown into a dungeon, to spend six months preparing for the French baccalaureate. After that, and after they have shaved," I added, as I kissed their newly grown stubble, "I will allow them to take me ice-skating, window-shopping, and to a pastry orgy at Demel's."

We were off, not alas, in a carriage or a chauffeur-driven car, as we would have been before the war, but still to a whirlwind of visits and outings shared with their university friends. For five days, I hardly saw the adults. My father is due to arrive after Christmas and so are Uncle Ian and Aunt Clara from Iglau. We solemnly promised to spend New Year's Eve at home — so long as we could go to Fledermaus at midnight and skating the next morning.

Before we left Vienna, the weather suddenly turned warm and balmy. Amidst the melting snow, my cousins and I walked up and down the suburban hills, feeling the melancholy of vacation's end. We came upon the rickety wagon of a gypsy woman who foretold my cousins' fates right out of the latest popular newspapers.

Giggling, they pushed me into her overfurnished shabby room. She looked at my hand and predicted that at first I would have many admirers, "none of whom would touch my heart." Then she squinted a bit and said that she saw me with a red kerchief over my head and something like a hammer in my hand.

"Do you have a brother or father who likes to do carpentry?" she asked.

"No, but I'm planning to build stage sets," I replied.

She nodded — I'm not sure she knew what I meant.

"I see a man approaching you now. He is tall and dark, very handsome, but there is something between you. It glitters — money? A wedding ring?" She looked up, but I didn't change my expression. "Now it's fading and you touch each other."

She paused for a moment, and added in a toneless voice, as if I was expecting her to say it, "You will be very happy."

She didn't say "forever" or smile. I guess she was tired of telling fortunes. When the others asked me what she foretold for me, I said it was the usual drivel. Superstitiously, I did not mention the red kerchief. It was so vivid that I half-believed in it.

16.

Mother did not return to Paris with us. The conclave of aunts and uncles persuaded her, as my father had tried earlier, that she should not go back to her job in the dressmaking salon. Instead, they thought that with the Hungarian economic conditions improving, she should try to sell some land that Father had inherited in his native province. She went and became involved in an amateur detective venture. She wrote to us:

> Your Uncle Theodore has convinced me that the fake Russian rubles and Countess Pulski are connected — Count Pulski is director of the mint. Could you possibly find out whether the bills we have are fakes? You know where I keep them — in the cigar box on top of the dresser. Then again, I may have put them in the pantry, under the baking paper or in my hairpin box. But be careful.

Father sighed when he got her instructions, but he did find out that the bills were forged.

The theory that Mother, Theodore, and my father put together is that the forgeries were thought up and carried out by organizations of rabid Hungarian nationalists who had been displaced from lost territories.

These men knew that inflation was endemic in post-war Europe and that it could be fuelled by the infusion of large amounts of paper money. Reactionary noblemen like Pulski had probably been persuaded to help by loaning machinery from the government printing office. Some police cooperation was clearly needed; not much went on under Horthy that escaped the eyes of the vigilante organizations that had merged with the national police.

When Mother came home, she and Father tried to convince their friends who were influential in French politics that the Horthy government was trying to ruin the French franc. But they had no real proof, and they could hardly persuade the French government to abandon Admiral Horthy, whom they considered a pillar of anti-Bolshevik reactions, because a silly Hungarian countess forged a few francs.

Stubbornly, I refused to get involved. I listened to the political discussions at Liane de Coligny's with a kind of anger and pain.

"If our parents had not been so liberal, so high-minded about suffrage and land reform, I would still be leading a charmed life at home," I said bitterly to my brother when we were alone. "The price of other people's happiness is one's own."

"I don't know," he said. "I think that you got burned in 1919 — what turned you off politics were those two Huns who tried to arrest you." I screamed and tried to hit him as hard as I could, but he laughed at me. I was furious, but he was quite strong. I couldn't beat him.

"Baby!" I said haughtily and stalked out.

17.

Springtime comes slowly to Paris. At first, only the lightness of the continued rain and the lingering glow of the late afternoons indicated that winter was over. Then the sky seemed to move up several notches, so that a high pale dome sparkled with blue while the wind chilled Odette and me on our Thursday walks. Parisian women changed into lighter colors before we could discover the smallest fresh buds. I felt the hope of renewal lifting my spirits.

I had a few friends now at school, a few professors who called on me and listened to what I said without correcting my pronunciation. Odette and I started to talk about the Easter vacation which she had invited me to spend with her family.

"You should see the Provence now! Gold mimosa, hot pink bougainvillea, and in the distance, the dark blue sea."

I wished they would invite my parents, but it didn't occur to them. Father had taken up some work with the League of Human Rights for almost no pay to balance the tedium of his everyday job. Mother had had a succession of jobs, none very exciting. She had started to entertain friends in our cramped quarters. They came for pastry and liqueurs after supper and kept Andrew from going to sleep on the living room couch, but she could no longer live as a hermit.

One evening I came in quite late. I had been to the theater with two girls I had met through Odette. The bus didn't come, so we decided to walk through the spring night. Paris was full of rustling leaves and walking lovers. I was glowing with intense awareness of the beauty of life. When I turned the key in the outer door, I could hear several voices from the tiny antechamber. Jean Richard Ponselee, my parents' playwright friend, might be here, Odoetov and his statuesque Russian wife, Odeotova, a few voices I didn't recognize. When I stepped in, ready to greet the assembled company, a silence suddenly fell, leaving me uncertain of whether to speak or not. Odoetov's wife started to laugh her deep contralto laugh.

"We didn't mean to startle you, child. It's just that the men suddenly realized that you are a beauty and being intellectuals, they are at a loss for words."

I blushed and protested, knowing that my parents would expect me to. But I was grateful to Odoetova.

18.

We were having dinner at an outdoor terrace when a newsboy passed by, shouting the latest headlines.

"Hungarian diplomat arrested with forged francs! Only the Evening News has the story! Buy it, buy it, Messieurs, Dames!"

My father jumped up; he could hardly wait until the boy finished giving change to another customer. We leaned over him as he read. The diplomatic pouch of the Hungarian ambassador had been opened at the border by the police; hundreds of thousands of fake French francs had been seized. My father looked at his watch.

"Excuse me, my dear — I think that this is the opening we've been waiting for." And he rushed off, his oysters untouched.

For the next days, he was ceaselessly active and yet he seemed wholly unhurried. Activity released latent energies in him that seemed to create more energy. He had time to explain to us what was happening, to prepare memoranda of meetings and information, and to bring people together who needed to meet. Already, through Uncle Theodore, he had arranged to talk to the Hungarian Socialist deputies in Vienna the following week and he had outlined political strategies for their use in exploiting this scandal against the Horthy regime. He instructed Mother on dealings with the French police and the bank, who were preparing an investigation of the origins of the francs, and who now relied on the clues she had collected on her trip.

During the last months of my school year, the investigation of the forgery took over our lives. Father had left his job and came and went between Paris and Vienna. He and Mother were full of talk and projects.

The trees turned green and I confronted a succession of elderly examiners with my staccato French. The French Sûreté continued to send investigators to Budapest, and they were wined and dined, like all foreigners who might present a threat. They retained sufficient sobriety, however, to identify the Hungarian chief of police as responsible for the forgeries. Much detail in the press was lavished on Count Pulski's romantic castle where the forged francs had been printed. My parents were not amused, although even we had to laugh when we read descriptions of their chaplain blessing the counterfeit notes. Then the story dropped out of the news and Mother said, "Our children look like French children — pale and bent-shouldered. Let's rent a house on the Riviera, the season is over and we can probably get one for very little."

We took a house in Sainte Maxime off a village square shaded by those strange, stubby plane trees that seemed to have corns on their trunks. The house had cool tiled floors and a terrace overlooking the village. In the evening, we ate outside, while the scent of herbs rose all around and swallows swooped over the tiled roofs. We loved it and stared unbelievingly at the telegram asking Father to return to Paris at once to discuss his case with Dr. Csolnoky.

"I'll be back!" I said to the swallows, to the old bike in the hallway, to the lizards in the wall.

This time, we held a family conference. I was polite to the old lawyer who seemed grayer in the gray Parisian light.

"I do not need to spend too much time recapitulating the political situation for you, my dear friends, since you are more or less au courant."

Father sat with his legs crossed, tall, elegant, and relaxed. Mother leaned back against the shabby sofa, her hands spread out by her sides in rare immobility — only nervousness could make them inactive.

"The White Terror is over," Csolnoky continued. "The resignation of the chief of police ends Admiral Horthy's ties to the Hungarian Race Avengers, to the secret interrogation, to the assassination squads. This was the principal demand of the Socialist deputies, backed by their French supporters, and it's the only one that was met."

"In other words, none of the laws have changed," said my father.

"That's right. But there has been some development in your personal situation."

The lawyer explained that the prosecutors were anxious to work out some kind of accommodation with Father, who was now both respected and feared in government circles. They offered to drop the charges of treason and not to stir up the emotional issue of the land reform bill. However, if my father wished to return, he had to stand trial on a minor charge, conviction for which would involve suspension of all his rights to be politically active in any way.

"They suggested indicting you for your proposal to abolish flogging in the navy," the lawyer said, with a faint smile. "The issue is dear to Admiral Horthy's heart and, since Hungary has no navy, they thought that to admit your error would not cost you too much."

"Of course, said my father, "to people who are incapable of having political principles, it is difficult to imagine what it costs to give them up — even minor ones."

My father spoke quietly, but we could feel the bitterness in his voice.

Mother asked tentatively, "But why do they want to deprive my husband of his political rights? I mean, in the present climate, he could hardly do very much, could he?"

"It's a matter of principle with them," the lawyer replied, conscious of the echo of my father's words. "It's the only principle they have."

We talked some more and he left, urging us to take our time in deciding what to do. We sat in silence for a while, then Father looked at Mother. She shook her head — "I won't influence you." She added, "I can only say, like the Roman brides — where you will be Gaius, there will I be Gaia."

I motioned to Andrew that we should leave. My last vision of Paris is of my father, sitting at the dining room table, his fingers slowly stroking his mustache, so deep in thought that he never heard us get up and close the door behind us.

PART VIII ~ FRIENDS

"Call me Elizabeth"

❧

City and Country (1922)

Elizabeth wrote:

My dear Anna, just a quick note to tell you that we're back in Budapest and very happy to be here. I am so busy with unpacking, doctor's appointments, getting the children registered at their various schools, etc. that I will only send my warmest regards to your family and my love to you, until I can do so in person.

Elizabeth Ignatius

Dear Honored Madam, I hope that you and yours are in good health, as we all are, thank God, as well as can be expected. I was very happy to know that you have returned home. No matter how wonderful those foreign places must be it is our own soil and our own sunshine that make us feel at ease.

Right now, we work from long before sunrise until dusk, but the summer's work is not as backbreaking as the spring's. Joska has put his heart into this harvest, and I can hardly stop him long enough for his medicine and his visits to the doctor, whom he must see if he is going to recover from the terrible damage to his lungs suffered in the war. How God could have allowed that devastation to rage for so long will always be a mystery to me. I keep thinking about it because nothing seems the same as it was before. When I was growing up, there was sadness and poverty also, but there were also bonds between parent and child, neighbors and neighbors, masters and servants, that no longer exist — there is greed and hardness now between all, and each of us seems alone.

Maybe I shouldn't say that — or judge from appearances. About my own children I can't complain. They are dutiful and hardworking. Stevie has put away his school clothes and he is working with us as if he never left the countryside. But I am terribly disappointed that a bright, strong child like him shouldn't be able to do more. It isn't just that I had such high hopes for him — I also wanted him to have the learning to understand wider horizons than ours .... Of course, if we had been able to get the extra land that the Honored Sir Attorney Frederic and his friends wanted to give to all, we might have had wider horizons and could afford more education. You see, dear Honored Madam, how contrary I am: Here I am complaining that the world is different, but I too want to change my son's position in it.

1923

Dearest Anna, please excuse my long delay in answering your letter. Frederic's trial has started, and all I can say is that the government has determined to make us pay dearly for our return — the bitterness of the humiliation he is subjected to is too painful to describe. You can read it in the newspapers, but don't. I sit there every day and watch the proud man I love forced to explain and apologize for actions that were altruistic and farsighted. I boil and rage every evening, but he shrugs and laughs. He says that the trial is unreal, that it's just a way of making him promise to "behave," a promise made to men who represent no one but themselves. His faith in the people who needed those freedoms he fought for is unshaken. I think that keeps him going. Anger keeps me going and the commitment not to let him down.

I thought about your letter and the problem you raised. Stevie is a bright boy, and it would be wonderful to allow him a full education. Would it be possible for him to live with us in Budapest? If he is with us, he can register at any secondary school, whether he chooses the classical or the scientific course, which is probably more useful for a boy. Consult your family — I know that we would love it.

Dear Honored Madam, the answer to your kind offer is no, and it grieves me more than I can say. I talked it over with Joska and there is no way we can spare the income that Stevie's work brings in. Prices have fallen again, we have very little cash, and medical expenses are high. Joska offered to go to the local doctor instead of the more expensive clinic at the county seat, but I saw what happened when we first went to this one and I couldn't agree to that. Even what we save with going to a less expensive doctor may not be enough. Stevie is a first-rate worker, already strong — I wish I wasn't so proud of my son, it must be sinful to think so much of one's own.

The only consolation in giving up this dream is that Joska and I talked it over with the old closeness and the old love. He would not want me to tell you about this, but there were tears in his eyes as well as in mine and foolishly, I kissed them away. We were both embarrassed, not being demonstrative in nature, like you, Honored Madam! But I am so glad he still loves and understands his family. I had reason to doubt it for such a long time. So we have to do the best with what we have, it's more than many have.

1924

Dear Anna, we all enjoyed your visit and I've enclosed the recipe that I couldn't find when you were here.

1925

Dear Anna, I have waited for too long to discuss this with you — could you please call me Elizabeth? Every time I read your letters I think of this, but there is so much else to talk of. Even if you hadn't fed and comforted us that terrible year when I was alone here, we would long ago have reached that level of closeness where to imply social distinctions is almost a betrayal of the warm affection of two loyal friends.

1925

Dear Little Madam — for that is what I shall call you — I can no more change the way I address you than I can change the color of birch bark or the shape of sunflowers. I sincerely appreciate the compliment of your request but I am stubborn and old-fashioned, as you know. I hope I have not offended you, nothing could be further from my intention.

I was out on the plain yesterday — you know how our village is situated, with woods and hills toward the west but once you cross the river, it's just the wide, dry plains as far as the eye can see. I felt again the immensity of God's world and the small place that each of us occupies in it. It's strange that in the city, where there are so many more people, each of us seems so important. But I don't resent our smallness in the great scheme of things. We are carried on the back of the broad wide earth as she turns around the sun (as I was taught in my few years of elementary school! for I certainly don't see the church tower spinning as I look out over the flatness), and we can accept what happens to us without fretting over every little event.

Having refused your request, I know that you are generous enough to say yes to mine — would your Honored family join us for our grape harvest next month?

1925

Dear Anna, here we are putting up our storm windows already and I have not thanked you for the fun we had at your harvest! The grape juice and the wine

were wonderful, but I think we also got drunk on the
roast ducklings, the wafer-thin strudel dough filled
with every kind of delight, the fresh bread, and fruit.
That warm October sunshine made our husbands as
happy, as relaxed as I recall seeing them for a long time.
Surrounded by friends, by healthy, tall young people we
have (goodness knows how) brought up, we may yet
enjoy middle age in harmony and peace....

Yes, Kate is strikingly handsome, I worry about it
all the time. The French call it "the fatal gift," and I am
not agreeing with them because of any jealousy — I have
gotten along very well with prettiness and vivacity. Nor
am I unrealistic about the value of her beauty. Kate will
probably have no dowry (her father says that even if
his practice prospers, he does not believe that a woman
should come with a price tag). Kate's looks will allow her
to marry as she wants to, as every woman must. But her
beauty confuses everything about her. You yourself, dear
Anna, used the expression — "You look at her and the
sun's rays don't dazzle you!"

The girl herself does not know what she is like. I have
a notion, of course — she is willful and passionate, but is
she self-centered or just spoiled? and how much of that
is my fault? Andrew is a relief compared to her — fitful,
unsure of himself, but bright and loving through and
through.

1927

Dear Little Madam, you are neglecting your faithful
correspondent. Is everything well with you and yours? We
are in good health, thank God, Joska is tolerably better.
My daughter Esther is a big help to me now, she works
from morning to night, and there is a song on her lips
for the same length of time, when she is not giggling or
shrieking from a teasing little boyfriend.... Stevie hopes
to get work at a mine. The company is restoring some
abandoned caves nearby and will pay good wages. I will

go to Budapest as usual in the late fall, but if you need me, I'll come sooner....

Dearest Anna, thank you for your concern, I am as usual involved in too many things and erratic in my letter-writing. We are well and look forward to your visit.

1928

Dear Anna, we very much enjoyed Stevie's stay with us. No he wasn't any trouble, and you have every reason to be proud of him. His manners are quiet and natural, and I couldn't think of any situation into which I couldn't introduce him with ease, but what is more important is a kind of suppressed energy which makes one admire him in spite of his modest disclaimer to any achievement. Andrew and he got along wonderfully, though they couldn't be more different. As Andrew said when they ended a heated debate on why the soccer team they both admired lost: "Even when you don't know the first thing about what you're talking about, Vas, you'll always be a technician and I'll always be a dilettante." I think what Andrew means is that Stevie has a sense for detail and patience for how technical details fit together that he wholly lacks.

Frederic was very interested in what he told us about the mine. I am not sure I like the management's attitude.

1928

Dear Little Madam, thank you so much for the kindness you showed my son during his visit. He came back with enough stories for a lifetime. When did the young people sleep? It sounds as if they went out every night of the vacation, and there was still a film that they had missed seeing! I guess the automobile show was the high point of the visit, but Stevie's account of the sports events, the cafes and restaurants, the excursions, and the time spent watching pretty girls by the river are going to empty our village. I go to Budapest every year, as you know, but the boys saw more in a week than I have in all my years!

The boy's work at the mine, as you said, is a mixed blessing. I think the company does not like too much ambition in the workers. They do things for the workers but in a funny way. Like the rent for their houses — it's deducted from the worker's salary, so they are tied to their job. The company's big mines are all in the north. Here, they only operate eight months out of the year, so they want to be able to fire everyone each year, with no questions asked. But at least we have our son home then, with the grime of honest work on his brow and arms, instead of that black soot that makes one man look like the next, just the eyes staring out at you.

1930

My dear Anna, yes, the rumor you heard about Kate is true, she is engaged to be married. I hope you will forgive me for not telling you earlier. It embarrasses me to have people hear from the paper's gossip column rather than from me. (What a small town Budapest is! And what a small country our little Hungary.) Frederic and I are not well known, as you know, but Kate's fiance, Philip, is a world-famous physicist and from a prominent family.

The fact is that Frederic and I are unhappy with Kate's choice, but of course we have to accept it. The times are long gone when parents chose spouses for their children, and I made my own choice myself to marry Frederic, a Hungarian, rather than a man of my parents' circle in Moravia. Not that anyone in my family could disapprove of Frederic and fail to love him!

It makes it worse that I was the one who introduced Kate to Philip von Reddich. It happened a year ago at a rehearsal of a play for which Kate had designed the sets. I was chatting with young Philip, whose father had helped me in 1921 when I was in Budapest trying to get help for Frederic, unjustly accused of crimes against our country.

A very unpleasant man by the way, the father, a Baron von Reddich who I'm sure bought his title of nobility, arrogant and reactionary, but he did help us as he was a former client of Frederic's.

Well, in the theater, Philip, came over to talk to me, and I could hardly be rude. He's about forty, balding, elegant, with the manners of the nobility I don't care for, kissing my hand and clicking his heels. Kate came bounding off the stage, in slacks and a kerchief over her head, and that's how they met. Do you remember our talking about the fatal gift of beauty? Philip was struck by Kate's, and I could feel the electricity between them — they couldn't let go of each other's hands, while talking for the sake of talking and prolonging the moment.

So it seems they started seeing each other even though Philip was married to a young woman from the old nobility. Andrew said it was like a bad play. It would have been hissed off the stage had it been anything but real life. But they were serious. Philip divorced his wife, and Kate wouldn't listen to any criticism of her fiancé.

I hope they will be happy, but Frederic wonders whether happiness is what Kate wants. She wants intensity, a life of wider scope and glamour than we can offer her. That doesn't seem to me to be a good foundation for marriage. I said so, and Kate is very angry at me. But you know me. I will try to accommodate myself, but not without saying my say.

1932

Dear Anna, I have just come home from Moravia— I mean Czechoslovakia — where my father is slowly losing his strength. My sister Hilda wants to take him to Vienna, where the great specialists are, but I don't know if there is time. I was looking for some letters from my mother, and I came across the one you wrote to me about being out on the plains and how unimportant one feels in the great scheme of things. Do we really matter as individuals?

Again, on this melancholy visit, I realize how much my father matters to me and — I shouldn't say this, it is not meant to reflect on my dear sisters — how much I, his favorite daughter, mattered to him. But — how it saddens me to say this: What bright hopes he had for me! Have I fulfilled any of them? It has not been hard to be a loving daughter to him, but what have I done with all the talents, enthusiasms, and ambitions that he encouraged in me when I was young?

He had hoped to have a son and he loved me as a person — no, he enjoyed my being a girl, but he did not ignore my personality. And then, of course, I fell in love with Frederic....Did the children ever tell you the story of Semele? I sometimes think I am like that girl, whom Zeus took while he was in the form of a shower of fire and who was consumed by love. I have not stopped being in love with my husband, but I wonder what else is left of me.

I was unable to finish this letter — you know my bad habit of starting several things at the same time — and I mentioned some of my thoughts to Frederic, including your acceptance of our infinite limitations. It seems to have opened up a vein of sadness I never fully understood, a depth of disillusionment in Frederic that I only suspected.

He said that high ambitions can never be fulfilled where there is no justice or political freedom. Not only do we not enjoy these, but he wonders whether people value them. All over Europe, he sees the very people who lacked the right to vote and to national self-determination before the war promote totally different aims: the unleashing of passionate prejudice, of brutal force over the unprotected, of cowardly sadism, and of conformity fueled by hatred. If he is right, what happens to the hopes and ambitions of our children? At least he and I had a chance to fight for what we thought was right....

1932

Dear Little Madam, I was grieved to hear that your dear father is so very ill. He is one of the most lovable people I ever met — your mother being the gentlest. On his visits to Budapest, there was no one, child, servant, chimney sweep, or friend, who did not find excuses to spend time with him. With all my heart, I pray for his health.

If I may be so bold, I cannot honestly agree with the rest of your letter. Dear Madam, did your father expect you to make the Danube run upstream or to move the Iron Gates? To dry one tear if one cannot dry them all is to value loving kindness above all else.

If I may come to visit you, I will take an early train on Sunday and should be there by noon.

1932

Oh Anna, my father died. So much goes with him. I am taking the train to Vienna to be with my sisters. I will be back on Thursday, come to see me.

PART IX ~ A DISINTEGRATING WORLD

"There is such a thing as serious journalism"

Andrew (1930)

1.

I started my career as a journalist when I was nineteen — a little more than a year ago. Of course, I've been writing ever since I started gymnasium — poetry, plays, an epic poem that nearly killed me, and articles for the paper I edited with my closest friends, who invariably let me down and forced me to cover sports, entertainment, and news. Everyone in my family thought that my childish efforts were terrific, and everyone was horrified when I declared after my graduation that I was going to make a career of journalism.

"Why can't you accept my choice of a profession that I will probably be good at? The university isn't anxious to have me — the Jewish quota is filled."

We were drinking coffee after our midday dinner.

"You wouldn't want to study in Budapest anyway, Andrew. What's wrong with Vienna, Berlin, Prague, or Paris?" my mother asked. Then she looked at my father. There were some strands of gray in her auburn hair, but her posture was that of a much younger woman, slim and erect. Her long fingers pushed away at the table. Kate, who had come by before her job at the theater where she designed sets, quickly refreshed her lipstick. My father looked grave. His hair and mustache were turning light gold with age.

"You talk of having chosen a profession — is journalism a profession?" he asked in that serious way that trapped his interlocutor to consider his point of view.

"Most people think of it that way," I replied. "Why not?"

"What most people think...." he said. "To me, a profession involves the systematic application of carefully accumulated knowledge. Your colleagues perform a service, I don't deny it, but I think that it would be accurate to characterize their method as the careless dissemination of unreliable rumors."

We laughed.

"I wouldn't accuse my friends of excessive seriousness," I admitted, "but there is such a thing as serious journalism. What about the Berlin papers, the London Times, your own publication, the Twentieth Century...."

"Which you never read," he said in a neutral tone.

"I plead guilty," I said, while I could sense Kate stirring impatiently.

"The great foreign papers that you mention operate in complete freedom. Could you publish an article here praising the accomplishments of the Soviet Union?"

"Frederic, you have to admit that he could learn to write here as well as abroad," said my mother. "My objection is more to the kind of life that newspapermen live. It's so...cheap."

"But when I think of the life of a respectable Herr Professor or Doctor you want me to become, I'm bored already," I said with heat.

"Your mother and I have not had a dull life," said my father, glancing at her in a way that made her reach over for his hand. "And believe it or not," he added with a smile, "we have enjoyed having a family and the material prosperity needed for one."

"We were just as happy when times were hard and the only good meals we saw came from Anna's garden," interjected Kate.

"All right," my father cut in." I don't want to be misunderstood. What really matters to me is that you should do good work that enables you to respect yourself. To do hackwork out of a sense of revolt against respectability is not a good long-range plan. "

"To destroy everything, to construct nothing," my mother quoted the romantic rebels' motto.

I was irritated and bit my lips as I played with breadcrumbs on the table. I live from day to day and don't like this kind of talk.

"Why don't you give yourself more time, Andrew," my sister said. "You really have no idea of what you want from life and you haven't given it much thought."

"Thank you," I replied. "Do you?"

"We're not talking about me," she said, turning to my mother to indicate how little respect she had for my opinion. "If he did go to the university now, wouldn't he just make a mess of it?"

"I can't agree with the point of view that somehow rebelliousness has to spend itself," said my father, more to her than to me. "It sounds like one of those psychological theories that are such a fad now. I would like Andrew to choose a profession and apply himself to it. But I agree that he has to make the choice, and whether he makes it now or later is up to him."

I remained silent because Kate's theory that I didn't know what I wanted gave me a way out. I knew what I wanted, but my mind was already off on other subjects. How long would my parents wait patiently? I checked my watch and excused myself. My father looked at me with a touch of irony. I think he saw through my strategy. Kate left with me. In the hallway, I took her arm. "Thanks, sister, I thought I'd never get out of there alive."

"Oh," she shrugged, "don't worry. They've got each other and that's all that matters to them."

Her tone was bitter. I stared at her. She adjusted her hat. "Come on, I'll take a taxi and drop you off."

2.

I went to see old Uncle Theodore, who had always been my special friend and who had edited a big daily paper in his youth. He offered me a cigar, which made me feel like an adult.

"I'm sure that I can find something for you," he said. "I have not lost all my old contacts in the newspaper world. I have to warn you, though, your first job will be a grubby one."

Within two weeks, I had a job as a copy boy, with enough money to pay for cigarettes, coffee, and one outing with a girl each week. I was in seventh heaven.

Journalism in Budapest is a whole way of life. Three-quarters of it takes place in the coffeehouses. You can collect your materials by stopping in at the political café, the artistic café, the miscellaneous little places along the boulevards and then you write your story, surrounded by the smoke, the noise, the comings and goings of the newsmen's favorite haunt, The Chicago. Of course, as a lowly copy boy, I had to spend more time in the office than the reporters did, but I could pick up stories at their "workplace," and while they finished scribbling, breathe in the atmosphere. Coming from the puritan liberalism of my home, the frivolity of my colleagues was delightful to me.

After I had been working for about three months, I got to know and like a young writer who was highly critical of the whole profession. His name was Tibor, and he had been in my gymnasium a year ahead of me. He was a scholarship student from the provinces, a thin dark guy who spoke very little. One day at school he surprised me by submitting a poem for publication in my private little paper, which was, of course, known through the school. The poem was excellent. I printed it, complimented him, asked for more, and never heard from him again until I met him at The Chicago. He apparently had gotten a few poems published and was therefore accepted as a writer. He watched our antics with somber disapproval while sipping cheap cognac. He recognized me and one evening asked if he could walk home my way.

"I am curious about you," I said frankly. "You come to our reunions, but you don't seem to like them. Am I right?"

He took a deep breath before he answered, "My blood boils over half the time. Do those clowns think that the poets of the last century created our God-given language to waste on the filth they call news?"

"Hmm. That's a bit strong, don't you think?"

"Our language is the greatest instrument of music and of sorrow. When a writer decides to borrow this lyre, he should use it for the real issues of the nation, not to say who was seen with whom on the Corso."

"And what are the real issues?"

"The fate of the countryside, of the Magyar peasant whom the regime exalts and allows to rot in poverty and disease."

"I guess it's true that the rural articles deal mainly with

vacation spots."

"Have you ever lived in a village?" he asked.

I told him about the summer Kate and I spent with Anna. I could tell that to him it sounded like Marie Antoinette playing dairy maid, but somehow we became friends. I asked to see his recent work, and he appreciated the sincerity of both my praise and my criticism. He was difficult. In spite of his resentment of Budapest society, he wanted to be accepted by it. I persuaded Kate to invite him to one of her parties. After sulking for half the evening, he walked a girl to her home and practically raped her. Ever after living in Budapest for years, he still could not grasp that a girl who danced the Charleston in a red silk dress was not necessarily available for the asking. Kate was furious and called to tell me to drop Tibor. That made me mad, so the friendship continued.

He introduced me to his circle of friends — the Onion Eaters. "They were all provincials, poor and ill at ease in Budapest, but they were more cheerful than Tibor. And they were all — I hardly noticed it at the time — Gentiles.

Their favorite meeting place, outside of The Chicago, which they also patronized, was a bistro where they played billiards and drank beer. One day we were discussing why they didn't write about their own background since they all felt so misunderstood. Géza, a large loutish man with a lively mind, spread himself over half the table and drew on his cigar butt. "They would be episodic, sentimental, not right, somehow. I'd like to do something more systematic, more scientific. Do you remember the sociologists at the turn of the century who collected rural statistics and created such a stir?"

"Of course," I replied. "That was my father's study group."

"Who would have thought that such a lousy billiard player came from a heroic background?" he said.

They developed the idea of a series of works on rural life. I had to leave soon after the beginning of the discussion because I was meeting a girl. I was not sure whether I wanted to be involved in their project or whether they wanted me. But their past led me to mine. I looked up old issues of the study group's publications at the turn of the century, and I was amazed at how modern my father's friends had been. I read articles about the protective tariffs that enabled the large estates to raise the price of wheat while the peasants starved, about the causes and effects of mass emigration, about unions, about educational policy. They were clear, dry, thoughtful articles. It's too bad that I get bored so quickly. I told my friends about my reading, and they were interested, but when I suggested that we ask my father to reminisce, the suggestion somehow sank without response. After Kate's experience with Tibor, I did not feel like insisting.

Late in the summer, Tibor suddenly had to visit his hometown of Bercze and invited me to go with him. The schoolteacher who had taken care of him since his parents' death was very ill. My paper was having a slack time — we called the stories the reporters filed "cucumber stories" because their ripening seemed to be the only news there was. I easily got two weeks off. I knew that Tibor was thinking of a book about his region, and I felt that some article idea was bound to come to me on the trip.

When Géza heard that I was going, he cornered me at The Chicago.

"Look, Andy, since you don't know what you are looking for, why don't you get some information for me? You know how much I dislike dragging my bulk from one place to another."

From his shabby briefcase, he pulled out long sheets of neat columns of numbers. I looked at these while I sipped my soda. They were entitled "Farm Labor Contract Wages, 1923-1929."

"What is this milk, bacon, firewood, grazing rights?" I asked.

"Farm laborers are paid in cash and in kind, mostly in kind. The trouble is, I don't know what the grain, firewood, etc. is worth in terms of money, and that keeps changing."

"So I should go up to the first venerable pipe-smoker I see and ask him to tell me what the conversion value of his non-cash contractual wage is?" I asked, to make him mad.

"You idiot," he said calmly, "all I want you to do is to hang around a few weekly markets. When peasants sell six eggs or a few pounds of potatoes, you can be sure that they came from their own table. Then try to see what they buy with the money."

"And what if they end up selling their produce to me? Can you imagine me returning to Budapest with a dozen kohlrabis, which I hate?"

"Oh, I don't know, stuffed with sausage meat, with a sour cream and dill sauce, it's nothing to despise..." he replied dreamily. Our plan was to spend three or four days in Bercze, depending on how Tibor's guardian was. Then I would explore by train and bicycle two other areas that were included in Géza's statistics, and I might look in at Anna's on the way home.

Tibor wore his black suit, on the train. He fretted about this a little. "It's my only good suit, and I hate to wear it out. On the other hand, my guardian might die and if I don't have it, how can I appear at the funeral?"

"What is the matter with him?" I asked.

"Cancer, I think," said Tibor, "or discouragement, or both. He is not an old man. When he taught me in elementary school, he had just arrived from teachers college, full of enthusiasm. It didn't take him too long to realize that nothing could be knocked into those hard peasant heads. That's why he did so much for me. I alone cared for words, for knowledge."

Tibor's parents had died when he was eleven. His distant relatives wanted to apprentice him to a trade, but the teacher obtained a scholarship for him at the gymnasium in Budapest. The relatives disappeared into the obscurity from which they had emerged, and the boy's report cards went to his guardian.

"Every year, he came to visit me. He stayed at a small pension, went to the dentist, and took me out to dinner. It was a red-letter day for both of us. I never told him of my disappointments, of my shame about my origins, of my big hands."

The train stopped at dusk at a little station where we got off. I got my bike from the freight car and walked it along Tiber's long strides. His suit matched the mood of the street. The first three houses we passed were boarded up. Even the ones with a broom by the open door or a child sorting beans on the stoop looked abandoned. Weeds grew between the stones of the foundations, shutters hung on one nail. I remarked that most of them were substantial in size.

"If the inhabitants are too poor to fix these houses, how could they build them so large?"

He explained that the owners weren't all that poor once. In 1848, when the revolution freed their great-grandfathers, they became owners of whatever land they worked as serfs. But they lost all their other feudal privileges: timber, fishing rights, and grazing land.

"So their hearts fastened on their plots, which they could never hope to increase, and a curse descended on the land."

"A curse?" Tibor was always rather melodramatic, I thought. He lowered his voice.

"It's the fear of childbirth, which shrinks the patrimony by subdividing it."

It was nearly dark when we reached the schoolteacher's house, a kind of lean-to adjoining a larger house. Tibor, who is tall, had to bend down to enter the dark little room.

"Pax vobiscum, Magister," he greeted the teacher in the church Latin, dear to educated men in the past. The sick man's eyes glittered. "Tibi! you haven't forgotten to come! Light a candle, my son, there should be one in the lower drawer."

We searched in vain and the schoolteacher became agitated. I offered to go out to see if the store was still open.

"There is no store in the village, but there is an old widow who will cook us some dinner, and she'll let you have some light to eat it by."

Tibor gave me directions, then sat down by the bed. The teacher had become relaxed again, and a faint smile lit up his face. I went out in the dark street, peopled only by the skinny stray dogs of the village. The woman looked at me distrustfully. "Noodles is all I have" she said. I waited outside. The stars started to glitter in the dark blue sky. I felt as if I was far away from everything I knew.

When I got back with a petroleum lamp and two plates of greasy noodles, the sick man had dozed off. We ate in silence. Tibor walked me back with the lamp and the plates to the "cooking woman's."

"I'll sleep on the floor here," he said as we left, "but you can

195

get a bed. The widow rents them out."

She showed me a large room off the kitchen. There were six beds in it. In all but two, men were snoring, fully clothed except for their boots.

"You don't have a room I can have by myself?" I asked. In the flickering light of the petroleum lamp, her stare and Tibor's emphasized the incongruity of my question.

"They'll be up in a few hours," she said. "They go to the square to see if they can get work for the day. Then the young gentleman can sleep as long as he wants to."

She said this without any resentment. I said goodnight to Tibor and to the widow, who closed the door. I felt my way to the empty beds and picked the least lumpy mattress. There was neither blanket nor pillow, so I rolled up my coat to put it under my head.

The room was warm and extraordinarily noisy. The men sighed, groaned, coughed, and shifted in their sleep. One of them spoke in his dream. I think he was arguing with a mule. When he quieted down, another got up and went out, presumably to the outhouses. I had just dozed off when he came back and woke me that moment. I jumped up with a shout. There were bedbugs biting my ears, hands, and neck. I shook out my coat and left, slapping myself as I went.

The front door had not been locked, and soon I was on the empty moonlit street. I did not feel like sharing the sick man's room with Tibor, so I just stood indecisively in the street wishing I had never come. The sound of a river started to separate itself from the other sounds of the night, and I decided to walk towards it. I had a piece of soap and a towel in my knapsack, and since it was a warm night, I thought I might get rid of the pests by washing.

I was soon out of the village. I felt better walking under the open sky. Dry stalks rustled in the wind, frogs croaked in melancholy unison. When I reached the river, I got off the path onto the shore. A hedge of bushes on a little mound gave privacy to the beach. I undressed and hung my clothes on the branches. My good humor returned and I wondered whether to reimburse the landlady for the bedbugs. I wasn't returning. I lay down on my coat in my shorts and went to sleep.

When I woke, it was still dark, but a faint grayness had diluted the blackness of the night. There was a damp chill in the air. I lay still, thinking that the change in temperature had woken me, when I realized that I was not alone. On the other side of the mound, hidden by the bushes, two women were talking quietly. I couldn't imagine what they were doing there at this time. They were in the middle of some conversation about fields and Swabians, when I heard a phrase that made me sit up.

"Why are you taking his clothes off?" one of them asked.

"I didn't last time and my husband called me a wastrel. It's true he won't need them where he's going. Pass me that rag, Viola, I'll wrap him in it."

Suddenly, a faint cry pierced the bush — it was an infant's.

"Jesus Christ, you mean he's not dead?"

"Oh shut up, you tadpole," the other said angrily. "I didn't feed him since Thursday, he should be gone by now."

I heard a blow and the crying intensified.

"No, choke him, not like that," and the crying weakened.

I jumped up. I realized they were killing an infant.

"What do you think you're doing?" I shouted through the bushes. I heard them scramble to their feet and flee. I ran after them, pulling on my pants as I ran. When one of them aimed a stone at me, it hit me hard on the ankle — another just missed my face. I stopped to rub my ankle and lost them. I could still hear them, but I could no longer see them. I walked around the bushes to inspect the other side of the mound. The river bank was empty. A faint glow on the water indicated the approach of dawn. A flock of birds rose on the other side of the river. I shivered.

4.

The sun had just risen when I got back to the schoolteacher's room. Tibor was up, and breakfast was waiting for me. Hot chicory coffee, rolls, and honey sat on a painted tray. The schoolteacher smiled at the brambles in my hair. "Tibor went to look for you where he left you, but you seem to have found better quarters sub astra — in the open."

I told them about my adventure and they looked grave. "You'd better take the next train out" said Tibor. "I can't vouch for your safety here. By now, everyone knows about you and fears that you will report what you saw to the authorities."

"You mean that woman's husband and neighbors all approve of killing babies?"

"In this region, it's a way of life. They don't want more than one child, and they don't care how they achieve this. But they know that it is a crime, and that others call it a sin."

I could see that Tibor was disturbed. I was especially struck by the hostility of the mother towards the innocent babe. The schoolteacher raised his hand from his bed gently.

"Ours is a dying race. Should we interfere with its wish to disappear? Look at those mugs, that tray. They belong to my landlady, who is Swabian — in other words, German. Her house is clean, her children are healthy, soon her husband will buy a house from a Magyar family that doesn't have the energy to keep it up. They say that they belong to a master race, and I'm beginning to believe it."

"That's your sickness talking, not you," said Tibor, straightening out the sick man's bed with tender hands. "Don't you recall what you taught in school — if the earth is the cap on God's head, Hungary is the feather?"

"And you refused to recite it when the inspector came," the older man said with a smile. "What a caning I had to give you!"

"I was insulted that you asked me such an easy question," Tibor smiled his sad smile. They reminisced about his schooldays until it was time for my train.

Although I liked Tiber's guardian, I was glad to leave Bercze. I got off the train at the next market town and hardly set foot indoors for the next week. On foot and by bike, I crisscrossed the low plain between the rivers Tisza and Danube. After my experience in Bercze, I did not try to get a bed in the villages and every night I slept in the open. If I close my eyes now, I can still feel the vibrant heat of those long, sundrenched days I spent on the Alföld, the great Hungarian plain. The days were as flat, as monotonous as the landscape itself. Even when I saw men at the markets or the inns I visited, it is their long silences that I remember because they went with the landscape. One day I saw a house with a well next to it that kept receding as I walked towards it — it was a mirage of the plains.

I guess I got some of the information Géza wanted, but I don't remember too much about my research. He had warned me not to question people closely because they were fearful of spies and labor organizers. The country militia, I was told, picked up anyone suspected of socialist agitation and beat them mercilessly. Once, by luck, I came upon a discussion comparing prices of that year and of two years ago in the yard of a little tavern. The speakers at green tables sized me up when I came in, decided I was just a kid, and continued. They were angry but did not know who to blame for the fact that agricultural prices had suddenly dropped so far behind the price of manufactured goods. They were clear about their predicament, however.

"Last year, it was the choice between meat or a pair of shoes. This year, it's between meat and getting further into debt than we already are." "And at least we've got our contracts," said another. "There are many who don't."

I knew what he was talking about. I had discovered the rural shantytowns behind the rural slums. Families of migrants hoping for extra work in the big harvests huddled there under the hostile eyes of the regular laborers, whose wages they depressed. Their encampments frightened me. I could imagine being murdered there for my knapsack or my Swiss pocket knife. The day after I went to one of these camps, I took the train to Anna's — I had had enough.

As I sat in the train going to Kisbánya, I diligently wrote down every figure I could get for Géza. I was not, however, inclined to write about what I had seen. I must have an instinctive need not to follow in my father's footsteps. I recalled the articles I had read in my father's publication about the "latifundia" the enormous entailed estates that I had found unchanged since he wrote about them, or the obstacles placed in the way of organizing the landless worker, which had not changed either. Politics and sociology blew right out of my mind when I pushed the little gate to Anna's yard, setting off the barking, then the enthusiastic welcome of old Bodri. A pretty girl with blond braids appeared at the kitchen door to see what the fuss was.

"Andrew!" Esther ran toward me, still wiping her hands on her apron. "Your letter just arrived yesterday!" and she threw her arms around my neck. I tossed away my knapsack and caught her around the waist. I used to pick her up and twirl her around; but when I felt her strong back against my hands, I realized that in three years she had turned from a girl into a young woman. She was nearly my height now, and she felt warm and muscular in my arms. She drew back from my embrace and pinched her nose with her fingers. Her blue eyes sparkled. "I'm awfully glad to see you, Andy, but you stink," she said through her nose.

"Esther, that is not the voice of true love." I said with mock indignation. "A woman overcome by passion doesn't ask a man to stop and wash his underarms."

"Stop what?" she asked, and then we both realized that the childish banter to which we were accustomed no longer suited us. She lowered her eyes, and I picked up my bag.

"You're right," I said. "I haven't washed for a week, and I'd love a bath in your big wooden tub. Shall I draw some water from the well?"

"Do you still remember how to do it, Mr. City Gentleman?" she asked, as we went into the summer kitchen.

"Sure," I said and I was going to add, "and I still know how to chase you up a tree, too," recalling how she sat in the big walnut tree till suppertime because I had stolen her underpants and refused to give them back. But again, I felt intimidated and I went to draw water while she put on a kettle to heat my bath. Pushing the heavy wheel that draws the well water calmed me down. It's hard work, which starts up easily but knocks your wind out by the time the pail of water appears over the brim. I carried it into the summer kitchen and asked, "Is everyone else out in the fields?"

"No," she replied, pouring out a glass of water for me. "Mother took Father to the doctor, and Stevie works in the mine."

"You mean that abandoned coal mine where we played hide and seek?"

"Yes, they've reopened it with some new machinery and it's quite prosperous."

I expressed surprise that Stevie would give up farm work, and she said that they had quite a family battle over it. Her father was opposed to the job, but it was his lung disease that made it so important for the family to have more cash than they could get by selling produce. Anna originally took Joska's side, but then she came around to Stevie's view. Some devil (I was beginning to guess which one) prompted me to say, "So the lucky fellow who marries you will inherit the whole kingdom?"

"Oh, I'd just as soon marry a miner," she said negligently, stabbing me right through the heart." All the girls do. The company gives you a house with running water, some of them even have radios. "

"I have a radio," I said, and I could feel myself turning red at what was probably the stupidest remark I ever made in my existence. Esther burst into a healthy, wholehearted laugh that made the chickens who had wandered in flee with flapping wings. "Oh, I'm so glad you have a radio, Andy, I was so worried about it! All is well, he has a radio! He can listen to the soccer scores!" and she burst into fresh hilarity. I don't know what I would have done if her parents had not appeared then.

Anna's smile when she saw me was a real home coming. "Our other mother," Kate and I used to call her, and she still felt like one. Joska gave me his guarded smile, and we shook hands. He looked terribly aged and sunken-chested.

I always liked Uncle Joseph, and it hurt me to see what the disease had done to him. I remember that Kate and I once compared him to Father's pipe. You would think that it had gone out, but then a spark would appear and glow.

Anna questioned me about my family and scolded Esther all in the same breath for not having finished the midday meal. I defended her, saying it was my fault, and hurried off to take the bath that had interrupted her work. I noticed that Esther did not tease me in front of her parents, and the fact that she was so spirited with me when we were alone drew us further together.

As I washed behind the summer kitchen, splashing water on the ground under the sun-dappled vine leaves, it occurred to me that there was something very innocent about the girl's provocative behavior. Esther had always been a lively girl, and she probably did not realize how quickly two and two made four in my mind. As a country girl, she had known the facts of life long before I ever did, but she had been raised as a virtuous Baptist virgin. I was only virtuous when I couldn't help it. My friends and I celebrated our graduation by our first visit to a brothel. Most of us didn't like it, but we were determined to have all the adventures we could between now and our far-off weddings. I suddenly felt guilty that my reaction to the natural change in Esther and my relationship was to wonder how soon we could sleep together.

5.

We were rarely alone with each other for the next two days. Anna took time off from her usual work to cook and bake special treats for me, and Stevie took me on a tour of his coal mine. I thought it was dark and dangerous, but he was very proud of it.

The household soon settled back to its normal routine after the disorder created by my arrival. I rose with the others at the ungodly hour of four or five to feed the animals with Joska. There was still some work available on the neighboring estate, and Anna and Esther took turns. They would leave after their scant breakfast and return at nightfall. There were heavy lines on Anna's face as I held a chair for her to sit down to the supper Esther had placed on the table.

"Thank you, my son," Anna said to me, as she glanced around for her real son.

"He's here," said Joska, "he's just washing off in the yard."

"Honestly, I don't know why I even go over there, sometimes," she said, dipping in her spoon after Joseph had said grace. "Good noodles, Esther, although they could use a pinch more salt. Every year the foreman gets harder on us. The count's men were not pleasant, but now that a tenant farms the land for him, the foreman counts every grain before he lets me leave."

"You shouldn't work there, wife," Joska said in a quiet tone. "We can live off our own land, and if there's less, we'll just make do with less."

"It doesn't bother me to go every day," said Esther, with a toss of her braids. Her brother had come in, and after a nod signifying his greetings, was wolfing down his dinner.

"I wouldn't do it if I wasn't worried about the future," said Anna in a conciliatory tone to her husband. "If prices keep falling, we might really need that salary, and once we lose our place, we'll never get it back."

Stevie asked his sister, "Does anybody over there bother you — I mean...."

She laughed and raised her fork like a weapon. "If they did, I'd show them a thing or two. I'm not one of the farm servants."

Our eyes met, and her expression softened, making my heart thump in my chest.

"Then let Esther go daily, and you stay home," Stevie said to his mother. "I can help out at home, too, before and after my shift. I'm used to the long hours now."

Esther and I groaned. We had planned to stack the hay together on her next day home. Anna said that she'd wait to quit till after I was gone, "Let the children enjoy each other's company," she added indulgently. I could sense Stevie's annoyance.

Early next morning, Esther left with her brother. The hay work was to be the following day, "provided we have no rain" said Joska, looking suspiciously at the lone cloud in a corner of the sky. He and I finished cleaning the stalls, and he hobbled off to the village. I washed and sauntered back to the summer kitchen.

"How about a second breakfast?" asked Anna.

"Great. Black coffee, buttered roll, smoked salami," I teased her, "with the morning paper, please."

"I was wondering when you would finally get homesick for Budapest," she said, smiling as she scrambled fresh eggs for me. While I ate, she walked back and forth doing various tasks, and we talked. I told her about my near-encounter with infanticide. She listened with interest.

"What do village women do here to prevent unwanted babies?" I asked.

"They go to the medicine woman or the 'wise woman' as they call her. She usually gives them herb potions to induce miscarriage, but sometimes they use more radical methods. Once, a girl came to me, bleeding badly and infected. I took her to the doctor at the county seat, and he said he was able to save her, but that he had seen a number of women die after such treatment. The authorities don't take much trouble to find these 'angel makers,' as these women are called."

She had heard that in the region I had visited, women used some kind of wooden device, covered with fine linen, to prevent conception. That, too, was dangerous because after a while, it could only be surgically removed.

I asked, "Do a lot of girls come to you for advice?"

She smiled, "More and more, lately. It's probably because I've been nursing Joska all these years, and God has helped me learn the way to do it. Your mother says I should study midwifery."

"I agree with Mother. At least you wouldn't give the girls herb potions."

"Well, you know, some of these 'wise folks' have their wisdom. They believe in the spirit, which doctors don't understand."

She paused for a minute, her potato peeling knife in mid-air, and to me, with her square and level brow, she looked like a sympathetic, intelligent man. It occurred to me that with the years, my mother's features had gotten finer, with a brittle strength, while Anna's had solidified. I wondered what Esther would look like as she grew older. I decided to go walking through the country, and Anna packed some bacon and bread for me.

This was my last wholly free day on this vacation, and as if to prolong it, I managed to get thoroughly lost. I still knew more or less where I was when I built a twig fire in a clearing and roasted my slab of bacon, letting it drip on the bread the way Joseph had taught me years ago. Then I fell asleep in the cool shade and when I woke up, every path seemed to lead deeper into the woods. Late in the afternoon, I finally emerged sick and tired of birdsong and wild flowers. A village perched on the nearest hill, and I went to it. For a moment I thought I'd get as lost here as in the forest because the streets went higgledy-piggledy in and out of yards, with dead ends everywhere. No one I asked knew the way to Kisbánya, when an inscription over a low thatched-roofed house caught my eye: "Pentecostal Baptist Temple" it said. Since Kisbánya had a Baptist temple too, I thought that I could get directions.

A whitewashed room with small windows contained a few benches, a harmonium, and a petroleum lamp on a table. People of all ages sat or stood with arms extended, like those of Christ on the cross, deeply immersed in prayers and mutterings. When they saw me in the doorway, they made room for me. I was tired and curious, so I sat down. Amid the mixture of sounds, from time to time a deep sigh or a loud outcry to God rose over the rest. The tension was like that of an orchestra tuning up, with snatches here and there of the melodies to come. Then a man got up and all turned to him. In broken tones, with tremendous effort, he talked about his sinfulness and his efforts to be saved. He drank, he explained, and when he was drunk, he hit everything in sight, his wife, his children, even his animals. But he knew when he was sober how wrong this was, and he strove for salvation, "because this earth is nothing but a dunghill," he repeated with the approbation of the audience. Voices rose all around, encouraging him in his efforts. Finally he broke down in heavy weeping. After a while, the leader of the congregation, whom I had not noticed earlier, led everyone in a hymn sung with great fervor. He was a small man with burning eyes and a broken nose.

When it was over, an older woman rose. She prayed, shook, and rambled in a tone verging on hysteria. My neighbor told me that she had been fired from an estate because she was too old for the work, and she lived with her daughter-in-law, who beat her. She was praying for help to find forgiveness. By the time I got it all, she was in a nearly beatific trance, babbling incoherently, her face raised to Heaven, her eyes rolling in their sockets. Her state acted as a catalyst on the other people present. Voices grew louder, some people shrieked, and a young woman fell down. I made a move towards her, but my neighbors gently restrained me.

I felt as if I was somewhere in purgatory, surrounded by writhing figures whose shadows coiled and uncoiled on the walls in the light of the lamp. I was not frightened, and somehow I was moved. I did not believe anything that the participants said about salvation and the other world, but they evoked the presence of a supernatural or unconscious spirit so vividly that I could almost see it, like some enormous black bird flapping its wings against the bars of reason. I stayed for a while more, but then, in spite of my vision, I lost touch with the others, like a non-drinker at a drunken party. I no longer felt anything but the desire to get away from the noise. I got up to go, and the preacher joined me at the door. He thanked me for coming and gave me directions to Kisbánya. Except for his eyes, he seemed as cool as the others were exalted.

The light of the long summer evening still hovered at the edge of the sky when I got back to Anna's house. My friends were familiar with the practices I had observed. They disapproved of them. I observed that the service seemed to bring some kind of comfort to the misery of the poor.

"Our religion teaches us to bear our ills with courage and dignity," said Anna severely. "These people get drunk on theirs."

That was my mother's friend all right, I thought. I could never be as sober and strong-minded as these women. Joska snickered as he added, "I've heard that they also indulge in other excesses when everyone is rolling on the floor, men and women together. The leader you met, by the way, is a former farm labor organizer. I heard that he found God when he was being beaten by the county militia. He saw stars and then he saw the light."

Steven glanced darkly at his father. It occurred to me that there must be some labor organizing going on in the mines. I could have asked him about it later, since Stevie had offered to share his room with me and had been disappointed by my refusal to resume the night talks we used to have. But my mind was elsewhere, and I was glad that ever since I arrived, I had insisted on sleeping in the hayloft.

The next morning was bright and clear, and Esther and I raised our glasses of milk in a toast to "our day." Piling up the hay was hard, satisfying work. The golden heaps rose symmetrically over the fields, with poppies, cornflower, and daisies sticking out all over. Esther made garlands for her neck, wrist, and hair, and then she insisted on crowning me too. I refused, but after Joseph, our supervisor, had gone off for his drink, she chased me barefoot from haystack to haystack. It was clear that the girl could outrun me, so I grabbed her by the wrists when my breath started to give out, "All right, I'll let you make a jackass out of me if you give me a kiss."

"Well worth the price," she panted, and her kiss smelled of sunshine and hay. I held her firm young body against me.

"Will you come out to visit me tonight?"

"Maybe, if I can manage to find the way," she replied. Her words were mocking, but her voice trembled. Only the presence of other harvesters kept us from collapsing into the hay like so many boys and girls before us.

That night, I stayed awake listening for her step and to the thousand noises of the country outside. Through a crack between the beams above me, a star shone. Finally, I heard her push the heavy barn door. I met her at the foot of the rickety ladder and with my arm around her waist, I helped her up to the loft. We laughed with joy before grave, hot desire overcame us. All night we tossed on the hay like on a stormy sea, sometimes fierce and passionate, at other times friendly and playful. When we fell back exhausted by love play, we found again the tone of our childhood. Esther babbled on about her school friends, her work, her excursions to the town which now had a movie theater. I enjoyed drawing her out. Her conversation was simple and cheerful but sensible. When she asked me about my life and plans, I couldn't remember them. I was lost in the present. Towards dawn, I dozed off and felt her turn my wristwatch to the light. I tightened my arms around her. "You don't have to go yet."

"Yes I do."

"No you don't."

We went on like that for a while, then she kissed me good-by. Determined, I said, "Esther, this is love, you know."

"Is it?" she asked. Her face was serene and a little sad. Swiftly, she slipped away. The next day I put my bike on the train to Budapest. My holiday was over.

6.

It was wonderful to see Budapest again. I am not an "onioneater" — home to me is busy city streets, the clank of tramways, the metallic bridges gleaming over the river. My parents had missed me. Even though all I do is breeze in and out of their apartment at all hours, they said it was too quiet when I was gone. I had to tell them all about Anna and her family. I don't know if my mention of Esther was casual enough to sound indifferent. But I must confess — men are heartless, as the popular songs keep repeating — that as the week progressed, I hardly thought of her. The paper was resuming its fall activity with a shudder of hungry presses and the ringing of telephones. Géza was grateful for the material I had collected for him and enthusiastic about my own article ideas. He suggested calling a series "Birth and Death in Transdanubian Village Life," and I dared to discuss it with my editor. The latter encouraged me without committing himself. My life of work, cafés, friends, tennis, and girls now included long Sunday bicycle trips to the villages Tibor had introduced to me.

One Sunday in early October was framed in heavy lines in my calendar. It was when Anna and Joska harvested their wine. We were all invited, although it was just a little harvest, enough to keep them in wine during the winter and to invite some friends and neighbors. My father seldom went. He was becoming very sedentary. Till the last minute, my mother was planning to come with me, but she worried about Kate working until late hours at the theatre. I ended up going alone on Saturday after work.

The moment I saw Esther, a kerchief around her hair, her bare feet trampling the grapes in a vat, all my love for her returned. We were surrounded by people: relatives, neighbors, unclaimed children. I never found out who all these guests were, but I heartily wished them to the devil. The loft was fully booked, as I found out when Stevie told me he had saved his room for me over the protest of two cousins. As time went on, and I could not get a second alone with Esther, I panicked. How did I know that she wanted to be alone with me? I hadn't even written to her since the last time I saw her. She was just then carrying a basket of grapes, walking with a friend Stevie had brought from the mine, and she was cheerfully listening to his sweet talk. I lost all self-confidence. My fellow workers urged me to help finish last year's wine, and I threw myself into this task with abandon. I had worked hard at the office all morning, rushed to the train, pumped buckets of water, and drunk liters of wine. When Anna announced supper, I went to

Stevie's room to wash up and fell fast asleep.

An hour later, in the house emptied of the harvesters, whose forks and glasses could be heard in the yard, I woke to see Esther's blue eyes and sweet mouth over me. Without a word, I pulled her down to me, and we made love with that reckless intoxication that makes one forget caution, respect for others' feelings, life itself. The banging of a door brought us back to reality. She went back with whatever she had come to fetch. I waited and joined the company for a long drawn-out supper, after which we danced with sweaters on in the cooling autumn night. Now the wine I drank only sharpened the triumphant glow I felt. I was shocked when Stevie and I turned in, and he called me a prize moron for not going abroad to study, "I'd give an arm and a leg for a university degree — now that it's too late."

His bitterness jolted me out of my self-satisfaction, but I really wanted to go to sleep. Stevie was only a few years younger than me. I looked at him — Anna's clear eyes in Joska's square face — and saw a mature man.

"Why is it too late?" I yawned as I pulled off my shoes.

"You have to get out of this cesspool life before you're ten and never set foot in it again. You have to disown your mother and father and the God that brought you into it. Otherwise, you can resign yourself to being a beast of burden."

He had a dream — of being a mining engineer. It wasn't new, either — as we talked, I could remember that when we played in the abandoned mine, he was always the engineer, the one whose brilliant imaginary machines rescued the rest of us, trapped in fearful dangers. (It wasn't so bad, hugging little Esther, even then....)

As Stevie explained the link between the mine and the local fascist organization, I could sense his seething energy and ability. I still could not fully understand why he was so trapped to remain as he was, but I fell asleep before he could explain.

The following week, I brought up his case with my friends, the onion-eaters. I couldn't have asked them anything to make them happier. There were so many answers to my question that I had to defend myself, my hands over my ears.

"In the first place, leaving the land to become a professional isn't encouraged, isn't rewarded, and in the last place, it isn't done."

"But," I protested, "public education is free, isn't it?"

"Yes, well, but books aren't, shoes aren't, train fare isn't, and neither is room and board. Not to mention the loss of a salary, which can be — let's see, Géza, what would it be for a 14-15 year old boy?"

Our walking statistic removed a pipe from his mouth. "On average, I'd say, 20 to 25 pengöes a year plus 400 kilos of corn and rye each, and kindling, as well as the use of some grazing land.... Kids that age aren't married, so no milk, no bacon."

"Anyway," interrupted another, "your friend is a real borderline case, a real tragedy, because a smallholder's son just might make it, economically, that is."

"But economics is just a part of it," said Tibor. "When I went to gymnasium, my scholarship was paid. I had no family to pull me back, but I felt like a fish out of water. City people make fun of your accent, of the way you wipe your nose on your sleeve, and hardly ever does a kind soul come along to say, 'Here, this is how it's done.'"

The most decisive factor, I gathered from what they said, was the fear of change that brooded over the land. Everyone had his place, the farm servants, the overseers, the gentry, with their sons in civil service, and all was to stay as it was.

"Since 1919, the upper classes are suspicious, humorless. In my district, a tractor driver was fired for driving with gloves on. 'What is the world coming to?' the foreman said."

I asked my father the same question when I saw the light still on in his study.

"It's neither coming nor going, as far as I can tell," he replied. "Europe is governed by an uneasy coalition of unstable governments — which means that no reform has a chance of succeeding. But you don't usually ask global questions. What is on your mind?"

I told him about Stevie and my friends' reaction to his plight. I could see the slight line that appears between my father's eyebrows when he really focuses on a problem.

"What did your friends propose after they described the dilemma to you?"

"Nothing, really."

"They may be smart," my father said, to my surprise. "Under a regime which outlaws any discussion of land reform, it may be safest to avoid discussing solutions to social problems, which all sound like Communism."

"Is that your view or is it the regime's?"

"It is not my view," he said. "I never believed that the just distribution of power and income can only be brought about by the dictatorship of the proletariat. Do you?"

I wasn't sure.

"Anyway, your friend is in danger. Once a young man starts questioning that kind of atmosphere, his rebelliousness is soon noticed. Tell him to come and talk to me. It's never too late to complete one's education."

I wondered whether that remark was meant for me, but I don't think that Father meant to be sarcastic because he added with a smile, "I remember Stevie's father at that age. He was no fool. He did not like the army or his poverty, but they were part of the way the world was made and there was nothing to be done about it."

7.

During the late fall, Esther and I managed to meet a few times at a country rendezvous that she could walk to and I ride my bike on the pretext of my research. We were not always careful on these Sunday meetings, and one cold afternoon, I decided to walk Esther back to her village. No one in Anna's family had any idea that I was in the neighborhood, and when Stevie overtook me, one hand on my bike handle, the other around Esther's sheepskin-coated shoulder, he just rode by, without a word, on the family cart. His sister and I looked at each other, and she said, "He won't say anything, I know."

As soon as I got home, I wrote a long letter to him describing my own position and his and conveying Father's offer to help him. He did not reply.

As winter set in, I took fewer trips to research my articles and became more engrossed in writing them. I had a lot of material from my field trips, and I thought I could organize it into a good series. Because of what Anna had told me, I had talked to rural doctors and to specialists in Budapest. Some of them really cared about the women caught in the conflicts that led to infanticide, abortion, sometimes suicide — the need and desire for more children, the loose morals of the countryside, and at the same time the stigma of illegitimacy and the difficulty of feeding extra mouths whether of legitimate or illegitimate children.

I could not help worrying about Esther after I read such stories. Once, I asked her what would happen if she got pregnant. She replied, "My parents wouldn't like it, but they would not turn me out."

When I was away from her serene confidence, troubling and fearful images haunted me — Esther on an operating table, Esther dying. It was when my love for her wrenched my heart most deeply that I started to examine it, question it, and undermine it.

Although our relationship was so physically passionate, there was always love in it. It was different from my other affairs where I always felt a slight hostility, a slight guilt at using a woman. Esther and I could establish such intense physical rapport because we knew each other and cared. Yet somehow, she played no part in my life. She probably knew this and suffered from it all along. But it must have become clear to her in March, when Anna and Esther visited Budapest to meet Philip von Reddich, Kate's fiancé. I no more approved of her romance with the famous physicist than Stevie did with Esther. At least, Philip, who had divorced his wife after falling in love with Kate, was about to marry her and had a brilliant future, while my future.... Better not talk about it.

Philip came for lunch, my father poured champagne, and we had a very pleasant meal. Esther, I remember, wore a city dress and heels, and her gold braids, twisted around her head. Philip awkwardly flirted with her. I thought that he was warmer, more concerned with Kate than I'd ever seen him. I invited everyone to the American circus to which I had a press pass.

I wish I could relive that afternoon because it was still

"before" — while everything else seems "after." My father, Esther, and I adored the circus — we could not believe how much was going on at the same time. The ingenuity of Barnum and Bailey was totally wasted on Mother and Anna, who talked to each other the whole time. I can't remember whether Kate and Philip came with us. We ate exotic things, at least Esther and I did: American candy and peanuts. We walked home in chilly clear weather. At Gerbaud's pastry shop, young and old parted company. I promised Anna to have Esther at the station in time for the last train.

"Come and meet my friends," I said, and dragged her off to a party.

My closest friends and I made a habit of getting together at one of our houses on late Sunday afternoons to recover from the obligatory family meals we all attended on that day. One after another, young people would come in, throw themselves in an armchair, and cry out, "Air! light! a cigarette! You wouldn't believe the lectures I listened to today!"

We were neither quite as frivolous nor as rebellious as we pretended to be at these parties. Even the girls were medical students or musicians or aspiring dramatic actresses. But all of us lived at home — none of us was "established" — and the rule on Sunday afternoon was not to become serious until we had shaken off the week's constraint.

That day, we met at Lillian's house. She was very modern and had prevailed on her father's valet to prepare "mixed drinks" for the company. Someone was winding up a phonograph when I came in with Esther. She shook hands all around and sat down primly, her knees together. She accepted a raspberry syrup and soda and from time to time, I could see her stealing a glance at the flat breasts and bold makeup of the women. She answered questions modestly and clearly but would not be drawn into conversation. I thought how much like Anna she acted. She knew who she was and had no wish to pretend to be different. We talked about movies, the latest books, and jazz. Although the subject of our conversation was foreign to Esther, I knew her well enough to guess that the cynical and critical tone probably offended her deep sense of propriety. She did not show her reaction in any way. It was only when we started to play charades and guessing games that some of Esther's spirit appeared for a minute, then was quickly smoothed down like a rebellious curl. She guessed an atrocious riddle and punched me in the side when I tried to mislead her. My friends gave her a round of applause and voted to escort her to the train station for a grand send-off. On the platform, my closest friend from gymnasium made a speech in Esperanto, or what he said was Esperanto, and presented Esther with a key to the city, which was also useful to open a suitcase he lost somewhere in Italy. The train left, he gave me a resounding slap on the back, and we all went to see a film.

Three days later I received a letter from Esther. I don't have it, but I remember every word.

> My dear Andrew: I hope this finds you well. Thank the Lord, I and mine are in good health. I am writing to tell you not to think of me any more. It gives me great pain to have to say this, for it would be my dearest wish to be a good and loving wife to you. But that cannot be. I always knew it in my heart, although I hoped otherwise. When I visited you and your friends, I saw that it was impossible. Our situations are too different.
>
> My parents have been thinking for some time of finding a suitable match for me. Yesterday I told them that I, too, think it is time for me to be married. After all, I will be seventeen soon and I don't want to be an old maid. So, again, I have to tell you not to think of me any more, and I will try not to think of you except in a brotherly way, although I know that I will shed many tears before I can do so.
>
> My best regards to Madam your Mother and Madam your sister and the Sir Attorney.

Everything in that letter hurt me, but her sweetness most of all.

8.

I threw myself into my articles on "Birth and Death in Transdanubian Villages." I was amazed at how easily the work progressed. I wrote with a kind of concentrated fury. I tried to be absolutely objective, but there was a bitter edge to my facts that I did not attempt to temper.

My onion-eating friends listened in silence to my reading. I realized that they had never taken me very seriously and that they were surprised. But then so was I. They made a few suggestions, which were excellent. "Good luck, pal!" Tibor said at the end of the evening.

My editor took my copy without comment. I think he had completely forgotten our conversation about my writing anything. For a month, I heard nothing. Then he called me into his office.

A short, pudgy man with heavy jowls, he glanced at me in an angry and anxious way as if he had never seen me before.

"Sit down, Ignatius. I'm sure that you will accept advice from an older, experienced man." He paused for a minute. "You seem to have a certain flair, some journalistic ability, I'd even say some style. But if you want to become a newspaper man, I'd suggest not writing anything until both of us have forgotten this — and his hands trembled as he flipped through my manuscript — this...." He exploded.

"You can just throw this straight on the garbage dump. These are not topics for articles and never will be."

"But," I said, "just a few days ago we published an editorial on the decline of the Hungarian birthrate, and it does seem to me that however unpleasant, the issues of infanticide and abortion are relevant...."

He interrupted me, "We did not publish an editorial, I did and I can figure out what's relevant, thank you. And let me tell you another thing" — here, he took a deep breath and all fatherly pretense disappeared as he exhaled — "We don't need a Jew, the son of a former émigré, to dredge up the problems and weaknesses in our social fabric to the delight of our enemies. This is a patriotic, Christian newspaper."

He pounded the table at each adjective. "And this degenerate, morbid curiosity, this obsession with negativism, doesn't belong in it."

He went on in that vein for ten minutes, which seemed like ten hours to me. I didn't say anything. I stared at the points of my shoes. When he finished, there was a silence. He had worked himself up into such a rage that he was nearly panting. But he had been so insulting that I felt neither the impulse to apologize nor the desire to placate him.

He said, "Well, since you don't seem to recognize your error, you may take this abortion" — he seemed pleased with his pun — "and yourself off these premises. Here." He handed me my manuscript.

I went downstairs. When I got to the street, I leaned against the wall. After maintaining my calm throughout the interview, I was so upset that I shook. I had been insulted and berated and thrown out, and, I now realized, fired.

I could not stay where I was because other copy boys or reporters might come by, and I didn't want to face them. I walked aimlessly with my heavy papers under my arm until I decided to go see Uncle Theodore. He could tell from my face what had happened and he whisked me past Aunt Helene. "We have newspaper business to discuss, my dear."

In his library, he poured a glass of Tokay for me, lit his cigar, and sat back, waiting for me to explain my pale face and the manuscript under my arm. My words came tumbling out, "But what is this business of being particularly outraged that a Jew should touch this topic? And how did I suddenly become so Jewish? I don't go to temple, I don't speak Yiddish."

He rubbed his ear, refusing to recognize any humor in the situation. "What you think you are is unimportant." He quoted the remark made by Karl Lueger, the first anti-Semitic mayor of Vienna: "I decide who is a Jew and who isn't."

I believed what he said, but I just couldn't see what it had to do with me. He didn't waste time arguing with me but told me to find a book while he read my stuff. He went through the whole series, puffing his cigar, while I leafed without interest through the travelogues that filled so many of his shelves. When he was finished, he asked me, "How long would it take you to translate these into German? Helen and I are going to Berlin next week, and I'd like to show these to an editor of the Ullstein papers."

I gasped — the Ullstein papers were the best in Europe, and he wouldn't show them anything he didn't like.

"It will take me all afternoon and all night to translate them. OK?"

He smiled, "I'm glad you never asked for my advice before you wrote these because I would have talked you out of doing it."

I felt better, but I was still reeling inside from the blow I had received. The reaction of my friends, the onion-eaters, did not restore my equilibrium. They were thoroughly sympathetic to me personally and heaped upon the editor-in-chief the colorful variety of curses that only Hungarians of lower-class origins can command. But on this tirade against Jews as social critics they were equivocal.

"You must admit, old fellow," said Géza "that the Jews occupy a position in Hungarian life vastly out of proportion to their numbers. There has to be some limit to their influence. In industry, in commerce, in the arts, you hardly find a Hungarian name anywhere."

"So what?" I asked. "They didn't take these positions from others. They created them. Where would we be without industrial development?"

In the Hungary of their dreams, it seemed. They longed for a feudal past in which nothing competed with agriculture, in which modernization had not shaken time-honored values.

I argued, trying to be as objective as possible, not realizing the folly of that position. I ended up defending the Jews as pillars of reaction. "What is progressive about old von Reddich, my sister's future father-in-law, who spent frantic weeks in Vienna raising funds for Horthy's return in 1919? And the overthrow of Bolshevism? And," I asked, "Why am I responsible for the actions of a man I detest? Who may be of my race?"

There was no personal animosity in our discussion, but afterwards, I felt one more support gone from the reality in which I had lived. I wasn't really one of them, that's all.

I told my parents that I had been fired over some stupid

altercation. I was more embarrassed by the truth than to pretend that I had done something dumb. My father, too, had spoken out on social issues and had been particularly resented for doing so because he was a Jew. It is true that his activities had been much more persistent and effective than mine, but I was loath to reopen old wounds.

Did I have a future in journalism? In spite of Uncle Theodore, I wondered. I was too demoralized to even look for another job. For weeks, I hung around the apartment, getting up late, sometimes without the energy to shave. I read. I listened to records. I refused my friends' invitations. I was staring at my disintegrating world, in which the loss of Esther's love throbbed like piercing flashes of pain. Somehow, I felt that if I had her with me, everything would be all right.

I avoided my parents, who tactfully refrained from asking me what was wrong but did not mask their real distress. I confided in my best friend from gymnasium. He told me that I was passing through a "crisis of faith," like Pascal's. "But I had not had any faith before!" I cried. His family observed the Jewish holidays, and he invited me to join their Passover dinner.

I shaved and went, curious to see whether it would make me feel more Jewish. It didn't. I found the service before the meal as tedious as the young children did. After a few minutes, the charm of the symbolic foods wore off, and we fidgeted while prayers in Hebrew and Hungarian praised the Lord, whose plagues on the Egyptians struck me as excessive. Maybe because it closed the service and heralded the approach of the steaming matzo ball soup, the last sentence alone made an impression on me: "Next year, may we celebrate in Jerusalem." I decided to find out more about Palestine. If I was being insulted for being Jewish, maybe I should find out about people who had elected to be as Jewish as possible.

I was becoming more and more curious about traveling to the Middle East when I heard from Berlin. My series would be published, and the paper was interested in other articles about rural Hungary. As Uncle Theodore remarked when I enthusiastically thanked him, the German public was not upset by the falling Hungarian birthrate.

I traveled to Berlin, and I became friends with Lothar, my uncle's friend there. I did three more articles on the Hungarian countryside. One of them was on the Hungarian population of German origins and its ties to the mother country; one on the unemployed agricultural workers, many of whom were Hungarian refugees of the territories lost in 1918; and the last one on religious and sectarian practices. When I handed in the second one, Lothar asked me what I would like to do next. Hardly believing my luck, I told him that I would like to travel to Palestine and do a series on the Middle Eastern French and British Mandate territories. He persuaded the management that that's just what they needed, and before I even left Berlin, he told me to go ahead. I knew now I would become a real journalist, and I was thrilled at the prospect of the trip.

PART X ~ THE MAIDSERVANT'S BOOK AGAIN

"I was a young fool"

CHAPTER 24.
Family Reunion (1933)

"Oh, those wretched deadlines!" Elizabeth thought, as she sat at her small desk, gluing herself to the chair. She had almost finished composing her review of the history book sent to her by the Viennese weekly to which she contributed a popular feature, "Serious Reading for the Frivolous Reader." She had started with art books but had branched out into history, biography, and travel. Her readers liked her vivacious and colloquial style, but she ground out the articles in agony, always at the last minute. She liked reading the books. She had gotten used to rapid reading of background material when she and Frederic worked together in their youth, but she would have preferred to talk to a friend about their contents while baking a cake or walking a grandchild or even catching up with Frederic's filing. But they needed the small supplement to his limited income, and Elizabeth had to struggle with the blank paper until she had fitted her views into the obligatory twelve paragraphs. What also irked her was that the companion feature, "Light Reading for the Serious Reader," was dashed off by a Herr Professor from the University of Vienna who dictated his comments to a secretary provided by the newspaper, who came to his flat every Saturday morning and was gone, review in hand, by the time the professor's lunch was served.

"But my dear lady," he complained to Elizabeth, when they met at the annual dinner of the contributors, "first I have to plow through a wasteland of broken hearts —not to mention the deep meaning of the modern novel!"

She offered to trade his broken hearts and secretary for the dishes she had smashed in desperation over her reviews, but the editor found their mismatch profitable and continued to ship heavy tomes to Budapest.

She really needed to get his work out of the way because she had a lot to do before they went to dinner at Kate's that evening. It had been a busy, happy week for her and Frederic because Andrew and his wife, Nicole, had come to Budapest to visit. Tonight's invitation was typical, Elizabeth felt, of the almost social nature of her daughter's relationship to her family since her marriage.

"How wonderful to hear your voice!" Kate had said to her brother over the telephone the evening of his arrival. "Won't you and Nicole come for dinner on Thursday? Just a small informal party — don't bother to dress. Mother and Father are invited too, of course."

"That means black tie but not tails and fifty people, with the maid riding on horseback around the table?" Andrew asked his parents. Frederic defended his son-in-law against Andrew's prejudice: He was really very interesting if you could follow what he said. Elizabeth reassured Nicole that Kate would only invite French-speaking scientists and artistic people of her circle.

It was certainly true, Elizabeth thought, that Nicole, a foreigner, fitted more warmly into the family than Philip ever did. Andrew's wife was a small gray-eyed woman with fluent gestures, who seemed to make Andrew very happy. Kate, who liked her, said she was the only Frenchwoman in France who did not know how to dress. Since her student days in Syria, where she and Andrew met in 1930, Nicole had become a professor of archeology. It was typical of her self-effacing tact that Andrew, who was still struggling with a degree in economics at the Sorbonne, looked like a contented, well-fed "intellectual," while Nicole made no impression at all until one of her rare smiles lit up her face.

Andrew's letter about becoming engaged to Nicole was funny and joyful but made Elizabeth and Frederic realize how rarely they would see their son.

The two met because a tour bus broke down, and Nicole had enlisted Andrew in coaxing or carrying some elderly French nuns on the tour to their destination, an oasis in the desert that would be part of Andrew's articles. Nicole, Andrew found out, had been working on an excavation in Petra as a student of archeology, and was guiding tours in Syria and Lebanon until a new dig could be opened. It was clear from his letter that Andrew fell head over heels in love with her.

The nun asked whether I had learned to speak French in Hungary. I told her of the two years I spent in Paris as a child and found out that Nicole grew up two blocks away, on the Avenue Wagram.

"So I must have seen you going off to school in your black apron and your heavy knapsack of books on your back! Did you have pigtails?" I asked.

"But no, Monsieur, I wouldn't have been caught dead in a black apron. We wore blue, dark blue, with white starched collars and it was wonderful for wiping blue ink...."

Her family were Protestant leftist, mostly scientists, "very serene," she said. Those were the people we never met in Paris, the upper bourgeoisie leading quiet lives behind the high windows over the trees of the boulevards. I didn't see much of Nicole during the rest of the tour, but she accepted a dinner invitation in Aleppo the day after it was over. She wore a short white tunic dress and when I asked her to marry me, she laughed, "How can you be so impetuous? We haven't even ordered wine yet."

But for the first time in my life, I am not being impetuous. I know that we will be husband and wife, and I'm not in any hurry either. When we are together, time stops and the small and large beauties of the world unfold for our enjoyment. Nicole has not agreed to marry me, but she passes her arm through mine and calls on the phone to wake me in the morning – a necessary task, as you all know.

I would love to persuade my friend Lothar to assign me to his Paris office. But if he doesn't, I'm going anyway. I wouldn't mind studying economics and political science at the Sorbonne if we can afford it. My mind weighs up my life as we discuss French politics on the terrace, and Nicole's white wrist flashes before me as she talks. Then, bless her soul, she listens to me explain myself — quirky, fitful, somewhat immature.

I understand the black bird, the desire to lose oneself into something greater, a collective unconscious that I wrote about in my articles. I understand it better than my father ever could as a motivating social force. But it isn't me. Somewhere between the high-mindedness of the last Victorians and the despair of the first barbarians, there must be a little place where I can breathe, laugh, survive.

I have lost my country, but I am at home with her — with her witty precise language, with the embattled European liberalism of my future wife.

* * *

The best part, Elizabeth reflected three years later, is that Andrew did enroll in the Sorbonne, did marry Nicole, and seemed not only happy but settled. She and Frederick had supported him financially to the best of their abilities during his studies, and he had continued writing articles to supplement his income. The worst part was that they could not afford traveling to Paris, nor could Andrew come to see them very often.

But, Elizabeth thought as she took her review into Frederic's study for typing, her son's happiness did not compensate for the uneasiness she felt about her daughter.

Neither Frederic nor Elizabeth had rejoiced at Kate's marriage to the brilliant physicist Philip von Reddich. How many times Elizabeth had had to tell herself that she was not to blame for introducing the two! She could remember vividly the spring afternoon when she had stopped at the National Theatre to see Kate. There was a rehearsal in progress, so she sat down in the empty auditorium. She had a message to give to her daughter, but it wasn't urgent. She watched the snatches of drama on the half-lit stage, interrupted by the comings and goings of the stage crew. Soon Kate appeared to supervise the placement of a balcony. Elizabeth was proud of the tall, lithe figure, clad in slacks, with a red kerchief on her hair. Kate had designed the scenery for this play. The director stopped an actress in the middle of a heartfelt tirade to talk to Kate. Elizabeth was pleased to see the serious tone with which he asked her daughter's opinion, while he dismissed the actress with a wave of his hand. She was almost annoyed to have her attention distracted by a young man who had wandered in earlier and now came up to her. "I don't suppose you remember me, Mrs. Ignatius – Philip von Reddich. I've been abroad for so long."

Of course she remembered Philip. His father, the Baron von Reddich, had helped Frederic during the difficult days of his return from exile, pompously, with slightly malicious glee. But he had helped, and she could not be ungracious to the son. Philip was a short, muscular man with a large nose and brilliant dark eyes. His thick black eyebrows nearly joined under his high forehead. Elizabeth had heard that Philip had studied mathematics and physics abroad and that his theories were the pride of the Berlin Technical Institute. She had also seen pictures of his marriage into a noble Hungarian family, but he acted as if Budapest were foreign to him. "I love this theater, but I don't know what the latest plays are, who the famous actors are — I feel lost."

They chatted, and he found out why she had come to see Kate. Then he did something that really annoyed her. He took out a monocle and observed the stage designer. If he had remarked on how striking the girl looked in her unconventional outfit, Elizabeth would have walked away, but he made no comment. Soon the director dismissed everyone for the day, and Kate jumped off the stage, hammer in hand, and came to greet her mother. She was flushed and pleased. Philip stood up and bowed slightly as he took her hand. Kate and Philip looked into each other's eyes, and apparently they could not let go of their handshake. Then Kate in her bold way, dismissed Philip and walked home with Elizabeth without a word concerning the encounter.

For several months, Elizabeth did not know whether the two had met again, but she suspected that Philip would try to see Kate.

It soon became clear that the girl was preoccupied, moody, and absorbed. She was also reckless by nature, and in a gossipy town like Budapest, it didn't take long for friends to let Kate's parents know that she had been seen in public, repeatedly, with a married man.

At the end of the summer, the Baron von Reddich, red and perspiring, stormed into Frederic's study, accusing Kate of being bent on "destroying a Christian marriage." Frederic asked whether Philip wasn't equally to blame, to which the fat man replied, "A few indiscretions by a married man are one thing. An open scandal, which may culminate in divorce, is quite a different story."

Frederic showed him to the door. "I may not like what my daughter is doing, but don't come here to call her names."

Elizabeth still didn't like to think about that period of their lives.

"I don't think that Philip will make her happy," she had said to her husband.

"I'm not sure that happiness is what Kate is looking for," he had replied.

She knew what he meant. Kate had had so many proposals, so many men were in love with her — there was no need to pick a married man with two children. It was the very difficulty of the situation that appealed to her, although she would not admit that.

"I love him, he loves me, and that is all that matters," she said with conviction. Elizabeth felt cut off from her daughter's view of passion. She could only love in broad daylight, with a peaceful conscience.

The drama went on for nearly a year. As Andrew said, it would have been hissed off the National Theatre's stage after one act. Only Kate's haggard look, wrenching her parents' hearts, reminded them that it could not be turned off at will. Finally, Philip and his wife got a noisy, acrimonious divorce, and Philip and Kate were married at the civil registry. Immediately afterwards, Philip took Kate with him on a lecture tour to Sweden. Her parents went to the train station to see the newlyweds off, Philip hatless with his rich black hair, Kate in a blue suit with poppies on her hat. They looked stunning — all the suffering of the last year seemed to have been washed away. Philip kissed his mother-in-law, and Kate made Frederic and the Baron shake hands. When a butler served champagne in the first-class compartment Philip had reserved, Elizabeth got a glimpse of the luxurious cosmopolitan life that Kate and her new husband were to lead for the next few years.

"Maybe it will be all right," she comforted herself.

"Of course it's all right, Mother," Kate laughed when Elizabeth once asked her how everything was between her and her husband, after Elizabeth had witnessed an angry exchange between the two. "He is a certified 'great man,' and sometimes it makes him into such an egotist that I could strangle him. At other times, I think he is the most exciting, attractive man who ever lived. But you know me — do you think living with me is a rest cure?"

Elizabeth smiled. "There is no analogy — even when I can't understand you, you are still my dearest stranger."

But of course she was aware of Kate's impulsiveness, moodiness, and pride. In herself, she had struggled against such characteristics to achieve greater inner harmony, while her daughter yielded to every passion as if it were a sacred command. Kate's beauty had encouraged others to indulge her. But Elizabeth also knew that Kate's character was part of her strength. She lived intensely, and she did not protect herself against possible suffering, knowing that after great crises and drama, she would probably emerge unscathed.

"How much these grown children, whom I hardly see, still fill my life!" Elizabeth thought, as she put the article in an envelope and carefully covered the typewriter.

CHAPTER 25.
Country Roads (1938)

In the pouring rain, Joska hitched the old mare to his wagon. The horse bucked to express disgust at leaving her stall, but he coaxed her out.

"Duty is duty. Although I'd hate to have you get sick on me. I can't afford it."

He pulled his hat down over his face, then limped back for a blanket and an umbrella for their visitor. Elizabeth was coming by train from Budapest to visit Anna. His wooden leg, which replaced the one he lost in the Great War, itched at the stump in this weather. The dog Bodri, the aging grandson of their first dog, followed him, tail down. Joska told him to get back into the house.

"I'd kick you if I could," he added.

The train no longer stopped at Kisbánya, so he had to drive on the muddy, rutted road to the next village, passing soaked fields and thatched roofs darkened with moisture. His own fields, only two acres, were not far from this road, but since his son's death two weeks earlier, he hadn't been able to muster the energy to harvest the beets and potatoes. "I'd better do it tomorrow before they rot, rain or no rain," he decided.

As soon as the train stopped, he saw Elizabeth fling open a compartment door and look around for him. A black cloche hat partially covered her fine, sharp features. In her long-skirted black suit, she stepped down with the quickness of a younger woman. While he hurried towards her, she waved, then struggled to open her umbrella.

"I kiss your hand, Honored Madam," he said. He reached out

to take her bag, but she dropped her umbrella and threw her arms around him.

"Oh Joska, I'm so sorry."

When she released him, he nodded, his broad shoulders joining in the motion. His narrowed eyes and tight mouth expressed resignation and anger. Rain drops fell from his long mustache. He picked up her flimsy umbrella from the platform.

"We'd better use mine, Honored Madam," he said.

They set off towards the wagon.

"How is she?" Elizabeth asked.

"Bad," he said. "She sits at the kitchen table, her fingers tracing the grain. Over and over. When she gets to a burl, she stops. She says that the burl is her child's death and that's where her life ends. When I ask, Wife, is dinner ready? she gets up and cooks it, but then she sits down again."

She looked at him in silent commiseration, her dark eyes softening. She understood that only a male was your child, in peasant parlance, because girl children didn't really belong to you.

He helped her climb onto the seat of the wagon and covered her with a heavy handwoven blanket embroidered in black. A quick "Tsk tsk" of disapproval escaped her.

"You don't want this to get wet," she murmured, as she pulled most of the blanket under the umbrella. She recognized the old "writing style" of embroidery that Anna had learned from her mother and grandmother. No flowers, no curlicues, only abstract designs in black or red.

Joska watched placidly. Her quick, nervous reactions were what he expected from city folks.

"How is the Sir Attorney?" he asked as they started.

"Frederick is troubled," she said, "very pessimistic. Since Hitler annexed Austria, he thinks we are in for war. Does Esther help you?"

"Oh yes, she's a good girl," he said. "But with little ones of her own and a house and a yard. Her man is in the mine too, may God give the owners the beating they deserve."

As he said that, he lowered his voice.

When they reached the house, Anna, stocky and straight-backed, was standing at the table, her hand on the dog's head. She must have heard the wagon and taken a step towards the door. Elizabeth could see the vacant look in her round face, whose features were pulled down like a tragic mask.

"Oh Anna," she said, and embraced her. They both started to cry and sat down at the table. Elizabeth's arm went around her friend, who sobbed louder and louder.

Joska waited for a while, then left quietly.

The two women wept for a long time. Elizabeth blew her nose and pulled a photograph from her bag.

"I know this will make you sad, but I thought you would want to have it. It's from the time Stevie visited us in Budapest."

Anna wiped her eyes and looked at the picture. Three young people, arms around each other's shoulders, leaned against the Danube's embankment. In the background, sunlight sparkled on the water. Stevie blond and sturdy, stood in the middle, between Elizabeth's children — Andrew, in his high school soccer uniform, and Kate, tall and elegant, a cigarette in her hand.

"He did enjoy that visit," Anna said finally. "For weeks, he talked about the movies, the cafes and the automobile show, the pretty girls everywhere. May I keep this?"

"Of course."

"It's the talking I miss more than anything," she continued. "You see, the mining company, they only work this mine for eight months, then they fire everyone, which is a hardship for the men. But for us, a blessing. Stevie would come back to work on the farm and that's when...."

She stopped and stared down for a while. Elizabeth sat silently.

"He and I started to talk," Anna continued. She was crying now, but she continued to talk through her tears. "Esther and I, we understand each other without words, but this was like having a new friend. He would make me laugh, tell me stories, ask about my life before he was born. All this, while weeding or hoeing or taking care of the beasts."

She lapsed back into silence.

"There is a picture of the four of them I wish I had," Elizabeth said. "Do you remember the time when you came to Budapest, after Frederic went into exile? I was so tired and discouraged. I was teaching my class at the museum. The students were so dumb and arrogant, I nearly wept. And patronizing. I came home to find you cooking dinner. I almost got run over by Esther, Stevie, Andrew, and Kate chasing each other all over the apartment. You remember?"

"Yes," Anna said slowly. "Layered cabbage with meat and sour cream, that's what it was I cooked for you. I found out that the peasants, to punish the leftists, would not allow food to reach city markets. I was afraid you'd starve. What a lot of hard times we've been through, Little Madam."

They continued to reminisce, with Anna occasionally relapsing into tears but more animated than she had been. She remembered her duties as hostess and got up to heat some bean soup. It was nearly four o'clock when they ate. Soon, Joska would be back to take Elizabeth to the train.

"Anna, do take care of him," she said as she got ready to leave. "If it weren't for Joska, we might have stayed employer and employee forever, instead of the friends we became. And work is good medicine."

Anna shook her hand self-deprecatingly.

"We were so young, Little Madam, we didn't know what life would bring."

* * *

On the way back to the station, Elizabeth asked Joska.

"So what happened at the mine? The Budapest papers talked about an accident, but they were vague."

He looked around. They were alone on the wet road.

"There was an accident, and the managers sealed the mine to prevent the gas from escaping, trapping the miners who were still down there. The others got mad because they believed they could have been rescued."

He stopped and only the horse trotting on the wet road could be heard. She waited for him to continue.

"So a group of them went to see the managers to protest,

Stevie too. Of course, it's illegal to strike, so the managers called the police, and they fired into them, hitting my son and one other. I'm not even sure they were on strike, but I think they had it in for him."

Once, when Stevie suggested an efficiency measure, he almost got fired, he told her. "If you're so smart, go to school, we don't want intellectuals here," the foreman had said.

Elizabeth shook her head in dismay.

"How awful," she said. "Do you know, repealing the anti-strike law was one of the charges against Frederic in his trial in the early 1920s. Of course, the government reinstated them."

"My leg, my lungs, and now my child, all gone," he said bitterly.

He never mentioned how proud he had been of his son, how much he loved Stevie's strength, his steadiness, the thoughtfulness that his two years of secondary schooling had emphasized. That was over and done with, and only womenfolk wasted words on the past.

At the station, Joska helped Elizabeth down from the carriage and, under the shelter of his large umbrella, walked her to the platform. After they shook hands, he turned to go, but she called him back.

"Does Anna still advise young women in the neighborhood about health care?"

"From time to time," he replied.

"A doctor I know has just been appointed to run a midwife training institute," Elizabeth said. "You might want to encourage Anna to get a certificate. I think that the activity would distract her."

"I'll think about it, Honored Madam," he said.

He was reluctant to have Anna go away and stop whatever she was still doing at the farm, and he was sure that the training cost money. He would mention it to Esther, he decided, see what the girl thought. The price of his farm products was so low that the midwife's fees — he had heard that a delivery brought ten, twenty pengöes — might be attractive.

The next day the rain stopped. Whether it was because of the comfort of her friend's visit or the change in the weather, Anna returned to her tasks. Mechanically, she went from one to another, in the order that she had learned as a young girl: beasts, house, garden, fields, house, beasts. But she remained taciturn, almost dour. Joska was pleased to find her working, but as soon as he could, he escaped to the tavern.

The rest of the fall was dry and sunny. They got their harvest in except for the grapes. Esther came to visit, herding her children before her like chicks. She had heard talk of war too.

"Mother, will you take the children if Laci gets called up? I want to go into service because the house belongs to the mine, and they'll take it back."

Anna put her hands on her waist.

"You'll move in with us, my girl, before you'd do that."

"But you loved working for Elizabeth!" the young woman exclaimed.

"Yes, but I was lucky with her. Most city women are slave-drivers. They don't even know what they want except to squeeze the life out of you. Even at Elizabeth's, the work was long and hard, and it wasn't for me but for others."

"I guess. You made it sound exciting, somehow."

"I was a young fool," Anna said, "with stars in my eyes."

War didn't break out, and Esther and her husband helped harvest the wine in October. Laci was a quiet, gentle giant, clumsy with farm work. In one generation of mining, his family had forgotten what country people had known from time immemorial.

Chapter 26.
The Black Bag (1939)

The stork came back to the house where Anna was born, but he came back alone. In the spring morning, he stood on one leg, his shape black against the sky.

"Where's your mate?" Anna asked, craning her neck. She was catching her breath after her long walk from her own village. Her forehead and gaze were clear and steady, but wrinkles had formed around her mouth and eyes. Her clothes hung a little looser than they did on the firm stoutness of her middle years.

Her brother, Alex, came around the outbuilding, a pail of whitewash in his hand.

"Sister! God brought you well, it's been a long time." His graying hair and mustache reminded her of their father, but without the dignity of the old shepherd.

"Why isn't the stork mother hatching her eggs?" Anna asked.

"She never made it home," he replied. "Someone shot her, or she knew better than to come to a place where no one welcomes the likes of them anymore."

"They used to say that they bring luck," Anna said wistfully.

"Babies, too," he said in a deprecatory tone. "This village doesn't want any more mouths to feed."

He picked up his pail and walked toward the kitchen. Anna followed, saddened.

"Martha's out in the field," he explained. "I had to finish whitewashing the barn, but the kitchen's her work. Sit down, rest. How is Joska's cough?"

"Not much better than it was in the winter," she sighed, as she unpacked the gifts she had brought: a pot of noodles with cabbage, cut with the famous noodle cutter Elizabeth gave her long ago, and a bottle of mulberry wine left from last summer.

"I wish I had something sweet for my god-child Theresa, but I'm all out of sugar."

"Martha's signed her up to be a little nurse-maid for the Messers," Alex said.

"Really?" Anna sat down. "Mrs. Messer is mean-tempered. "

"You didn't expect us to keep her home all summer, did you?" he asked.

"I'll go to see her on Sundays, it's closer to my house than to yours," said Anna, avoiding his question.

"Thank you, sister, it's true that one should keep an eye out on children going into service."

Brother and sister were silent, thinking of an old family tragedy. Shortly after Anna was born, her oldest brother died, mangled by a thresher on a large estate. The owners never called a doctor and only notified the family when it was too late. Anna only knew Mike from her family's reminiscences.

"Of course, Mike was much older," Alex said, to dispel the unlucky thought. "What a nice, cheerful guy, though! He taught me to carve my first wooden flute. I liked him much better than Rosza , who shrieked all the time."

"Of the dead, speak only well," said Anna, although she recalled what her mother had said of her sister — "I never got a kind word out of that girl. A little one like you does more to warm my heart than she did all her years here!"

"I remember us all getting a hiding the day Rozsa's in-laws came for her engagement. We all shrieked too. I had to sit on the neck of the fireplace to eat because there was no room on the benches. But I got the best view!"

"My kids still do that," said Alex, looking up at the large fireplace standing in the middle of the room. It joined the wall with a thick, whitewashed outlet, made of fired clay like the rest. Martha came in, a small wizened woman, glad to see her sister-in-law.

"I'll leave you women to each other," Alex said as he got up.

"Anna, I heard you've been delivering babies. You might talk to that superintendent about doing that on the estate. That is one place where people still have babies — in fact, they breed like mice. Don't forget to grease his palm, though."

Anna had been slow to warm to the idea of midwifery, although Esther encouraged her as soon as Elizabeth broached the idea with Joska.

"Old Bözsi is lazy and slovenly," Esther said. "They say that a woman died in childbirth in the next village because Bözsi was too drunk at the delivery to call the doctor in time."

Anna had consulted her minister, more because of Esther's prodding than because of any real desire to undertake a new job.

"You don't need a certificate," he said. "God's help, strong legs for walking, and common sense are all that are needed. You have enough experience tending the sick and newborn."

"Would God help me?" Anna thought at once, with painful doubt. Since Stevie's death, she had gone to services, as always, sung the hymns, and mouthed the prayers. But there was a hollowness, a deadness in which the words reverberated, giving off their own echo. She never felt that opening of the heart through which, in the past, she had grasped God's love, like warm sunshine. She believed that God would not support her in her efforts, and she told Joska that to invest in her training would be a waste of time.

However, after hearing Joska brag about his soon-to-be-certified wife, families started to ask Anna for help. They were not put off by her refusals because they thought that she was just trying to increase her price.

But after refusing to help several families in distress because of illness, Anna finally rushed off, full of fear and doubt, to an imminent birth, the day Bözsi was found half-frozen and drunk by the side of a road. The messenger who had come for Anna was an eight-year-old girl. She led Anna away from the village, towards the forest, to a small hut.

"They're acorn pickers," the girl explained, "and mean and stingy. The old man made the daughter-in-law go out to work, although her load nearly reached her nose."

Anna quickened her steps on the hard ground. The hut seemed awfully far.

"So the baby might be here by now?" she asked. Her guide nodded.

"Second babies come fast, especially girls," she said wisely.

"How do you know it's a girl?"

"My mother said that the young woman craved white sugar, a sure sign."

Anna hurried on as the child told stories of the sex of infants being predicted by the mother's love of pipe smoke, of lean meat or sewing needles. Anna said sternly,

"Whether it's a boy or girl is in God's hands and not for us to speculate."

They reached a scene of consternation at the hut. The young woman was lying on the floor next to a newborn infant, who was covered with blood.

"Quick, cut the cord. I don't know how to do it," the old man barked at Anna. The neighbor whose daughter brought Anna stood with a pail of clean water in her hand, afraid to touch the child. Anna brought out two ribbons from her apron pocket and tied the umbilical cord and cut it with clean scissors. The infant moaned and, when she slapped it, gave a feeble cry.

"Has she expelled the afterbirth?" Anna asked.

"Yes, my son is burying it," the old man replied.

"All right, help me put her to bed," Anna said. She was surprised at her own harsh tone, but what the little girl had said about the father-in-law made her angry.

"I'll clean off the baby after I take care of her."

She put the young woman in a clean shirt and tried to stop her bleeding with the pressure of her own apron, fearing all the while that she would die in her hands because the body felt so inert.

"Do you have something strong to give her?"

Reluctantly, someone gave Anna some brandy with which she roused the young woman.

"Go to sleep now," Anna said, "but don't go too far. You've got a son to care for."

The mother gave a faint smile.

"I made some diapers for him," she said, pointing to a large chest. They were torn out of an old shirt, not even hemmed. Anna washed the baby in the rainwater the neighbor had brought. She checked the tiny body for deformities. When she finished, she put the baby next to the mother on the bed. The dark hut, with its smell of blood and lack of air, was beginning to make Anna feel faint. She looked around and only then did she notice the other family members, cowering behind the father-in-law. There was no other bed, and Anna started to worry that her patient might be displaced.

"What is your fee, Mrs. Vas?" the old man asked. "Of course, you're not a real midwife, just a stand-in, so you can't charge the regular amount."

Anna ignored his rudeness.

"The better you take care of her, the less work I'll have and the less you have to pay me. I'll be back tomorrow, and I'll expect to find her in bed. She is to stay in bed for two weeks and eat the best of everything."

She left before they had a chance to protest.

"She's a feeble little thing," Anna thought of the mother. "She won't stick up for herself."

She was surprised to see how involved she had gotten in the situation and pleased to be able to exercise some power over the surly acorn-picker. Anna knew that in less than a week, the young mother would be out again, her baby tied to her back, with a brandy-soaked pacifier in its mouth. But she felt that if she could get the young woman a few days' rest, she would have accomplished something.

For a week, every morning she went to clean and change the new mother and child at the edge of the forest. If any of the other children were present, she washed and fed them too. The old man resented her presence and, as soon as he could, dismissed her with a miserly fee. But old Bözsi's reputation suffered further from the incident, and hardly a week went by without someone asking Anna's help. There weren't that many babies, but many old people who were bedridden needed her. Anna tried to improve their diets, which often consisted of stale bread soaked in water, since their teeth were mostly gone, and she tried to get them clean and massaged. Some of the families felt she did too much, but others were glad to pay.

"After all," they would say, "it won't be for long."

Anna was ready for more work when her brother suggested the estate, but she didn't have much hope of getting work from the superintendent, who had refused in the past to employ her, except as a harvest worker. When she went to see him, he pocketed her proffered bribe and said, over his shoulder, "It's none of my business, really, you go to see the district doctor and see if he needs help in this area. If he doesn't, don't come back to complain — it's the law that requires medical care for the farm workers, not me."

Anna had met the district doctor once or twice — she herself took Joska to a private doctor in the nearest large town. She remembered him as a young medical school graduate who had been appointed to that post in 1929. The man she saw reading a newspaper in a dusty office seemed to have aged more than ten years during that time. He swatted away some flies as he listened to her in a bored manner.

"So you say you live near the estate?" he asked.

"Right nearby, Honored Sir Doctor. I've worked on their harvest nearly every summer."

She had not dared to bring him a bribe, but she put a basket of cakes and flowers on his desk.

"And what do you know about delivering babies?" he asked. She gave him a letter from her pastor praising her work, and she told him what she had done during the past year. She also mentioned that old Bözsi had become nearly useless.

"I know, I know. And I don't much like trekking out there for every stomachache that a snotty peasant kid gets from eating stolen, unripe fruit. How would you treat that, by the way?"

She thought that an emetic of soapy water would usually purge an upset stomach if a cold compress didn't help.

"You seem to know what you're doing," he said with a yawn. "And could you get them to wash from time to time? It keeps down the infection and makes them smell sweeter."

She asked if he could give her a note to the superintendent of the estate approving of her visits — one couldn't just come and go to the estate to do business without his permission.

"You seem to be a very literate peasant woman, with all these certificates. Don't worry, I'll mention you to him the next time I see him. Also, get some quinine at the pharmacist — when you don't know what ails them, it's usually TB, malaria, or early pregnancy, and malaria is the only one we can treat."

She pushed the flowers forward with some hesitation.

"Could I leave these for Madam your honored spouse?"

He laughed cynically.

"When you hear of a girl of good family who is anxious to become Madam my spouse on my miserable salary, let me know. Here, let me find something for you to put your quinine in."

He scratched his head and after rummaging in several messy closets, he came up with a worn black leather bag. Anna's eyes shone. She knew that it was as good as a certificate.

She enjoyed picking out her equipment at the pharmacist. She had always liked the dark store, with the gleaming porcelain containers along the walls and the bottles of colored water in the window. She could pick and dry her own herbs, but her rough fingers delicately packed into her bag a thermometer, some disinfectant, and a bottle of aspirin, which the pharmacist let her have on credit.

Treating the farm workers was different from her work in the village and its outskirts. Here she did not know most of the people, especially since many were transient. Although the workers did not pay her — she had to submit her bill each month to the superintendent, who paid after deducting his "commission" — her patients were sullen and uncooperative.

"Bark at them," the doctor said, when she complained that they didn't follow her simple instructions. "They're deaf and dumb, mostly."

Reluctantly, she developed a brusque, authoritarian tone, which she sometimes forgot to abandon at home. Many times she wanted to give up. The workers seemed to her so dirty, so downtrodden, so lacking in peasant dignity. But the pay was good, even after her expenses. From time to time, she met some transient workers who had owned their own farms, as she did, and had sunk through their losses to work as paid laborers. That was the fear that really kept her going — that she and Joska would not die in their own house.

.

CHAPTER 27.
The Maidservant's Book (1939)

"Oh my God," Anna cried, as the militiamen threw Joska's inert body at her feet. "What happened?"

Her husband was covered with blood. A tooth hung out of his mouth, and a swollen eye was barely open.

"Keep an eye on your man, old woman, and perhaps he won't get into trouble again," one of them said. He gave Joska a parting kick with his spurred boot, and they left, their long plumes shivering over their helmets.

"Can you move?" she asked Joska. He moaned. She couldn't lift him, so she had to wash him off just as he was, lying by their gate. They must have beaten him with truncheons. There were bruises everywhere. She was grateful for the vine that grew along their fence. At least no one would see him in this condition.

When Joska came to, he cried out in pain.

"What happened?" she asked. "Did you get into a fight?"

"No," he said, "not he, she. Water."

She brought him some and covered him with a blanket. She remembered that people can bleed inside as well as outside.

"I'm going to fetch the doctor," she said.

"Don't, please," he said. "Don't shame me."

After a while, he got feverish and incoherent. Anna sent a message through a neighbor to her brother to help her because Joska had fallen off a ladder. Alex came early in the evening, and to her relief, asked no questions. He made a stretcher from two boards and slowly they lifted him to the bed. The move exhausted him, and he fell into a deep sleep.

"Everything will be all right now, sister," her brother said as he left. She wondered what he meant.

Very slowly, Joska started to recover. He couldn't get up from the bed, but the fever left him. He thought that he had a broken rib and a shoulder bone, but he didn't bleed or throw up. Neighbors expressed sympathy without asking questions, and she was sure they knew something she didn't. The first evening that Joska spent quietly staring ahead, she sat down by the bed.

"You'd better tell me what happened."

"I got mixed up with a woman," he said, "and people had too much respect for you to gossip about it."

"And did her husband get the militiamen to beat you up?"

"She told him I was after her when she got tired of me. I knew, but I couldn't leave her alone. I skulked after her like a beaten dog."

"You poor old fool," she said.

He lifted a hand and placed it over hers. She was moved.

"So who was this young trollop?"

He told her it was the tavern keeper's wife.

"But she's old and ugly!" Anna exclaimed.

She stormed out, without even checking as she always did that he had water by his bedside. She went to the vegetable patch and angrily pulled out weeds. The tavern keeper's wife was a squat woman, swarthy and pockmarked, with eyes like coals. The tavern keeper was her third husband. She moved lightly from table to table, and her throaty laugh kept the noise and spirit of the place alive. That must have been what attracted Joska. Men don't like gloomy wives, she thought, and I have always been serious, even before Stevie's death made me withdraw into myself. She wondered how long this had been going on.

She pulled out a pale blue flower with white pistils and noticed its beauty even though it was just a little weed. The smell of earth and grass rose in the fall evening. Her anger gradually abated. Joska had been a fool, but so had she. A wife should know what her man is up to. Maybe God had protected her, although she hardly deserved it, by shielding her from the knowledge that Joska wanted another woman until he came back to her. She felt her old belief come back that there was wisdom hidden in the sorrows and disorders of life.

She brought him a glass of wine.

"If your taste runs to old hags like her, next time you won't even have to cross the street, we can do as well here."

He smiled at her rare attempt at humor.

"You've been a good wife, woman," he said.

* * *

While Joska was recovering, he stayed around the house, helping Anna to the extent he could with the garden and the animals, but he was unwilling to face the world beyond his home. It reminded her of the way he was when he came back from the war, but now he was embarrassed before the village rather than cold to her.

He wouldn't have been able to work in the fields yet anyway because of his injuries. Anna earned enough as a midwife to enable the couple to hire two workers from the estate, who completed the harvest and prepared the fields that wouldn't lie fallow for fall sowing. Farm workers expected to be fed, at least once a day, and Anna had to arrange her schedule so as to cook at least one dish for her menfolk. Both workers were older, taciturn men, who kept Joska company without making him self-conscious about his injuries. If they knew how they came about, they never let on.

One of the rare conversations at Anna's dinner table took place when Admiral Horthy announced that he had arranged for a treaty of friendship between the German Chancellor Hitler and the Fascist dictator of Italy, Benito Mussolini. Horthy declared a national holiday, and the farm workers went to the village square to hear the speakers and the band. Anna and Joska stayed home, but the next evening the workers talked about the event.

"Well, it was quite something," the younger of the two men, Paul Agi, said. "This Hitler is going to return the lands we lost during the last war."

"Just like that?" Joska asked.

"What do you mean?" Janko, the older man asked.

243

"Well, I'm not against that," Joska said, "but that land belongs to someone else now, and if you take it, that someone else might get mad and go to war."

"The speeches in the square were all hot to go to war," Pali said. "They were hot about everything, the Jews, the Bolsheviks, people I've never heard of."

"Was Üstoki there?" Joska asked.

"Oh yes, he's a commander of the Arrow Cross, and he and his followers wore green shirts and spurred boots and helmets with rooster feathers."

"Rooster feathers?" Anna laughed. "What for?"

"To frighten people," Joska said. "The Arrow Cross is the new militia, and you don't want to mess with them."

He got up from the table, unwilling to continue the conversation. Anna could see that Joska was disturbed. The others, having spoken more than usual, calmly finished the meal and went back to their work.

Anna cleaned up the kitchen. She saw that Joska sat down on the bench before the house, deep in thought. She joined him. The men bade them good-night and went home. The sun had set and the sky was still light.

"So what about this Üstoki?" Anna asked.

"He's something else," Joska said. "I heard him talk in the tavern when he was a nobody. He said he'd been a journalist or soldier or politician, I'm not sure what, but a real rabble-rouser. I didn't pay much attention. I don't care about the Jews or Bolsheviks, but he kept harping on them, how they've sapped our country's strength, and we have to fight and kill to get it back."

He was silent for a while, then he continued.

"So that's how it started, with that woman. That's why I don't like to talk about it."

"Tell me anyway," Anna said.

"Well, one day, Üstoki got arrested because he criticized Admiral Horthy for being soft on the Jews. His sentence was commuted, and he came back from two weeks in jail a hero. He started riling up the people at the tavern on how they ought to drag all the Jews and Jewesses — whom he blamed for his arrest

— into the brick factory yard and beat and torture them until they confess where they had their gold, banknotes, diamonds, all the money they have hidden somewhere. The women too. People were drunk and shouting, competing on who could come up with more vicious tortures."

"How awful," Anna said.

"It was. I felt I was back in Siberia. I couldn't breathe, my heart was pounding. I went out the back way to the yard, and my uncle's wife, that woman, came after me. 'They're going crazy in there,' I said. She calmed me down by holding me, and that was the beginning."

"You haven't gone back there since," Anna said quietly.

"No, and I won't," Joska said. "But that Üstoki and his kind are more powerful than Horthy now."

"Doesn't bode well for Elizabeth and our other Jewish friends," Anna said.

"Not for us either," he said. "These people who want to clean the world with blood and fire, they don't know what they're talking about."

* * *

When the war broke out, Esther was pregnant again. She accepted her parents' help, insisting that she would contribute her husband's service pay to their small cash earnings. She was distressed to lose her own little house, and Anna told her she and Joska would move out of the big bedroom into what had been Stevie's room.

"That way, if Laci comes home on leave, he has a place to rest his head."

Joska acquiesced without discussion. Since his recovery, he thought of himself as an old man. So Anna started to empty the heavy wooden chest with the tulips, which had belonged to her parents and in which she had stored her trousseau. There were embroidered sheets and pillow cases in it, softened by many washings, some of which she put back for Esther's use. In an old leather pocketbook, she had stored documents: Joska's military discharge, tax receipts, the children's birth certificates, and her maidservant's book.

"Dear heart," Anna thought of Elizabeth as she took the little book in her hand, "how much trouble she took over my entry."

She could still see the young woman at her desk, her silk skirt in waves around her chair, her back straight, as her pen scratched over her draft because she said she didn't want to make any erasures in the book.

The title page contained Anna's name, age, and address in her own, laborious handwriting. Under these was a printed excerpt from the Servants' Law.

"Paragraph 3140 of the Servants' Law provides that contracts between masters and domestic servants are covered by the Anti-Strike Act of 1892 under which such contracts are public obligations, enforceable by the master with the assistance of the police. Under no circumstances may the servant fail to perform his or her duties except in the case of non-payment of wages persisting for more than one year...."

She wasn't sure she understood all of what she read, but she recognized the words "Anti-Strike Act" with horror.

"Joska!" she cried out. "Wasn't that why they shot Stevie?"

She remembered that he was out in the fields, and she was alone. The cold, official words chilled her. How could this awful law have anything to do with her? Her former mistress had been her friend for years now. While she admired Elizabeth for her loyalty, warmth, and vivacity, she also felt that her friend had been sheltered by her social status, while her own had aged and hardened her.

Her eyes skimmed over the rest: "...duty of the servant to perform conscientiously whatever duties are assigned... the master may fire the servant without notice if the servant's behavior gives rise to an accusation or suspicion of theft, disobedience or venereal disease...." Just as I told Esther, she thought.

She looked at the handwritten entry:

"Anna Nagy performed her duties conscientiously, efficiently, and skillfully. She was respected by all members of the household for her hard work, good temper, sound judgment, and high moral qualities. She leaves my employ to my regret, after ample notice, to be married."

That's nice, and she meant it, Anna thought. But still, we were maid and mistress, with that law in there. And now the same law had come to take her child away. How ignorant we were, Elizabeth and I, that we thought we could avoid this system that makes us so unequal – so that any word of Stevie against his "betters" results in his death.

A wave of anger swept over her.

She would never want to see that book again. Never again would she go into service, even if anyone wanted to hire an old woman like herself. Angrily, she ripped up the maid's book and then continued to sort her possessions, taking comfort in being able to help her daughter in her need.

PART XI ~ Desperate Errands

"This was our home"

CHAPTER 28.
Helping Kate (1938)

Of late, Kate's husband, Philip von Reddich, didn't join her and Tom and Zsuzsi for Sunday lunch with Elizabeth and Frederic. His excuses grew thinner, and Kate's parents guessed that all was not well with her marriage. The young couple led a busy social life in Budapest. Even Tom and Zsuzsi, their children, seemed to move in a different world, Elizabeth felt, with ponies, governesses, and birthday parties with hired clowns.

Nevertheless, it was a surprise when Philip called up right after the Munich agreement in 1938 between Hitler and Great Britain, which many thought would not prevent war, to ask whether he could come for dinner one Sunday.

"I'm going to America," he told Elizabeth, "and I'd like you to help persuade Kate to join me. With the children, of course."

He had never asked for their help. As soon as Kate arrived, elegantly dressed, her mouth set, Elizabeth knew that her role would be difficult. She wished that Andrew, who was working as a journalist in France, were home.

After dinner, when the children went to play in the next room, Philip explained that the colleagues who had invited him on a lecture tour of the United States had told him to bring his family.

"Whether or not there's war in Europe," he said, "there's no future here for my work."

Kate lit a cigarette and looked down at her high heels.

"All the people in my field who matter worked in Berlin, and now they're in America," Philip continued. "I want Kate and the children to come with me, so that I can provide for them if I decide to stay."

"Because your colleagues are Jewish, right?" Elizabeth said irritably. The von Reddichs were converted Catholics, but they had been Jews once.

"You can stay there or come back," Kate said in a strangled voice. "I'm not going."

"I'll give you a divorce in America," Philip cried. "We've been through this before."

His hand trembled on the table. Kate got up to close the door.

"I don't believe you," she said as she sat down. "You won't give me a divorce because you don't believe that I no longer love you. I did but I don't."

Elizabeth's heart leapt. My beloved child is coming back to me, she thought.

Frederic put his hand over Kate's.

"Whatever you do, my dear, there's a better future for you in America."

He described the pressures on Admiral Horthy since Hitler's invasion of Austria and the possibility of a more radical Fascist regime, the Arrow Cross Party's coming to power in Hungary.

"All that doesn't concern me," Kate shrugged. "Philip leaves, I stay, the whole problem is solved. And the children are better off with me and my friends and family."

From the way she mentioned friends, Elizabeth believed that Kate loved someone else. Although she didn't like her son-in-law, she felt sorry for him.

Philip postponed his trip to the United States hoping Kate would change her mind, but she didn't. He left a few weeks before war broke out. Kate looked very pale for a few months, then she started to bloom.

In the months after Philip left for America, Elizabeth discovered that she had been right about Kate having a lover, although she was uncharacteristically discreet about him. He was a musician, slight and energetic. Kate didn't bring him to her parents' home, and when they went backstage to congratulate him on a performance, her introduction was perfunctory. She once explained to her mother that although Ernest was important to her, as far as her children were concerned, she was married to their father and that was that.

It was Ernest who got her involved in organizing the Jewish Opera after the firing of Jewish actors and musicians from state institutions. And it was when Ernest was drafted in 1942 into one of the Jewish "work brigades" that Kate asked Elizabeth to help her raise funds for the drafted men's equipment, which they had to provide for themselves. This was odd. Jews, who had served in the Hungarian Army for generations, were not allowed to do so now. But why weren't their own brigades supplied with equipment, Elizabeth wondered.

Elizabeth, going to the offices of the Jewish Rabbinical Council of Budapest, expected something resembling her memories of the Red Cross in Geneva, where she had gone to try to locate Joska in 1917. Instead, the place was crowded and frantic, a far cry from the quiet efficiency of the Swiss organization.

"Did you come to contribute?" a bearded man barked at her.

"I don't have much money...I thought that maybe my time would be useful," she said. In fact, she had no money, since so many of Frederic's Jewish clients were unemployed.

"Everybody has time nowadays," he replied coldly. "Go and ask your rabbi what the assessment is for your congregation."

Elizabeth didn't explain that she didn't belong to a congregation, and she set out to find Kate. Everywhere, she was greeted with the same anxious, unfriendly response of people who were being asked to do more than they could. Finally, someone suggested that she try downstairs.

In the hallway she saw a long line of men waiting at a teller's window. Each one answered the same questions in a low, embarrassed voice.

"Why can't you supply your own equipment? How much can you contribute to it? Who are your dependents? Come back tomorrow, we'll decide on your application.... Next. Why can't you supply...."

Each man had the same fearful, resigned expression. Not one of them, she thought, looked like a soldier. And how many already had the hunched-over bearing of old Jews! Of course, she thought, these are the poorest of the draftees, since anyone who could afford to do so bought or borrowed boots, blankets, and warm clothes. Since, as Jews, they weren't allowed to serve with the regular army, they would do subsidiary work such as trench digging.

Elizabeth realized that she kept saying "them" in her mind.

"Aren't these my people? Wouldn't Andrew be among them if he were here?"

The thought only increased her longing for her son. She knew too little of what was happening to him to know whether to be sorry or glad that he wasn't on that line. Troubled, she finally found Kate at a telephone, surrounded by papers and harried people.

"What do you mean, under guard?" Kate was asking someone on the line. "And what do you mean, no weapons? Aren't they going to the front?"

She ended the conversation in disgust.

"They need another fifty thousand pengöes for shovels. But why do they assume that our men would desert?"

She finally acknowledged her mother.

"What are you doing here? Never mind, I'm glad you are. There's another problem. The refugee Jews from Poland, Yugoslavia, Czechoslovakia, all the German-occupied territories. Now they're being drafted, and if they say that they're refugees, they are being deported with their families. What we need are Hungarian Gentiles willing to say that these people are friends who are visiting them or to supply papers or anything. Do you remember all those contacts you made while we were in Paris?"

With a list of "cases," as Kate called them, Elizabeth started to call on her former acquaintances. Some refused to see her, giving a transparent excuse or a haughty referral to "present circumstances." But others treated her sympathetically as a fellow Hungarian trying to help foreigners. Her visits were so social in nature, and she was so eloquent and unassuming as she pleaded for these strangers from Rumania or Yugoslavia, that she almost forgot that her errands were desperate for the people involved. She could even console herself by thinking that the people for whom she had not found sponsors would succeed in staying somehow in the confusion over their papers.

"After all," her friends repeated, especially when they refused to help, "there's a war on."

But she didn't see any signs of war as she got into the tram to take her home. The sun was shining. People were busy shopping or eating ices at restaurant terraces. The family she had just visited had a twenty-five-year-old son, who had interrupted his listening to the wireless to open the door for her. During the Great War, he would have enlisted in the army out of patriotism even though a man of his background could usually buy his way out of service. The euphoric, oily miasma of the government news, which Frederic and she did not believe, but which they could not compare with any accurate information, added to the unreality of the war. Only that line of men in the Jewish Council offices gripped her with an intimation of destruction.

She found Frederic at his desk, working.

"Did a case come up?" she asked hopefully.

"No, my dear," he said. "My friends have asked me to draw up a declaration for Hungarian Jewry. This may be our last chance to protest being treated as enemies before we are made stateless, like the German Jews. Listen."

With the eloquent words of the language created by the great nineteenth-century poets, he talked about the Hungarian Jews, some of whose ancestors had slept in rural cemeteries since the seventeenth century. They did not long for new or distant lands. This was their home. But if their sons were to fight for their country, they should be sent out with honor, with arms, to die if they have to, like others....

Chapter 29.
Evening Light (1943)

The afternoon sunlight streamed through the living room windows onto the yellowed ivory keys of the piano. Elizabeth and Frederic sat at the round table listening to their guest playing a Mozart fantasia. The pianist was blind, but right now his eyes could have been closed in concentration on his playing. His wife sat next to the piano. Her gray suit, gray hair, and colorless face were those of a woman who could not be seen by the person closest to her.

The couple, Ferdinand and Paula Feld, were Hungarian-speaking Jews from Yugoslavia, who had been smuggled over the border into Hungary to escape deportation by the Germans. Elizabeth and Frederic had arranged for Hungarian residence permits to legalize their stay in Budapest, and the pianist wanted to thank them.

A year ago, Frederic had suffered a heart attack. His blond hair and mustache were a pale gold, and his blue eyes seemed lighter under their heavy lids. Elizabeth's shoulder was slightly bent by rheumatism, but her bright glance, her fine face structure, and her quick hands seemed unchanged.

Elizabeth leaned back, letting the music engulf her with its sensuous beauty, but Frederic sat upright, puzzled and thoughtful. The fantasia was in a minor key and a somber mood. It seemed to Frederic — he should remember to ask the pianist about this — that Mozart had not abandoned the formal structure of the sonata to achieve some kind of freedom, such as the romantics sought later, but to revert to a primeval dark mood of chaos and of death.

Frederic felt overwhelmed by a sense of defeat such as he had never felt before.

When the last chords had come down and the pianist let his hands fall by his side, there was silence. All were reluctant to let go of the feeling of grave beauty left by the music.

"I can't thank you enough for this beautiful, beautiful piece — I've never heard it," Elizabeth said.

The pianist lifted his head in her direction.

"The gift is yours. And if these anti-Jewish laws enabled us to make friends like you, maybe they are not all bad."

"They are very bad laws," Frederic said. "Ferdinand, tell us a little bit about this music — what do you think Mozart was thinking of when he embarked on such modernism?"

The pianist discussed keys and organ precedents and reversion to polyphony. The terms in which he was thinking were not in Frederic's vocabulary.

His wife led the pianist to the table. Elizabeth poured coffee and cut up a cake.

"But of course, Hungary is not at war now, so maybe we only have to think about bad laws, not terrible fates, as we did in Yugoslavia," Ferdinand said.

Hungary was allied with Germany, he meant, and Germany now ruled most of Europe unopposed.

"But there is a war against us as Jews," Frederic said. "You may be safer here, but I have to tell you about all the restrictions."

There were laws prohibiting their employment in the civil service and in the army. Jews could not attend public meetings, theaters, movies, or public schools. There were restrictions so ridiculous that they were hard to remember — Jews couldn't get fishing licenses or ride in first-class carriages. The penalties on possessing arms or explosives were now death by hanging. And above all, there were the laws, administrative decrees, and ordinances, defining a vast multitude as Jews, ranging from the orthodox through the recently converted to nuns and monks of Jewish origins. They were all Jews now.

"What makes it so hard for me is the loss of all choice, of all self-determination. I don't feel Jewish, I feel Hungarian, but others decide what I am and the consequences," Frederic said.

"When you lose your sight, you probably get used to that," Elizabeth said quietly.

"I'm sorry if I offended you," Frederic said. "Maybe it's because I had such high hopes for my country that it's so hard for me to accept going back to living in ghettos, as we did in the Middle Ages, despised and restricted, deriving all comfort from escape into a meaningless orthodoxy."

"Music is better," Ferdinand said with a smile. "Even the dark moods are beautiful."

Paula asked after Andrew and Kate.

"Kate is very busy, working and caring for her two little darlings," Elizabeth replied. "Mail from our son is irregular, unfortunately."

She was not sure whether it hurt her more to think of Kate, worrying desperately for news of Ernest, or of Andrew, cut off from them in Occupied France.

* * *

Ernest disappeared in Russia long before the battle of Voronezh sent home the staggering casualty lists of the defeated Hungarian Army. Kate mourned him as soon as his letters stopped coming. If he was alive, he would write to her. Not being a relation, she knew that she would not be notified of his death, and she could only make discreet inquiries of his family through the Zionist organization for which she worked.

He had been gone ten months when they received a notice that he was killed on the front. She wept again. Their happiness had been so young, so fitful, there was an infinity of future for her to mourn. She organized a memorial concert for him. The orchestra played without a conductor, trying to remember the taut, lively pace that was so typical of his style of conducting. The music swirled around the empty podium.

After the audience left, a man Kate had never seen before came up to her. He was small and freckled, with powerful shoulders. He had served in the same brigade as Ernest and asked whether she wanted to know more about his death.

Later, Kate came to her parents' house, pale and shivering. They went into the bathroom and turned on the faucets to talk.

"He was killed on the front, but not by the Russians, by ours. The moment they got there, the brigade leaders took away their clothes, their blankets, their money, and sent them out to pick up grenades, barehanded, from a minefield. They were assigned to a Hungarian Army unit for which they performed the most menial tasks, without food, without rest. At night, the brigade guards meted out punishments on any and all excuses. Beatings, hangings, dousing with icy water, and letting them freeze were daily fun for the Hungarians, who started to compete in cruelty and sadism. The men died but slowly. One of them overheard the unit leader say that he would bring back the whole work brigade in his briefcase, where the dead were listed.

"After that, Ernest managed to get himself killed by running half insane towards a Russian regiment. Daniel, his friend, is a Rumanian peasant, tough and crafty, who managed to escape when they got close to the Rumanian border. Of course, he had no papers, and the Rumanian Nazis were rounding up Jews, so he fled back into Hungary. He is sure he will be picked up soon, so he said he wanted someone to know what happens to Jews in the work brigades."

They sat in silence, while the water ran on and on.

"Does the Jewish Council know this? Does anyone?" Elizabeth asked.

"No one's coming back," Kate replied. "And the few who do don't want to talk about it because after a year they're liable for service again."

Kate went to the Jewish organizations, to the Swedish Embassy which represented the Red Cross, to the Papal Nunciate, to publicize the fates of the Jewish work brigades.

"There's a war on and these men are soldiers," she was told. She was reckless and noisy, and her friends asked her to stop. Through the people she badgered, she found out something even worse. The Germans had summoned Hungary's foreign minister to Berlin and complained that Hungary's anti-Jewish policies were arousing Hitler's wrath by their leniency. Why was Horthy dragging his feet?

In January of 1944 Kate had taken her children to her in-laws to spend the day. When she walked towards her office, she saw two official cars stopped in front of the entrance and a crowd. Someone brushed past her.

"Well, well, so they're finally arresting the Zionists," Kate heard.

She never found out whether that was a friendly warning or lucky hostility. She looked in her pocketbook, and as if she had forgotten something, turned back. On her way to her parents' apartment, she left a message for Daniel to meet her there.

"Mother, you will have to decide whether the children will be all right at Philip's parents," Kate said, breathless. "I want to live — I don't want Philip to bring them up alone after the war."

When Daniel arrived, she gripped his wrist. He and Kate discussed in low tones how they could get through Rumania to a Black Sea port.

"Come with us," Daniel said to Elizabeth and Frederic, as the latter emptied his wallet into Kate's pocketbook. "The Germans are going to occupy Hungary soon. I'm sure of it. The Rumanians consider the war to be lost, and they can be bribed."

"I'll stay with the children," Elizabeth said. "If things get worse, I can take them to Anna."

"The two of you will have enough trouble crossing the border" said Frederic. "What will you do when you get to Turkey?"

Kate explained that the Hungarian Jewish Agency held six hundred immigration permits issued by the British to Palestine — for one hundred thousand Hungarian Jews — she added bitterly. Since Hungary was not giving Jews exit visas, she would try to get one from the Jewish Agency in Istanbul. If she couldn't, there were boats taking illegal immigrants into British Palestine.

"Go my dear," Frederic said, embracing her. "We're too old to swim the Hellespont."

"I'll come back, Mother," said Kate, and they left by the service entrance.

Chapter 30.
Alone (1944)

The sun had set when Elizabeth got off the train in Budapest, having taken Tom and Zsuzsi to Kisbánya to stay with Anna. Immediately, two militiamen asked for her papers.

"I don't have any papers, I just went to the country because an old friend suddenly got ill. Here's my round-trip ticket."

"Everyone has to have identification papers at all times," one of them said in a harsh tone. He was dark, with sharp features. In his Arrow Cross uniform, he seemed eager to do his job of arresting and beating Jews. His companion was pale, with a small mouth — probably a city policeman recruited into the militia. Behind them, Elizabeth could see a group of Jews with yellow stars, guarded by a group of militiamen. It would only take a few seconds to make her a part of that group. Frederic! she thought. She had to get home.

With the courage of desperation, she turned like a fury on the more hostile of the men.

"Will you tell that policeman to leave me alone and to stop rifling through my pocketbook? Are you taking me for a Jewess? How dare you?"

She thought she was dreaming when he motioned her to go on, to get lost. She had to walk because he had not returned her pocketbook, and she had no money for the tram.

She could not walk fast because she might be stopped again, and her luck might not last.

She now wondered at her recklessness in yelling at the Arrow Cross man. Her instinct in avoiding the policeman, who seemed more sympathetic, had been right but also lucky. If the Arrow Cross man had felt challenged or defensive, he would have dragged her away, even shot her.

"I said you were brave," Frederic had said to her long ago. Her bravery, she reflected, was of the most reactive kind. In a crisis, she acted, for better or worse, usually on behalf of her family.

She grew hot and tired on the long way from the train station to her home. She was glad to think that Zsuzsi and Tom were with Anna. Her old friend was not only reliable but had grown in self-confidence and competence. The children were as safe with Anna as they would be anywhere.

Of her own children, she knew nothing. Kate and Andrew couldn't write to her — letters didn't get through between Hungary and Allied or neutral nations. She could only hope that they were both safe. But Frederic worried her terribly. How would she get medication for him in the ghetto? How could either of them survive further deportations?

Maybe this is the end of being brave or reckless, Elizabeth thought. Resignation, acceptance, patience, those are the useful virtues. In the hot late afternoon, she felt a release, a serenity in accepting the fact that the forces against her were overwhelming. I'm not sorry I fought all my battles, internal and external, she thought, but maybe it's time to lay down my arms. There was meaning in my fierce love for all those around me, but there's none in the darkness threatening all of us. Whether I accept it in the faith that Anna has that in the end light will defeat darkness, or without it, I would be foolish to contest reality.

Her serenity quickly gave way to anxiety when Frederic didn't open the door to her ringing. She rang and rang, assuming that he was asleep and might have closed the doors to the hallway and his bedroom. But she heard no steps and couldn't open the door because her latchkey was lost with her purse.

She ran down to the superintendent, who was having dinner with his family.

"May I have the key to my apartment, please?" Elizabeth asked. "I've lost it, and Frederic is ill inside."

"Get it for her," he said to his wife, without acknowledging

Elizabeth.

The woman got up reluctantly and walked ahead of Elizabeth up the stairs.

"Anyway, you're going to the ghetto soon, aren't you?" she asked, as she looked through her keys for the right one.

"Will you take care of our things while we're gone?" Elizabeth asked. "We've lived here so many years ...."

"The new tenants will take care of your belongings," the superintendent's wife said coldly.

"Who are the new tenants?" Elizabeth asked.

"People displaced to enlarge the ghetto," the woman answered as she turned the key. "They've got to go somewhere too, don't they?"

She left, and Elizabeth flung the door open.

"Frederic? Frederic?" she called.

In his study, she stopped. He was lying on the floor as if he had fallen from his armchair.

She felt his heart and pulse-dead, cold. Weeping, she turned him over.

She took his hand in hers. A letter had fallen with him.

My dearest — By the time you come back from Anna's, I will be gone. You know that I have never believed that there is anything after death except emptiness and void. My own absence will not hurt me, only you. I hope that after a lifetime of friendship and affection, you can forgive me. It is the only choice left to me in a world that has taken from me all power, all dignity, all hope.

I debated for a long time whether I should ask you about this, but I decided not to. Your vitality, your good health, your optimism have reached out long enough to my failing heart. Also, I have thought of a way in which you can save yourself.

Get Anna's maidservant's book and go to the Sacred Heart Hospital. There is a shortage of cleaning women and of nurses aides. I know it from my own stay at the Jewish hospital. Tell them that you married early, and you did not need to work for years. You know Anna's history well enough to reenact hers, and she, good friend that she is, will never betray you. Do not ask for shelter, but lie boldly. People expect Jews to be frightened.

That this is the best that I can offer you shows how weak I am. To shelter and protect those we love, not necessarily against all the storms of life, but still more than the arm around the shoulder — that to me is being a man. Long ago I lost the power to influence society to be more just and free. What was left was the clean shirt, the quiet tone, the personal ties that are not left to us now.

As to our children, if they survive the war, I will live in their memory. If they don't, be grateful now.

PART XII ~ EPILOGUE

"How can I live with this"

Chapter 31.
Susie and Andrew (1958)

When Susie Reddich graduated from high school, her father, Philip von Reddich, gave her a summer trip to Europe. She had changed Zsuzsi to Susie and had dropped the "von" from her last name soon after she and her brother Tom joined Philip in the United States in 1946. "It's ridiculous to be a baroness in America," she declared, "especially a fake one." Her father kept the particle because, he said, that was how he was known world-wide as a physicist. Tom didn't change his name because he liked to tell his college classmates how his grandfather bought his title, and Edith, their stepmother, wouldn't dream of changing her married name.

For a stepmother, Edith wasn't bad. She was fashionable, kind, and easy-going. While Susie packed for her trip, Edith kept her company, filing and painting her nails.

"I wish I could leave my suitcase in Paris," Susie said, "and just take a backpack to Italy. I won't need city clothes while I'm hitchhiking."

"There's always your aunt and uncle in Paris," Edith said.

The girl stopped pulling clothes from her closet.

"My mother's brother, Uncle Andrew, and his wife Nicole. We haven't heard from them in ages."

"Yes, well, your father and Andrew had some sort of falling out during Philip's last conference in Paris," Edith said. "It was about politics, I think, so you could ignore it. I'm sure Nicole would take you to a really good Parisian hairdresser," she added, casting a look at Susie's messy ponytail.

It was Andrew who had come to get both children from their hiding place when the war ended, and Susie rarely thought about that time. But she consulted Tom, who was working in Los Angeles, as she usually did about family matters.

"Absolutely," Tom wrote back. "Andrew is a great guy and Dad is being a jerk about him. And Sue, ask Andrew about our mother and Grandmother Elizabeth. When I finished high school, he wrote to me and said he wanted to tell me what happened to them, but then I decided to go to California and Hawaii instead of Europe, so I never followed up."

This was in a letter full of older-brother advice, such as Don't hitch rides with truckers; hostels are great for meeting people; and go and have drinks in the posh hotels, it's cheap and fun. Good advice, all in all, except that Susie found truckers safe and paternal on her rides.

She was ready for a French haircut and a reliable shower by the time she arrived, sweaty and tanned, in late August at Andrew and Nicole's door. This was her first visit because both had been traveling when Susie arrived in Europe — Andrew as a journalist and Nicole on an archeological expedition.

"So this is my grownup American niece!" her uncle, short, paunchy, and bearded, exclaimed as he gathered her up in a bear hug. "Have you forgotten me, together with every word of Hungarian?"

She gave him a kiss.

"Dad and Edith pretend we never speak Hungarian at home, but of course we do, she said. "And of course I remember you, you came to get us. After the war."

And she burst into tears.

Andrew held her close and then wiped both his own and her eyes with a handkerchief.

"The time for memories is after lunch, not before," he said. "Say hello to your Aunt Nicole, in any language."

Susiei apologized and shook hands with a slim, graying woman, who had been waiting in the doorway.

"He's very French about meals, isn't he?" Susie asked.

"After years of marriage to me, I should hope so," Nicole answered.

Andrew and Nicole made her feel completely at home, laughing at her travel stories and asking about Tom — "That great letter writer," Andrew said. "I treasure both of them."

Lunch ended with cheese, red wine, and espresso. Nicole excused herself to do some work, and Andrew lit a pipe as he and Susie settled down in the living room.

"You don't smoke yet, do you?" he asked, waving a pack of cigarettes at her. "Filthy habit."

"I'm waiting for college," Susie said. "Only a month."

"Tom told me that you wanted to tell us about Mom and Grandmother Elizabeth," Susie said after a silence. "I assume they both died in the camps, but he thought there was more."

"I should have done that a long time ago," Andrew said. "But those are terrible memories, and maybe I wasn't ready either."

"I last heard from our family in Budapest in 1943. That was late in the war, France had been occupied for a long time, but Hungary, an ally of the Germans, was still pretty peaceful. Your father, of course, was in America, but he and your mother had agreed to a divorce. Did you know that?"

"Yes, actually, Mom told us, and we almost forgot our father. So it was a shock to get together with him again."

"He's your father, so I don't want to malign him," Andrew said. "But he and I had a huge fight over Hungary and the Jews, which we wouldn't have had before the war, when I wasn't all that Jewish myself. After what happened to us, for no reason except for being Jewish, I couldn't tolerate his loyalty to our native country and his Catholicism, which he bought, together with that ridiculous title. I was proud of you for changing your name."

"But wasn't it all the Germans' fault?" Susie asked.

Andrew puffed on his pipe.

"Some, not all of it. They killed your mother, the Germans did. She had to flee Hungary because she worked for a Zionist organization, and the Nazis would have shot her. As it was, she managed to get across Rumania to Turkey and boarded a ship to Palestine. She was a brave woman, my sister. I thought of her

as spoiled and chi-chi, but I never knew her when she became a
Zionist and a fighter for other Jews."

"And then?" Susie asked.

"The Germans torpedoed the ship. The SS boarded the sinking
boat and machine-gunned all the passengers."

"Oh my God," the girl said.

"A few people fell into the water but survived. They swam
ashore and later made it to Palestine. It took me years to find them.
They remembered Kate."

Susie covered her face with her hands, but she didn't cry, and
after a few seconds, she removed them. She was bracing herself.

"What about Grandmother Elizabeth? Was she deported to a
concentration camp?"

"I don't think so," he said. "I'll never know exactly what
happened to her, but none of the scenarios are comforting."

He got up and walked around the room.

"When I got to Budapest after liberation — and it was hard to
get anywhere right after the war, no trains, no gasoline, I hitched
rides with various occupying troops — it was a frozen graveyard.
People were wearing socks on their hands, cutting chunks of frozen
meat from dead horses. Russian soldiers everywhere. They didn't
bother me, but they were often drunk and would shoot you for a
watch or a look.

"I went to our old house, and no one knew anything. No,
Frederic and Elizabeth weren't in the bomb shelter with us. Jews
weren't allowed in the shelters. The Jews went to Germany to
work, lucky them. Then they would all complain about the war
and the Germans, and I didn't have any patience for them.

"Finally, I thought about finding Anna. When she saw me, she
cried and cried, so I knew. It was almost a miracle that you and
Tom had survived, thanks to her. You know, I hardly remembered
you, and you didn't know me at all."

"So what did Anna think happened to Grandmama?"

"My father took his own life, she told me. He saw the coming
darkness and felt helpless to save anyone he loved. That hurt him
more than anything. He told my mother to borrow Anna's maidservant book and forge a new identity, since everyone had to have

papers to escape deportation. Anna cried harder than ever when she told me about this. She no longer had her maid's book — she had destroyed it. So my mother went back to Budapest after asking to borrow it. And a few days later, to the ghetto.

"Oh Andrew," Susie said.

"Anna tried to see her after she learned that my mother had moved to the ghetto. She stood outside for hours with food for my mother, but the guards beat her away."

"So maybe Grandmama died in the ghetto?"

"Maybe," Andrew said. "I told Anna I'd cable Philip in the United States — she had his address — and I'd come back for the two of you. I went back to Budapest to wait for his answer, and then the trial of the Arrow Cross Nazi leaders started. In the Opera House, no less, the only public building with a roof left after the bombing.

"As a journalist, I could cover the trial, and that's how I learned about what happened, to us, us Jews, at the end. It was horrible.

"You see, the Germans were losing the war so badly that after a while, they couldn't get trains to deport Jews to concentration camps anymore. So they marched them to death, in the cold and snow. But by the time my mother moved to the ghetto, I'm not even sure the death marches were going. I couldn't find her name on those lists.

"Then the Hungarian Arrow Cross took it on itself to kill as many Jews as they could before the Russians troops, who were already in Buda, crossed the river and occupied the city. There was heavy fighting, and the bridges had been blown up. The German troops were retreating but had left some units behind to cover the retreat. Even when the Russians came in, there was door-to-door fighting. All this I learned from the trial.

"And all this time, every night, Arrow Cross men would break into the ghetto and drag Jews out, shooting, knifing, or beating them to death. Sometimes they dragged them down to the river, which was nearly frozen, tied them together, shot one because they wanted to spare the ammunition, and threw them in the water to drown."

"How horrible!" Susie cried. "But why don't you think she died in the ghetto?"

"She might have," Andrew said. "People there died of disease, malnutrition, accidents. The ghetto wasn't destroyed, thanks to the German consul, who wouldn't let the SS blow it up before they left although those were Hitler's orders. That was some kind of miracle, one decent man among the Nazis. But my mother's body wasn't among those left, at least that I could see."

They were silent for a long time.

"What happened to Anna?" Susie asked. "She was so nice."

"She is. We still write to each other," Andrew said. "Her husband, Joska, died during the war. When I saw her right after the war, she was planning to run as a delegate of the Small Holders Party. My mother would have been proud of her. I think she won, but when the Communists took over in 1949, they outlawed the Small Holders Party. She told me that her grandchildren all go to school. They won't be peasants when they grow up, but she still grows what she can on her own little lot."

"Do you think I should go to see her?" Susie asked.

"Of course, you'd enjoy it. And we owe her a lot even if she couldn't save your grandmother. You're here, Tom's here. Or there."

"Oh, Andrew, how am I going to live with all this?" she asked, turning her pale, tear-streaked face to him.

"You will, somehow or other," he said. "After all, it's life that matters, not death, no matter how painful."

"Do you think my mother and grandmother had a good life?" Susie asked, sobbing. Nicole came in from the next room.

"If you had asked them, I think they would say yes," Andrew said. "There's a lot I don't know, but I'll try to tell you and Tom what I do remember."

Her aunt sat down next to her and put her arms around her shoulders.

"All life is good, Susie."

Sophie Cook

Sophie Cook, an attorney and mediator, was born in Budapest, Hungary, and immigrated to the United States with her family in 1951. She has a Master's Degree in fiction writing from Johns Hopkins University. In 2009 the Hungarian-language edition of *Anna & Elizabeth* was published in Budapest. Cook divides her time between Washington, DC and New York City and two sets of grandchildren.

CPSIA information can be obtained at www.ICGtesting.com
Printed in the USA
LVOW04s2040070715

445328LV00006B/10/P